Praise for *TEXAS ROADS*

"C   nt's **Texas Roads** is one I want permanently on my
bc   Her writing talent is outstanding as she blends sweet
Te   1, a Mayberry-like town, wanting a place to belong,
an   vill all together in one amazing read. Cathy adds
hu   e mix making it sure to be a best-selling inspirational
sta   ving series. Worthy of five-star praises!"
         Edwards, Book Reviews by Buuklvr81

"**Texas Roads** is one of those books that captures your
attention from the first and doesn't let go until the last page.
Cathy cleverly paints a picture that draws the reader into the
story. While reading, I was no longer in my home, I was in
Miller's Creek. I walked the streets of the town and relaxed in the
shade of the trees that dotted the countryside. I smelled the food
cooking and enjoyed conversations on Mama Beth's porch. I
struggled with the characters in their trials and rejoiced with
them in their victories. This is one book that you won't want to
miss! I can hardly wait for the next book!"
    ~ Donna Morris

"I couldn't put this book down! The story moves quickly, with no
wasted words. Dani's struggle to find a true home and get over
her past abuses spoke to my heart. But God is still in the healing
business, and watching and living through the healing process
with these people in Miller's Creek brought a healing to my own
heart. May God bless you as you read this book. And may God
continue to bless Cathy Bryant, so we can read more of her
works!"
    ~ Valita Randolph

"**Texas Roads** by Cat'   is a wonderful and thoroughly
enjoyable love story.   and the book was hard to put down
each evening at a dece   to see what
would happen next. I   chuckling
aloud and her plot twi   rs through
all their trials and emc   will touch
your heart and make you long to live in the lovely Texas setting
with the realistic and heroic characters that Cathy has created.
Five stars and "two thumbs up!"
    ~ Marlayne Giron, author of *The Victor*

TEXAS ROADS

a Miller's Creek novel ~ Book One

Cathy Bryant

WordVessel Press

Texas Roads
© 2010 Cathy Bryant

Published by WordVessel Press
P.O. Box 971
New Boston, TX 75570

All scripture quotations are taken from the HOLY BIBLE, NEW INTERNATIONAL VERSION ®, NIV ®. Copyright © 1973, 1978, 1984 by International Bible Society. Used by permission of Zondervan. All rights reserved.

Grateful acknowledgment is made to Brian Lary for the cover photography. Used by permission.

This novel is a work of fiction. Names, characters, places, and incidents are either the product of the author's imagination or are used fictitiously, and any resemblance to actual persons (living or dead), business establishments, events, or locales is entirely coincidental.

....

Library of Congress Control Number: 2010921118

ISBN: 978-0-9844311-0-6 (pbk.)

....

In memory of my daddy,

Bill England,

who taught me to love Texas roads.

"If anyone loves Me, he will obey My teaching.
My Father will love him, and
We will make Our home with him."
~John 14:23

Acknowledgments

Any writer who's honest will tell you no book is ever birthed by one person alone. Instead it is born and reborn through the efforts of many.

~ To my beta readers and extra sets of eyes: Carolyn, Virginia, Jimmie, Tessie, Mernie, Marlayne, Vanessa, Judith, Camille, Barbie, and Veronica. I can't thank you enough for the enormous help you provided. Thanks for being such a blessing!

~ To numerous friends who have helped spread the word about this book. I'm overwhelmed, humbled, and grateful. God bless you all.

~ To my church family at FBC, New Boston for your prayers and encouragement. Your kind words and intercession carried me through the writing of this book.

~ To my awesome critique partner, Ralene Burke, writer and friend extraordinaire. Thanks for telling me what I needed to hear instead of what I wanted to hear. I'm so grateful to God for allowing our paths to cross.

~ To Mom, who taught me to believe that I could do anything if I worked at it hard enough. I love you. Thanks for cheering me on.

~ To my amazing and supportive family. Josh, your legal and business expertise has been invaluable. Jase, it was your determination to stay true to your dream that gave me the courage to pursue mine. Megan, my daughter-in-love and the daughter of my prayers, I praise God for your sweet spirit and heart for Him. Harrisen, my beautiful grandson, in three months' time you've not only blessed my life, but captured my heart.

~ To my husband, Travis. The song you wrote for the book is perfect, but there aren't enough adjectives and adverbs in the world to describe how I feel about you. Your love, encouragement, and support kept me going when I wanted to quit. You have all my love, with all my heart, for all my life.

~ To my Lord and Savior, Jesus Christ. You are the reason for it all ...

∽1∾

Longing For Home

Dani's blue Honda Civic lurched and sputtered, drawing her attention to the neon-orange needle on the gas gauge. Empty. A frustrated growl rushed from her throat as she maneuvered onto the tufts of new spring grass at the side of the country road, turned off the ignition, and leaned her head back against the seat, berating herself for her forgetfulness. She'd love to blame this on the fight with her mother, but it wouldn't explain the hundreds of times she'd made similar mistakes—just one more to add to her collection.

She rubbed the dull ache building between her eyes and stared at her surroundings on this Texas back road. Why did she choose today, of all days, to visit her aunt, a woman she knew only from chatty letters and a brief phone call?

Escape.

She longed to escape. To disappear, to travel so far away that painful memories became yesterday's ashes.

A stray tear wandered down her cheek and she banished it with a swipe. Today marked the one-year anniversary of Richard's death. Death had robbed her—not only of her husband, but her dream—and stamped her heart's one desire with angry red letters: REQUEST DENIED. Thanks to the life insurance and inheritance of her father's company, a ridiculous sum of money now graced her bank account, but not enough to buy what couldn't be purchased. A house, yes, but not a home.

Stop wallowing, Dani. She grabbed her cell phone and flipped it open. No signal. Of course. She climbed from the car to scan the horizon. Nothing but tree-dotted pastures and a few cows. Breathing deep to quell the rush of panic, she closed her eyes and envisioned a sweet grandmother-type driving up to offer a ride. Her eyes fluttered open. Yeah, right. She wasn't Cinderella. Godmothers didn't exist. And Prince Charming? The biggest fairy tale of all.

Her marriage was proof.

Waiting to be rescued just squandered precious hours of daylight. She snatched her purse from the passenger seat, slammed the car door, and stamped toward Miller's Creek. Like a scratched CD, Mother's hurtful words from the earlier phone conversation replayed in her mind, and none of it made sense. Why did her mother oppose this visit to see Aunt Beth? And what had caused a rift the size of Texas between the two sisters?

A cramp commenced in her toes and inched into her feet. With a frown, she eyed her shoes. Heels weren't exactly the footwear of choice for hiking country roads. Balancing her discount-store purse in the crook of her arm, she rifled through its contents, searching for the keys as she marched back to the car. A sudden realization forced her into a stilted run, and a strangled sound ripped from her throat. "Please, no!"

The keys dangled from the ignition, teasing her like chocolate candy behind a counter of glass. With a guttural groan, Dani tilted her face toward the cloud-darkened sky. "What do You have against me?"

The isolated countryside responded with silence.

On the continued trek toward Miller's Creek, the hush enveloped her, the only sound an occasional bird's song and the rhythmic thud of her heels against the pavement. So peaceful, and so unlike the city's unending drone. The bluebonnets and

Indian Blankets of early spring painted the countryside, stretching beyond the barbed-wire fence into open fields, and the breeze tangled her hair. As she breathed in the fresh air, her shoulder muscles unknotted. Then a low rumble pulled her gaze to the clouded sky.

Heavy raindrops pelted Dani's face and dotted her consignment shop designer jacket. Within minutes she was drenched, the metallic taste of make-up dribbling into her mouth. She kicked at a rock, self-pity seeping through her like the rain through her dry-clean-only suit.

With a shiver, she hunched over and pulled the soggy jacket closer in an effort to get warm. Burning pain in her left little toe hinted at the formation of a blister, but she hobbled on, her thoughts on her aunt. Could the woman provide the sense of family she so desperately needed? She attempted to toss the question from her mind. One thing was· for certain. Her drowned-rat-appearance would make a memorable first impression. Just not in a good way.

The faint roar of an engine sounded behind her and intensified. Finally. She turned to see an older model pickup top the hill, and waved her arms in an effort to make herself seen in the rain and approaching nightfall. The beat-up truck slowed to a stop and the window lowered.

She tried to swallow, but her throat clamped shut. This was no grandmother. With one finger, a dusty cowboy pushed up his sweat-stained hat, his other arm draped over the steering wheel. "Can I give you a ride, ma'am?"

Dani brushed the drippy hair from her eyes, resisting the urge to correct his grammar. "I, uh . . . r-ran out of gas."

The cowboy smiled, his teeth white against his dirt-smudged face. "That's not what I asked."

With a glance in the direction of her car, her brain accelerated into high gear. "Actually, if you'd be so kind as to get me some gas—"

A soft chuckle resonated from him, and his eyes twinkled.

She hoisted her chin. How dare he laugh at her.

"Look, ma'am." His picture-perfect smile disappeared behind the long line of his lips, his voice laced with impatience. "I know you're concerned about accepting a ride with someone you don't know. Can't say I blame you. But by the time I get to town, get gas, and get back out here, it's going to be dark. Then you'll have plenty of reason to be afraid."

She raised a hand to her lips. What he said made sense, but could she trust him?

His mouth curled at the corners. "Coyotes are pretty bad in these parts. Sure wouldn't want to be out here after dark. Especially alone."

Coyotes? Dani yanked on the door handle and hoisted herself onto the grimy seat. After one breath in, she wrinkled her nose and sniffed. What was that smell? Eau de Sweat? She swiveled her head toward him and found his gaze trained on her, his face lined with suppressed laughter.

He needn't be so amused. She fidgeted with the seat belt and held it with one hand to keep it from riding across her nose. "I think someone up there must not like me."

"What makes you say that?" He stared at her like she was mentally unbalanced and put the truck in gear.

"It's just been a rough day. Like God has it in for me or something."

He raised one brow. "I think God must love you a lot, or I wouldn't have come home this way. Not many people use this road anymore."

Dani drew in a sharp breath. Did God love her? She gave her wet head a shake, sending droplets of water to the worn seat. No one could love her. Not even God.

Conversation lapsed as the rain continued its steady stream, thundering against the roof, yet unable to drown out the hum of the truck's engine. What would've happened to her if he hadn't driven by? The only coyotes she'd seen were in science videos at school. A surprising shudder scuttled down her spine, followed by a shiver that rattled her teeth.

The cowboy shifted her direction, his dark eyes focused on her ruined jacket. "You must be cold."

Brilliant deduction, Sherlock. Were all small-town people as intelligent as him? "What clued you in? My dripping clothes or blue lips?"

He laughed out loud, a hearty sound that made her somehow feel better. "Feeling a little testy, huh?" His eyes sparkled with amusement.

She hung her head, half in shame and partly to conceal the smile that crept onto her face without permission. "Sorry."

Dani started as he reached toward her, but relaxed when he pulled a brown suede leather jacket from behind the seat. "Here. This ought to warm you up."

"Thanks." She gripped the stained coat with two fingers, and examined it for signs of vermin. None that she could see. "Looks, uh . . . nice and cozy." She snuggled into its warmth and breathed in the light scent of men's cologne.

Richard.

She closed her eyes, the unwelcome memories and emotions clawing their way through her insides. The feelings still took her by surprise, crawling into her consciousness at unexpected times. Had she not been a good enough wife? Is that why he'd betrayed her, not just once, but several times? Her mind revisited their last fight. Richard had been more than happy to point out how many girlfriends he'd had during their ten-year marriage.

"By the way, I'm Steve Miller." The stranger's silky baritone interrupted her thoughts.

She opened her eyes to find his hand extended toward her. "Dani." She clasped his hand. Not as rough as she expected for a cowboy.

"You really shouldn't be on the back roads without enough fuel, you know." The look he gave her was stern, but kind.

Dani swallowed the sarcastic reply that popped into her head, and instead sent him a pasted-on smile.

His gaze rested on her wedding band. "Your husband not able to come along?"

The irony of his question made her grimace. At least the ring had served its purpose. She shook her head and focused on the passing terrain, some fields completely covered in wildflowers. How many more miles?

He leaned forward and made eye contact. "Been to Miller's Creek before?"

"Once when I was little, but I don't remember much about it."

"It's a nice place." His voice held a hint of pride. "Any family there?"

She slid a hand over her wet hair and cleared her throat. Time to change the subject and let him enjoy the hot seat for a while. "An aunt. What about you? Have you lived in Miller's Creek long?"

His eyebrow cocked into a furry question mark. "All my life."

"No surprise there," she muttered to herself. She glanced at his filthy blue jeans and tattered shirt. It had probably been that long since he'd taken a bath. Immediate guilt rained over her. *Ease up, Dani. At least he offered you a ride.*

"Excuse the way I look. We had a fence to mend today at the ranch."

Heat built up steam under her cheeks, and she averted her eyes. Okay, he wasn't supposed to hear that last comment.

His expression held nothing but friendliness. "I might know your aunt. What's her name?"

She rubbed fingers against her damp pants. Was it wise to divulge that information?

"Never mind." Steve held up a hand, a thin layer of black showing beneath his nails. "I know you city folks have to be careful about stuff like that."

What was it with his ability to read her mind? "City folks? You make it sound like a disease or something." She hugged her arms to her chest. "Besides, how do you know I'm from the city?"

"'Cause people from around here don't dress up in such fancy duds." His dark eyes glinted and her nerves unraveled more.

"True. They wear cowboy hats and drive beat-up trucks."

His throaty laughter reverberated in the cab. "Guess I had that coming."

Resting her elbow on the door, Dani leaned her hot face against her fist and wished for a punching bag.

"Which city?"

She stared at the tattered pickup cab ceiling and drew in a breath. "Dallas." If they didn't get to Miller's Creek soon she was going to blow.

"Should-a guessed that." Steve's face scrunched up.

"How can you stand living in the city with all that noise and traffic?"

"I suppose the same way you live with stinky old cows and a lack of civilization." Her voice rose in frustration. Dani immediately wished the blurted-out words back in her mouth.

She started to apologize, but Steve spoke before she could get a word out. "You in business for yourself, or you work for a corporation?"

Where'd he get that idea? "I'm an elementary school teacher."

"Really?" His brows notched up and he snickered.

Irritation seeped through the cracks of her frazzled nerves like floodwater penetrating a leaky dam. She twisted her head to glare at him. "Is that so difficult to believe?"

A smirky smile snaked across the cowboy's face. "Guess not. It's just that Miller's Creek teachers don't dress up like you. They get down on the floor with their kids."

The dam burst wide open. "Well now it's my turn to be amazed. I didn't know small towns like Miller's Creek had schools." She huffed out the words then yanked her head around to clamp a hand over her mouth. What was wrong with her today?

Broken only by the swish of the windshield wipers and the pit-pat of rain drops, the silence hung between them, thick and sultry. Suffocating. She let out a slow breath and ducked her head to study him from beneath her lashes. Steve faced forward, the dark hair at the nape of his neck curling upward, his stubbled jaw locked. Most of her friends would classify him as handsome, but she wasn't looking for a man. Not ever again.

He began to whistle, a shrill sound that chafed against her raw nerve endings. She pressed a hand to her temple. How much farther could it be? "Is there a convenience store in Miller's Creek by any chance?" She tried to infuse her tone with kindness.

His cinnamon eyes turned on her, dry hot winds that withered everything in their path. "Of course. Right next to the community outhouse."

A nervous giggle escaped before she could stifle it, but Steve's daggered glare brought it to a quick halt. After a few minutes she peeked at his face, now chiseled from granite. *Way to go, Dani.* She'd already offended one member of Miller's Creek and hadn't even made it to the city limits.

The rain ceased as they pulled into town, and she sat up straighter at the sight of country cottages lining the street. Homey. A little tired-looking, but nothing a fresh coat of paint couldn't fix. Tree branches arched across the road to create a living canopy. The sun, sandwiched between cloud and earth, changed the leaf-clinging raindrops to diamonds.

And children everywhere she looked. They splashed in puddles and chased each other across spring green lawns, their shouts and laughter a symphony of careless joy. So *Mayberry RFD*.

The hunger for home haunted her, and a familiar ache settled over her heart like ancient dust. "Unbelievable." Dani whispered the word and relaxed into the seat. The fear of never finding a home clung to her with razor-sharp talons, but she pushed it aside and glanced at Steve, his face impassive.

In one deft movement, he jerked the pickup into a parking lot and came to a whiplash stop. She avoided eye contact and allowed the sign above the door to capture her interest. B & B Hardware? Dani peered to her right where two lanes of gas pumps stood, and a smile wiggled onto her face. A hardware-store-slash-gas-station. Only in a small town.

She plucked a hundred-dollar bill from her purse and offered it to him. "I appreciate—"

"Keep it." Steve spat out the words and leaned away, his mouth a taut slash.

Surely he needed the money. His ragged jeans and this rattletrap he drove suggested as much. She squeezed her eyebrows together. For whatever reason, he wasn't about to take the money, so she stuffed the bill back in her wallet, shrugged off the coat, and handed it to him.

"Thanks for the ride." With a release of the door she lowered herself to the ground.

Without looking her direction, the cowboy put the truck in reverse, barely allowing her time to shut the door. As he tore out of the parking lot, his rear wheels spewed gravel.

Dani sucked in air and blew it out in a gush. Thank goodness that was over. Now to call Aunt Beth and end this nightmare. She faced the store, her heart pounding like a child on the first day of school.

∞2∞

Friends or Foes?

Steve pressed the accelerator and spun out of the parking lot. Rich, snooty city women worked their way under his skin quicker than a tick on a dog. He'd seen enough of them to make him gun-shy for eternity. With a grunt he slumped against the dingy cloth seat. Every fifty-something woman in the county tried to hook him up with that type of she-cat. Even around his own sister a man wasn't safe. Trish had joined the attack months ago, bringing in old college buddies in an effort to get him hitched. Just because the big four-oh loomed in front of him like a black hole didn't mean he needed a wife.

His attention shifted back to the blond city woman he'd just let off, looking down her nose at his town, as if Miller's Creek fell short of her high-falutin' standards. He leaned forward, crossed his arms on the leather-wrapped steering wheel, and let out a disgusted snort. And people wondered why he'd never married. No thanks. He'd gladly live out his days in blissful bachelorhood. Besides that, he'd already had his chance at love.

The rumble in his stomach raised his eyes to the dashboard clock. Almost supper time and behind schedule, thanks to the run-in with that Dallas prima donna. Mama Beth would be worried. The older woman practically raised him, and he'd learned not to be late, especially for her mouth-watering meals. He punched the gas pedal with a plan to phone her once he reached the ranch. Then he'd clean up and come back to town for supper.

A few minutes later, Steve braked to a stop in front of the small frame and brick house he'd called home for ten years, one of several standing behind the main ranch house. It might be small, but at least it was private. He slammed the truck door, breathed in the rain-cleansed air, and let it out in a puff of satisfaction. Nothing like coming home after a long, hard day of work. Manual labor always helped him relax. Sam, his golden retriever, stretched and yawned. Tail a-wag, Sam padded toward him, a doggy grin on his face.

He knelt and ran his fingers through the dog's soft fur. "Hey, Sam, old boy, how are you?" The gray around Sam's nose caught his attention. More signs of old age. None of them were getting younger, and reminders surrounded him—in the mirror, his parents, Mama Beth—and especially in Miller's Creek.

"Come on, buddy, let's get you some grub."

The dry chunks of food rattled the bag and then clanked against Sam's metal dish. He gave the dog one more scratch behind the ears before he headed to the kitchen. Just as he reached for the phone, it rang. Steve snatched the phone to his ear. "Hi, Mama Beth."

Her familiar cackle brought a smile to his face. "How'd you know it was me?"

"'Cause no one else calls this time of night."

The laughter stopped short. "Hmm, we need to do something about that, don't we?" She sounded determined.

Steve shifted his weight to the opposite foot. Great, Mama Beth had on her matchmaker hat again. Not what he wanted. He cleared his throat and redirected the conversation. "Sorry I'm late. I'll be there as soon as I—"

"Actually, that's why I called. I'm not quite ready myself. I'll give you a ring later."

"Okay. Bye." He dropped the phone into place then scratched the stubble on his chin. What was she up to now?

Mama Beth lowered the phone then rubbed her arms, her thoughts focused on Steve. Something had to be done about that man's lack of a social life. He might fool others, but he couldn't fool her. She knew him too well. The long hours he put in as mayor of the town were just an attempt to fill the days and cover his loneliness. And marriage to Miller's Creek was a sure-fire recipe for disappointment.

She moved to the front window of the old farmhouse to search for headlights. Finally after all these years, Dani was on her way for a visit, an answer to prayer. A prayer she'd almost given up on. The mahogany mantle clock chimed the hour, and her brows knitted. Dani should've been here an hour ago. Surely she hadn't changed her mind.

Lightning slashed a scar across the sky, its jagged edges white-hot. She flinched at the following blast of thunder, while the old house rattled and trembled, a persistent prayer tumbling from her lips. "Lord, keep her safe."

She turned and trained her gaze on keepsakes from the past, now perched on shelves Steve had built for her birthday. The cast iron horse Daddy gave her when she was a girl, the porcelain washbasin and pitcher which once belonged to Gramma Jo, the lace doily Mama crocheted. She trailed her fingers over its bumpy edges. These earthly treasures meant so much, but she'd trade them in a heartbeat to untangle this knotted mess in her life.

The rain started again, heavier than before, pinging against the tin roof until the sound escalated to a rowdy roar, bringing with it a reminder that her life had changed forever on a stormy night much like this one. Time-worn doubts surged to the surface and pounded against the wall of her heart, the familiar temptation so strong her breath caught in her throat.

Mama Beth squared her shoulders. *No.* She wouldn't break the promise she'd made, no matter the cost. But where did that leave Dani? She deserved to know the truth.

A cowbell above Dani's head clanked out her entrance into B & B Hardware, the stale smell of day-old coffee assaulting her nostrils. She shivered under the weight of the rain-soaked jacket and waited for her eyes to adjust to the darkness inside the old store.

To her left, the worn oak floors led to an array of gardening tools, paint, and aluminum bins of assorted screws and nails. A smaller section of candy, chips, and canned goods lined the shelves to her right, an ancient soft drink cooler standing guard nearby. Beside the checkout stand near the middle of the store, a group of men congregated, their man-talk accented by guffaws and snorts. The conversation fizzled as she approached, the floor creaking beneath her, and like one giant organism they shifted away, gawking at her like she'd grown an extra head.

She flashed the man behind the counter her best smile. "Excuse me. Do you have a public restroom?" Her voice wavered as visions of the community outhouse invaded her mind.

The man said nothing, only stared, his mouth half open. Then he motioned with a jerk of his head toward a door at the left corner of the store, his eyes fixed on her face. Had she grown a wart on the end of her nose? Still shivering, she made her way to the back, trailed by the creepy silence.

A single bare light bulb hung in the dark and tiny poor-excuse-for-a-restroom. At least it looked clean. She closed the old wooden door, latched the hook, and moved to the mirror. One glance at her appearance elicited a wheezing gasp. Like a clump of overcooked noodles, her hair lay plastered to her head, and mascara rimmed the flesh beneath her eyes. No wonder the men in the store had stared and the cowboy had been on the verge of a laughing spree.

Dani grabbed a paper towel from the dispenser and used it to twist on the ancient tap. This first meeting with Aunt Beth was too important to look like a rogue clown. She set to work, attempting to remove the offensive black circles. After a vigorous scrubbing she stepped back to view the results. Hopeless. With her fingertips she attempted to rearrange her wet hair, but nothing helped.

Her stomach somersaulted as she released the door latch and marched back to the counter. Let them stare if they wanted and take pictures if they dared. She raised her chin to muster a semblance of dignity. "May I borrow your phone and phone book, please?"

"This a local call?" The man spoke with a slow monotone drawl.

Her fingers curled into tight balls. Fighting the urge to tell him she planned to call NASA, she slowed her breathing and replied calmly, "Yes. My car ran out of gas. I need to call my aunt to let her know I'm okay."

One of the men spoke. "We'd be happy to get your car for you, ma'am."

Yeah. Uh-huh. Like she'd trust her car to a bunch of local yokels she didn't know. "Thanks, but I'll take care of it later. Right now, I just want to call my aunt."

The man behind the counter shoved the phone and directory across the worn Formica counter, while the men to her left nodded with whispers and nudges. The Miller's Creek welcoming committee could use a lesson or two on manners. She cradled the phone between her head and shoulder, located her aunt's number, and dialed. The phone beeped as she punched the key pad with shaky fingers.

"Hello?"

She released a grateful sigh. "Aunt Beth, this is Dani."

"Thank goodness! Are you okay?" Her voice crackled through the phone.

Tears pricked Dani's eyes. At least somebody cared. She coiled the phone cord around her finger and turned her back to the men. "Sorry to worry you, but I ran out of gas. I tried to call on my cell phone, but couldn't get a signal."

"Good gracious, how'd you get to town?"

"I walked part of the way, and then a man gave me a ride."

"Where are you now?"

She glanced over her shoulder at the staring men. "I'm at a place called B & B Hardware."

"Okay, here's what you do. There's a group of men..."

A frown puckered Dani's forehead. How did she know?

"...tell them what happened, and they'll take care of your car. I'll be there in a few minutes to pick you up."

"I told you she was kin to Mama Beth," blared the man with the bright orange, pot-belly-stretched-out suspenders.

Dani pulled the receiver away from her ear. Mama Beth? They called her aunt Mama Beth? Whatever for? She hung up the phone and faced them.

A thin elderly man with kind eyes stepped forward and extended a hand, his voice a gentle Texas drawl. "I'm J. C. Watson, ma'am. Couldn't help but overhear your conversation."

Couldn't help but eavesdrop? She raised her eyebrows, but held her tongue and shook his hand.

The rest of the men gathered around to introduce themselves, and J.C. spoke again. "Would you like for us to get your car?"

Her shoulders slumped as tension rolled off. Everything would be okay after all. "I'd be so grateful." The keys. She'd almost forgotten. "But there's, um . . . a slight problem. I-I locked my keys in the car." Dani tensed, anticipating their laughter, but no one smiled or snickered.

"Zeke, call Ernie." J. C. sprang to action, his tone suddenly business-like. "I'm sure he'll have a way to unlock the car. I'll get a gas can."

She placed her hand on his arm and offered him an appreciative smile. "I'd be happy to pay you for your time and trouble."

"Oh, no ma'am." He ducked his head, his voice low. "That won't be necessary."

A couple of minutes later, a balding police officer with a prickly-looking moustache and bushy eyebrows entered the store. J. C. stepped up beside her. "Ernie, I'd like you to meet Mama Beth's niece. This is Miss Dani."

The officer, his expression warm and genuine, clasped her hand with a two-fisted squeeze. "Nice to meet you, ma'am. The whole town thinks the world of your aunt."

Dani forced her gaze from his porcupine moustache to his gray eyes. "You, too." Surprise skidded through her. All things considered, these were the friendliest people she'd ever met.

"I understand you need help with your car. Where's it located?"

She gave him the details, and the policeman and J. C. left to retrieve the car. The rest of the men chattered at once, one offering her a folding chair, and another, a scratchy blanket. Their thoughtfulness rained down on her like soothing balm after the tense drive into town. Steve's angry expression intruded into her thoughts. She'd take thoughtful over tense any day.

The man who looped his thumbs through his orange suspenders, the one they called Coot, spoke. "So you're Cecille's girl." His chewing-tobacco breath blasted her in the face, his blaring voice in competition with his loud suspenders.

Her heart skipped a beat. This was a small town. Of course they would know her mother. She shifted in the chair and pulled the blanket closer. "Yes. You know her?"

He nodded once. "Yep. Grew up with her. Heard she married some rich city fella."

Dani offered him a close-mouthed smile, unsure of how to respond.

The men began reminiscing about the days of their youth, painting her mother in fresh colors. She marveled at their stories. They couldn't be talking about her mother. The person they mentioned sounded like a fun-loving country girl, not the cold and difficult-to-please woman she knew.

The rattle of the cowbell above the door drew her attention. An older woman approached, her face glowing. Dani's neck tingled, an indescribable feeling rushing over her. She stood and moved toward the woman, her hand out. "You must be—"

"A handshake just won't do, Dani. I'm so glad you're here." Her aunt waved away her outstretched hand and blanketed her in an embrace.

Unexpected tears spilled down Dani's cheeks, their saltiness sliding onto her lips, as tension and fatigue gave way to relief. She pulled away and used her hands to wipe dampened cheeks, brushing at a wet spot on her aunt's shoulder. "I'm sorry. I got you all wet."

"Oh, pshaw." Her aunt's voice hitched for a moment then leveled out. "Won't kill me. But we'd better get you into some dry clothes before you catch your death of cold. Let's go home."

Home? Was that where this road led? *Please let it be true.*

❧3❧

An Unexpected Guest

Fear curled snaky tentacles around Cecille Hammond's heart and squeezed like a vise. She placed one elbow on the table near the ice-skating rink at Galleria Mall and rested her face on her palm, careful not to smudge her makeup. The joyous laughter of kids on Spring Break and the smell of freshly grilled burgers swirled around her, but did nothing to lift her spirits.

The accountant had been blunt and to the point. She was broke, and had no idea how it had happened. The amount Daniel left in his will should've been more than enough to last the rest of her life. She nibbled the edge of her nail. Now the money was gone and bankruptcy loomed, an open-mouthed shark with deadly teeth.

How could she keep her friends from learning the truth? They turned on their own when they tasted blood in the water. She should know. She'd done it herself. Unfortunately there was only one way out of this mess. Danielle. Richard's unexpected death made her a millionaire many times over, not including what the company was worth.

She watched a young mother help a tow-headed toddler balance on ice skates. Like a leaf spiraling downward, Cecille's heart fluttered. How long had it been since she and Danielle were that close? Had her daughter forever closed and barred the door between them?

Now Danielle was in Miller's Creek. Anger billowed inside, washing ever nearer to the surface. Somehow Beth had once again managed to worm her way into the picture. Little Miss Perfect. The one everyone admired and respected. The one she could never compete with, not even in her parent's affections.

Would Beth win Danielle over too? The thought blasted immediate panic through her body.

With a deep breath, Cecille closed her eyes and tented her fingers in front of her lips. It wouldn't be pretty or nice, but she had no choice. She'd do whatever it took to keep Beth out of Danielle's life. Forever.

Was Mama Beth going to keep him waiting forever? Steve flopped back in the leather office chair, his arms across his chest, and brought his feet up to rest his boots on top of the desk. An overloaded brain and underfed belly made work a wasted effort. Hunger set off a grumbling complaint in his belly and moved his gaze to the clock. Seven o'clock. What was taking her so blasted long?

A familiar heaviness pushed aside his frustration. Its well-timed attack hit every evening when he was tired and alone. Would there ever be a day when he didn't think of Lauren and wonder what might have been? He leaned forward to punch the power button on his stereo, the haunting strains of Mendelssohn's *Violin Concerto in E minor* wafting through the silence. It relaxed his tense nerves and muscles, but only intensified the loneliness. *God, help me get through this. Again.*

He rose to his feet, moved to the window, and peered toward the main ranch house. The Texas spring storm had passed, and one small light glistened from a window on the ground floor, Mom's room since Alzheimer's made stairs too dangerous. His heart constricted, and a wad of guilt lodged in his throat. He hadn't seen her in over a week, but with good reason. Every visit only reminded him of what would never be. No more chances to have a real relationship. Not that it had ever been likely.

An ache took up residence behind his eyes, pounding out an aching rhythm. Part of him knew his mother's lifelong unhappiness had nothing to do with him and everything to do with being a city girl transplanted to his father's small and close-knit community. Another part—the little boy in him—still longed to be close to her. He rubbed a hand across his neck and banished the painful thoughts from his mind. Enough. Time for another stab at work. After all, the grant proposal for the renovation project wasn't going to write itself.

Steve jumped when the ringing phone split the silence half an hour later. He grabbed it and brought it to his ear. "It's about time." He growled out the words, but not as loud as the growling wolf in his belly.

Mama Beth sighed. "You've got to get a life."

"Forget my life. What about supper?"

"Omelets okay?"

His mouth watered. "You're on. I'll be there in a few."

Within fifteen minutes he let himself in her front door, the aroma of sautéed bell peppers, onions, and mushrooms triggering another rumble in his stomach. He followed the smell to the kitchen, his favorite room in the house. Original bead board paneling served as a back-splash to the country white cabinets, and the heart of pine floors spread their honey-colored warmth across the room. A sudden childhood memory flooded his mind. The one of Mama Beth offering him gooey-warm chocolate chip cookies every time his frequent bike rides landed him at her door.

The sizzling skillet and Mama Beth's happy hum mingled in an impromptu concert and brought him back to the present. She flashed a smile from across the room and bustled to the cabinet where she kept the plates. His eyebrows shuffled up his forehead.

Mama Beth looked better than she had in weeks. Fresh color tinted her cheeks and happiness sparkled in her eyes. His heart lightened. She must be feeling better. He sauntered over and kissed her cheek.

She wiped her hands on her apron and beamed at him. "How was your day?" Her voice lilted in the sing-song fashion he'd grown to love.

"Good. Finally got the fence finished on the east side of the ranch." He straddled an old stool at the counter, and it wobbled under his weight, another item for his to-do list.

"I know you're glad that's over." She cracked open an egg with one hand and emptied the contents into an antique bowl, tossing the shell into the trash with one hand while she reached for another egg.

"Yep. As warm as it was today, I can't imagine mending it in the summer heat." Steve scanned the counter for a snack. At this point grass would taste good. He spied a few pieces of chopped bell pepper, popped one in his mouth and crunched it, the sweet flavor rolling over his tongue.

Mama Beth's humming resumed while she whisked the eggs, forcing his eyebrows to climb higher. "You sure seem happy."

She smiled but didn't comment, the whisk whirring and scraping against the side of the bowl.

What was she hiding? "How was the doctor's visit? Did he say what was causing the dizziness and headaches?"

Her eyes clouded over. "No, he just ran a bunch of tests and told me to start acting my age."

Steve chuckled and shook his head. "Well, I could-a told you that." He waited for her to elaborate, but she went back to humming instead. "Did he say what was wrong?"

Mama Beth poured the egg mixture into the skillet where it sizzled and popped, sending vapor spiraling toward the vent hood. "Nope, but he wants to run more tests."

His pulse quickened. "More tests? Why?"

She raised a shoulder and made a wry face. "You know doctors. They think they have to poke and prod every square inch of you." Her infernal humming started again.

Time to get to the bottom of this. "Okay, what's up?"

"What's up?" Her eyes widened.

He crossed his arms across his chest. "Yeah, I haven't seen you this cheery in forever. Now you're prancing around the kitchen like a filly—"

"I feel so much better, Aunt Beth." The words sang out from the top of the stairs. "Whatever you're cooking smells delicious."

That voice. No, it couldn't be. He whipped his head around so fast his neck twinged.

A creature descended the stairs, clad in pink from head to toe. A turban-style towel encircled its head, a frilly bathrobe wrapped the body, and fat furry house shoes covered the feet. The only visible part of the creature was a face. One he had hoped to never see again.

When she noticed him her mouth flew open, and she stopped in the middle of the stairs, frozen. A charming pink tinge christened her cheeks. Except for her baby blue eyes, the city woman reminded him of a big sticky ball of cotton candy.

"I'm sorry. I didn't realize you had company." She pivoted and headed up the steps. "I'll go upstairs until my car gets here."

Mama Beth snorted. "You'll do no such thing. Supper's ready and you need some hot food. Dani, this is Steve Miller." She held one hand toward him like he was some kind of prize on a game show. "Steve, I'd like you to meet my niece, Dani Davis."

Niece? What niece? "We've already met." His voice sounded flat in his own ears.

"Mr. Miller was kind enough to give me a ride into town." A polite smile rested on Dani's face as she descended the last step.

"Why, Steve Miller! Why'd you just dump her at B & B like a stack of wood?" Mama Beth waved a wooden spoon in the air, nothing righteous about her indignation.

His jaw flapped open, and he fumbled words. "B-but—"

Dani stepped forward. "It's my fault, Aunt Beth. I asked him to let me off. I didn't realize he was your friend."

Well, at least she was honest. Or was she?

Mama Beth clicked her tongue like she always did when she scolded. "That's no excuse. He could've at least gone in with you." She faced him, hands on her hips. "My goodness, Steve! Didn't you stop to think about how nervous she must've felt going into a store full of strange men? I thought I taught you better than that."

He stared over Mama Beth's head at the city woman and clamped his jaw shut. Dani's gaze held triumph. Or was it a challenge? Either way, he wasn't about to let some petite piece of cotton candy make a fool out of him. He cleared his throat and stepped forward. "I apologize for my behavior, Mrs. Davis." There! He could be cultured too.

She took his outstretched hand, wide-eyed, her mouth rounded to an O.

Steve glanced down at her dainty fingers, so small in his big paw, like a child who needed protection. The soft scent of a fruity soap swirled in the air around his head. He gulped in air and struggled to concentrate on her words, his mouth as dry as the creek-bed in July. Dani's inquisitive gaze sent a jolt of electricity from his eye sockets to his toenails, leaving no doubt the woman could see straight to his soul.

Mama Beth bustled past with a basket of biscuits. "Steve, would you ask the blessing?"

He swallowed the cotton in his mouth as they gathered at the sturdy farmhouse table. "Dear Lord, thank You for Mama Beth and for, uh . . ."

"Dani," whispered Mama Beth.

". . . and for Dani. Give her a safe trip home." *And soon.* "Thank You for the food. In Jesus' name we pray. Amen."

He lowered himself into the ladder-back chair, grabbed the basket, and yanked back the blue- and white-checked towel. Steam drifted from the hot bread, and his salivary glands went into over-production. Nothing like Mama Beth's biscuits to feed a half-starved man. He claimed three and moved to deposit them on his plate.

"Why do you call my aunt Mama Beth?" Dani's bell-like voice raised his head. Her clear blue eyes focused on him.

"Uh . . ." The biscuits began a slow burn, and he dropped them on his plate, tempted to blow on the tips of his fingers. He tried to answer, but her eyes got in the way. Good grief, she was married. What was wrong with him?

Mama Beth shot him a questioning look and chimed in with the answer. "My name's actually Mona Beth, but when Steve was little he thought people were calling me Mama Beth. The name stuck. Now that's what everyone calls me."

Dani angled her head and directed a dazzling smile his way. "What a sweet story."

A flash of heat rushed to his face, and he tugged at the collar of his shirt. *Food. Focus on the food.* Why were his palms so sweaty?

Silence made the tick of the clock ear-splitting. Thoughts barrel-rolled in his head, and he grabbed at the first one that tumbled by. "What brings you to Miller's Creek, Mrs. Davis?"

"Please call me Dani."

"Okay, Dani. What brings you to Miller's Creek?"

"I already told you. I came to visit my aunt."

He cast an accusing glance at Mama Beth. "I didn't even know you had a niece."

Mama Beth smiled, but not at him. "We haven't really had the opportunity to get to know each other, but hopefully that's all about to change."

A silent communication took place between the two women. Time to break up the city woman's game, whatever it was. "Dani sure is an odd name for a girl."

Stern furrows plowed their way onto Mama Beth's forehead, but the younger woman chattered away and added a biscuit to her plate. "My name's Danielle, but that's a little too pretentious for me. The only one who calls me by that name is Mother." Her face momentarily darkened.

A steady stream of conversation soon ensued, and Steve could only marvel. Women could talk about anything. He pushed a puff of air through his mouth. Dani hadn't been near as chatty with him on the drive into town. More like tight-lipped.

What would make a city woman like her want to visit an aunt she didn't even know? He studied the question from different angles while he shoved down the hot food, no closer to understanding than before. His fork clattered to the plate and he leaned back to rub his full belly. There might not be a way to decipher Dani's intentions, but he wasn't about to let Mama Beth get suckered into a scam.

Steve stood and carried his plate to the sink, not certain why the city woman came here or how long she planned to stay. But one thing he knew for sure. He was ready for her to leave.

ᑧ4ᑫ

Hard Questions

If she had to rate the effectiveness of her visit thus far on a scale of one to ten, she tipped the charts at minus twenty. Of all the dumb luck. Dani sank into the cushioned softness of her aunt's overstuffed sofa, the smell of supper still permeating the air. How could she have possibly guessed the dirty cowboy who chauffeured her into town was her aunt's friend?

Aunt Beth peeked through the open doorway into the living room, her youthful face aglow. "How 'bout some hot chocolate while we talk?"

"Sounds great. Anything I can do to help?"

Her aunt waved a hand. "Nah, made it earlier today, so I'll just warm it up. You sit there and relax." Aunt Beth's shoes clicked against the hardwood floors in the kitchen.

Relax? Easy to say, but not so easy to do. She gnawed her bottom lip. Miller's Creek might prove to be the escape—no, the home—she longed for. Away from memories. Away from the pain. Away from her mother. Had she already mucked it up by alienating Steve Miller?

Dani viewed the high ceilings, exquisite moldings, and antique furnishings. A place that felt like home, unlike the house she'd grown up in, a museum of a place used to impress and intimidate.

She rose from the sofa, made her way to an array of photographs displayed nearby, and picked up a barn wood frame. Steve's handsome face grinned back. Her cheeks flamed at the memory of the ride into town. Judging by his demeanor at dinner, he had no intention of forgiving her for being so snarky on the trip. Not that she could blame him.

With his thick dark hair and eyes the color of cinnamon, he seemed a completely different person than the smelly man who brought her to Miller's Creek. She returned the photograph to its place and repositioned herself on the couch. A thirty-something man friends with a fifty-something woman? Wasn't that a little odd?

From the kitchen came the slam of a cabinet door and the rattle of dishes. A minute later her aunt entered, carrying a tray with a teapot and two steaming teacups.

"I love your house, Aunt Beth. It's so warm and inviting."

The older woman placed the tray on the coffee table and handed her a cup. "Thanks, sweetie, it's home to me. One of the oldest houses in Miller's Creek."

Dani inspected the contents of her cup, taking a deep whiff of the creamy mixture. "Is this white chocolate?"

A smile carved her aunt's face. "Yep. My secret recipe."

She shut her eyes as she sipped, savoring the warm rich liquid, her tangled nerves unwinding. "Mmm, this is delicious."

"Thanks. Want to move outside and enjoy the beautiful evening? I think the storm has finally passed." Aunt Beth picked up the tray and moved toward the door.

"Sure." As they stepped onto the wraparound porch, a fragrant breeze caressed Dani's skin. She inhaled deep and let out the breath in audible delight. "What's that heavenly smell?"

"Honeysuckle." Her aunt moved around the corner of the house. "You can smell it better over here."

Aunt Beth sat the tray on a nearby table, and they both settled onto the cushioned porch swing in comfortable silence. The gentle rocking motion, in combination with the hot chocolate, scented air, and soft chirp of crickets, lulled Dani into a state of relaxation. She leaned her head back. This is what she wanted. What she needed. Home.

She lifted her head and took a sip of the chocolate mixture before turning to face the older woman. "I apologize if I offended Mr. Miller at dinner. He seemed . . ." What word should she use? Distant? Aloof? Downright icy?

Aunt Beth swatted the air. "Don't worry about it. Steve's pretty complex. The deep-thinker type. I've known him all his life, but I still don't know what's going on in that head of his most of the time."

The deep-thinker type? Really? More like moody. Friendly one minute and sullen the next. Either way she had the distinct impression he disliked her. A question rotated in her mind, and she searched for the best way to ask it. "You two seem very close."

A tender expression softened her aunt's features. "His parents brought him and his sister to the daycare where I worked, and we saw each other at church. When he got older, he rode his bike to town for my homemade cookies. He's like a son."

A picture of a young Steve formed in her mind, and piercing envy stabbed deep. She could almost see him, sitting in Aunt Beth's kitchen, devouring fresh-from-the-oven cookies. The *Leave It to Beaver* life she'd dreamed of every day of her existence.

Her aunt's cup dinged against the saucer. "I haven't had a chance to ask how everyone's doing."

She shifted uncomfortably. The moment she'd dreaded. Crossing an arm over her waist, she clutched the opposite elbow, her dangling foot twitching. "The past couple of years have been a little crazy."

Aunt Beth slurped a sip, smacked her lips, and rested the cup and saucer on her lap. "What do you mean?"

Dani studied her aunt. She seemed almost oblivious. Surely her mother . . . well, maybe not. "You knew Father died?"

Her aunt's eyes registered shock, and she brought a fluttering hand to her chest. "What?"

"I'm sorry. I thought Mother would have told you."

"No." The word came out in an agonized whisper.

Why hadn't her mother called? The two sisters might not be close, but a death in the family deserved at least a mention.

Aunt Beth's wise eyes probed her own. "It's a long story, Dani. One I'm not prepared to share. But I want you to know I've tried."

Dani gave a brief nod and peered out into the darkness. "I know. I gave up on trying to understand Mother a long time ago." And gave up on trying to earn her love.

A breeze stirred the leaves of the large red oak tree that anchored the corner of the porch, and the full moon shining behind the remaining clouds turned them a silvery white. "Your father was a wonderful man. If I'd known, I would've been there." Her aunt's lips pressed together in a sad smile. "Were you close to him?"

She shrugged. "At one time, I guess. He wanted me to take over his business, but I wanted to teach."

"Sounds painful."

"It was. Things were never the same between us after that." An ancient wound that would never heal, the hurt of his betrayal as raw as the day it happened. She searched the sky. The moon tried desperately to penetrate the clouds. How could a father completely cut off his own child just because her plan didn't match his own?

"But you enjoy teaching?"

"Very much."

Aunt Beth's face lit from within. "That's why I run a daycare. I love being around the kids."

Dani turned her head to hide the rush of tears that sprung to her eyes. Finally someone who understood, someone who got who she was.

"How'd Cecille take Daniel's death?"

Almost as if nothing had happened. "Better than expected." Her social schedule barely interrupted and on a cruise with her friends less than a month later. She rubbed the nubby fabric of her housecoat as a horse whinnied in the darkness.

"And your husband? How is he?"

A wave of hurt broke against her heart. Why was it still so difficult to speak the words? She met her aunt's gaze. "Richard was killed in a car accident a year ago."

Aunt Beth's face turned deathly white, more pale than the gray curls framing her face. "Oh, you poor child! I had no idea." Her voice thick with emotion, she scooted closer and embraced her.

A thousand needles pricked her eyes. What was wrong with her? She teared up at kind words, but felt only contempt for her dead husband? Would she ever be able to forgive him and move on?

Her aunt pulled away. The compassion in her eyes prodded Dani forward, but the words dammed up in her throat as the numbness returned. If only she could cry and grieve like other women who'd lost their husband.

The older woman searched her face. "There's more?"

Dani stared into the almost empty cup. How could she explain? "Let's just say my marriage wasn't a happy one."

Aunt Beth didn't speak, but a knowing look washed over her face.

What was she doing? Dani uncrossed her legs and looked away. She'd come to Miller's Creek to establish a relationship with her aunt, not scare her away. "I'm sorry. I didn't mean to burden you with my problems."

"That's what I'm here for. Have you talked about this with anyone?"

Talk about it? She chewed the inside of her cheek. This wasn't something you shared with colleagues in the teacher's lounge. Too embarrassing. Too painful.

Aunt Beth grabbed her hand. "Please let me help."

Fear chained the words inside. Not yet. It was too soon. She was tired of being hurt, tired of trusting only to be betrayed. "Maybe some other time." Dani drained the rest of the creamy liquid then forced a smile. "Did I tell you I'm thinking about leaving Dallas? Starting over?"

Her aunt's features clouded. "I understand about wanting to start over, but make sure you're not running away. Problems have a way of following you wherever you go."

"Sounds like you speak from experience."

"I do. Pray about it first."

She set her cup on the wicker table and released a half-laugh. "Prayer doesn't seem to help me much."

"What makes you say that?"

A bitter taste uncoiled in her mouth. "My prayers seem to go unnoticed."

"That's not true." Her aunt's sharpened words sliced the air.

"Then you must have more faith than I do." Not that it would take a lot.

Aunt Beth's eyebrows wrinkled in the center. "You don't believe in God?"

"I believe there is a God. I'm just not sure he cares about me. All I ever wanted was a home and family, but ..." Her throat clogged with a salty lump of tears.

Sorrow-filled pain flared in her aunt's eyes. "I know what you're feeling, Dani. Trust me, I've been there. Life's confusing and hard, but running away from God only makes it worse. He'll help you through this if you let Him."

"I wish I could believe it." She blinked against a rush of emotion.

"Do you blame God for what's happened?"

Would her aunt understand? Would God? "I guess in some ways I do. If He's God, then why doesn't He bring a stop to evil in the world?"

"There's not an easy answer to that question." The older woman pursed her lips and leaned forward to refill Dani's empty cup with the cream-colored liquid. "Not that it's any consolation, but people have been asking the same question for thousands of years."

Dani waited for her to elaborate.

Her aunt didn't let her down. "Ever heard of Job?"

She rotated toward her aunt and pulled one knee close to her chest, relieved the conversation had moved in a different direction. "The guy with all the patience?"

Aunt Beth's hearty laughter rang out in the still night. "You mean all the impatience." She silenced momentarily, a chorus of crickets filling in. "Oh, I guess he was patient in that he endured the horrible things God allowed in his life."

"Like what?"

"He lost his children and livestock, his wealth. He was even covered from head to toe with painful sores."

A shudder crept down her spine. "See? That's my point. If God loves us so much, why would He allow that to happen?"

"He had confidence in Job."

"I hope He never gets confidence in me." She muttered the words and bent down to retrieve the cup of hot chocolate as a giggle erupted from her aunt.

"At least the story ends on a happy note. God healed Job and restored his fortune."

Dani shook her head. "Still don't buy it."

"Why not?"

"Because the story doesn't explain why God allowed it to happen in the first place. Does He enjoy watching me suffer?"

"We've all suffered, Dani. You're not the only one." The words were soft, but firm. "Maybe this will help explain it. What would the world be like if everything was wonderful all the time? No bad weather, no sad events, no ugliness or pain. No sorrow."

Well, that was a no-brainer. "Perfect."

"Oh, really? You know any perfect people?"

Her eyebrows shot up. "No." What was Aunt Beth after?

"Exactly my point." Her aunt leaned closer. "Even if things were perfect, we'd mess it up because we're not. That's what happened at the beginning of time. Everything God made was good. Man's the one who messed it up, and we've been blaming God for it ever since."

A rounded edge of moon peeked above the wispy clouds. She sensed the wisdom in her aunt's words. "But why can't bad things just happen to bad people?"

"You ever watch a butterfly hatch?"

"Of course. We watch them hatch in science class every year." The memory of her students' fascination with the process brought a smile to Dani's face.

"You know what would happen if you cut open the cocoon so the butterfly didn't have to struggle so hard to get free?"

"It would never be strong enough to fly."

"Exactly." Her aunt looked skyward and Dani followed her gaze, the moon now completely clear of clouds. Aunt Beth rocked the swing, drawing her attention. "Victory and growth don't come through an easy life, but from struggle."

The words still rang in Dani's mind later that night as she crawled into bed, the crickets crooning their nighttime lullaby. What a day. She pulled the soft cotton sheet to her chin and snuggled into the feather pillow that smelled of fresh air and sunshine. Aunt Beth was right. Trouble did follow you wherever you went. The trip to Miller's Creek proved it. But maybe God had a reason for everything. If things hadn't fallen apart, she'd probably never have made the trip to Miller's Creek and wouldn't have met her aunt or J. C. or Steve. What if God had a bigger plan than she was aware of?

Steve's angry distance at dinner made its way into her thoughts, and her heart sank. She had to apologize. Whatever it took, she needed to make it right between them for Aunt Beth's sake. Besides that, she needed to start things off right between her and the people of the town. After all, they might be her new friends and neighbors.

Overwhelming joy billowed in her heart at the thought. All these years of longing for home. Had she finally found it in the back roads town of Miller's Creek? Already she felt an unexpected bond with her aunt, a connection she couldn't explain, family.

A soft patch of moonlight filtered through the window and laid a silvery blue streak across the chenille bedspread. Would a move to Miller's Creek work out? Dani flopped to her other side, folded an arm beneath her head, and pushed the question from her mind. She'd make it work. Any lifeline, even in small-town Texas, allowed her the one thing she'd been missing.

Hope.

⚛5⚛

The Problem with Miller's Creek

S teve smiled down at her, in that sweet place between slumber and awakening. Even after all these years, she still beguiled and enchanted him. Breathing in her light fragrance, he closed his eyes and reveled in the serene moment of bliss, his heart burgeoning with gratitude. No doubt about it—he was head over heels in love with his hometown!

Miller's Creek, named for the little river meandering through the heart of town, lay before him like a sleeping princess in the rosy glow of a new day. A sense of wonder arose in him as it often did when he viewed his hometown. From the perspective of the rocky bluff where he stood, the land looked like a giant patchwork quilt. Outside the town, squares of green showed where the wheat, coastal hay, and peas were planted, while rich chocolate brown dirt revealed the future location of soon-to-sprout peanuts, cotton, and maize. Barbed-wire fences with rough cedar posts provided the quilt's stitching.

The crisp nip to the morning air issued a warning that cold weather could still kill off the chance for fresh plums and peaches, and the homemade jams and jellies which always made their way into his pantry. Sorrow descended as he searched out the town square, bordered by the creek on one side and Main Street on the other. Except for City Hall, a couple of businesses, the church, post office, and firehouse, Miller's Creek had become a ghost town.

Not for much longer. Not if he could help it.

He squinted against the rising sun and surveyed the rolling hills and pasture land, his memory taking him back in time. In some ways, his childhood seemed liked yesterday. A time when Ledbetter's Furniture, Watson's Drugstore, and the Piggly Wiggly grocery store thrived in downtown Miller's Creek. Saturday afternoons had been spent at the picture show with Lauren and Clay, followed by a trip to Watson's for the best root beer float in the county.

Could the town be brought back to life or was it too late? Steve shifted his weight to his left leg and tugged the brim of his cowboy hat to bring it lower on his head. Times had changed. The train came through town back then, and brought all-important commerce with it. Even though the tracks and old depot building still remained, the cry of the train whistle and the bustle of business was nothing but a distant memory. The town's buildings now stood in disrepair, a daily reminder of what used to be.

His jaw tightened. He'd find a way to turn things around or die trying. Not just for the town or himself, but for the people. They clung by a wispy thin thread to a place which could no longer sustain them. *God, help me. I know You can make a way.*

He turned and strode to his truck, forcing his mind from the town's dilemma. Should he make his usual stop at Mama Beth's? The last thing he wanted was another run in with Dani, but he'd at least drop in to say "howdy" and grab a cup of coffee.

A few minutes later Steve arrived at Mama Beth's house, the fragrance of her flower garden hitting him as soon as he opened the pickup door. Perched in her usual spot on the front porch, she smiled when he approached, but the smile on her face did nothing to conceal the sadness in her eyes.

He frowned and leaned over to kiss her gray curls. "Morning. How we doing?"

"You're handsome as ever, but I'm getting older by the minute." A wry expression flattened her lips.

"Aren't we all?" As if he needed another reminder he was aging. He folded himself into the other rocker and stretched his legs out in front of him, his boots resting near the white porch railing.

"Isn't today your big meeting?"

"Yep." Conversation about the meeting with Brighton could wait. "You okay?"

"Fine."

The dark circles under her eyes told him otherwise.

"Would you quit worrying about me?" Her sideways scowl rebuked him. "You look a little tired yourself, you know. By the way, why were you so cranky last night? Even Dani noticed."

He lowered his head and chuckled. Leave it to Mama Beth to call him out on his bad behavior. "Where do you want me to start?"

"The beginning's usually a good place." The droll words rolled out in a monotone.

"Okay. First of all, I was starving to death. Second, I'd already had a bad experience with your niece. Third, I didn't expect to see her in your kitchen."

"And that put you in a foul mood?"

Steve rested his elbows on his knees before looking over at her. She wouldn't let him get by with anything. "And I was jealous, okay? I know I shouldn't have been, but I'm not used to sharing you with anyone else."

"So in other words, you were acting like a spoiled child."

He lifted one corner of his mouth in a wry grin. She'd never been one to mince words. "Yeah, I guess you could say that. Sorry. I'll try to do better."

A smile erupted on her face. "You know I love you."

Rising from the chair, he nodded. "Yeah, I know. I'm going in to get some coffee. Want some?"

"Good gracious, no. Already had enough to keep me awake 'til Christmas. Be quiet going in. Dani's still asleep."

The reminder of her niece brought him to a hurried halt. Maybe he should forget the coffee. With a second thought he shook his head. So what if he woke her up? Her problem, not his. He needed another cup.

The screen door squeaked when he let himself in the house, and he purposely let it slam. The smell of coffee greeted him as he entered the door. Nine o'clock in the morning and the woman was still asleep, obviously accustomed to a life of luxury and self-indulgence.

Back on the porch, he voiced his thoughts. "I'm surprised your niece is still sleeping." He couldn't stop the accusation that crept into his tone.

"Her name's Dani and I'd thank you to remember it."

He raised his eyebrows and let out a soft whistle.

"She's had a rough few months, and yesterday's ordeal wore her out." A troubled look darkened Mama Beth's blue eyes. "The part she told me was bad enough, but there's more she's not telling. On top of that, she blames God."

She twisted her head away from him, but not before he caught the emotion inscribed on her face.

Guilt?

Steve chewed on the information while the squeak of the rocking chairs filled the silence between them. How could he voice his doubts without offending her? Easy answer. He couldn't. "How long is she planning on staying?"

She hoisted her shoulders. "A few days. It's her Spring Break."

"Surely she's not going to stay the entire week?" Her glare sent him stumbling for an explanation. "I mean, there won't be much around here for a city woman to do."

"City woman?" The warning look she hurled his way made contact.

"Sorry. I meant not much for *Dani* to do." Steve sipped the rich black coffee. Touchy subject.

"She needs rest more than anything, but I told her I'd show her around town later today."

Why the interest in a country town that had all but dried up? Steve rubbed his chin. Would Dani know someone who could help him find investors? He summarily dismissed the thought. She was just a school teacher. "Why didn't you ever mention her?"

Mama Beth didn't look at him, but rolled her lips between her teeth before speaking, a pained expression creeping across her face. "No reason. Nothing I can explain anyway. Suffice it to say, there hasn't been a day in her life I haven't thought about her and prayed for her. I'm glad she finally came for a visit. I just hope it's not too late."

"Too late? Too late for what?" He studied her clamped jaw and changed direction with his questions. "You could've told me she was coming."

"I was afraid she'd change her mind at the last minute." She pelted out the words like spit wads.

A million questions rolled through his mind. Why had Dani waited so long to make contact with her aunt? And what happened in the past that was too painful for Mama Beth to talk about? All good questions, but she looked in no mood to answer. He checked his watch and pulled himself to a standing position. Time to get a move on. Brighton would be here soon, and it wouldn't hurt to look over the proposal one last time. He leaned down to plant a kiss on her cheek. "I'll be back later to check on you."

She clicked her tongue with mock disgust. "You don't need to check on me. When you going to find you a woman your own age?"

Steve laughed and clomped down the wooden steps. "Not 'til I find one as purty as you."

With her laughter ringing in his ears, he clicked the picket fence gate into place, hauled himself into the truck, and ran a hand across his mouth. Actually it wasn't a laughing matter. Women like Mama Beth were rare—kind, loving, selfless—everything he admired and wanted in a wife. No one measured up.

Only Lauren had come close with her country girl charm. He'd been convinced they'd marry some day, but that was before the accident, before his carelessness caused her death.

He swallowed, his Adam's apple frozen in his throat. He didn't deserve to find anyone else. And being single was much better than ending up like his parents, unhappily married to the wrong person. An Atlanta debutante with a Texas cow-poke made about as much sense as a pig in a tutu.

With a premeditated push, he dismissed his thoughts and began to whistle. God would have to plop a woman down in his lap if He meant for him to be married. Until then, he planned on running fast and hard in the opposite direction.

His cell phone rang out its tinny song and he flicked it open to view the number, a slow grin spreading across his face. He punched the talk button. "What do you want now?"

"Where in tarnation are you?" Wanda Cates, the city secretary, sounded panicky. "Did you forget the meeting?"

"Take it easy. I have the situation under control. The meeting's not 'til ten. I have plenty of time."

"Well, for your information, Mr. Big-Wig's already roaming the streets, poking his nose in every nook and cranny."

His stomach rolled. "I'll be there as quick as I can."

He clicked the phone shut and gripped the steering wheel. So much for having the situation under control. What was it Mama Beth always said? Something about pride before a fall. Well, this fall could affect the whole town. He gunned the motor and sped down the hill toward City Hall, praying Ernie wasn't nearby. Just wouldn't look right for the mayor to get a speeding ticket.

Steve found Brighton in downtown Miller's Creek, prowling the streets in his expensive black suit. He grimaced and glanced down at his own khakis and polo shirt. Casual wear to a man like Brighton. He steered the truck into a parking space, braked hard, and jumped out to greet his guest. "Mr. Brighton?"

"Yes?" The man spoke in a cultured voice and shook Steve's hand as if it were a smelly fish.

"Steve Miller. Sorry I wasn't here to welcome you, sir, but I wasn't expecting you 'til later."

The man elevated his nose. And sniffed.

Great. Just what he needed. Another city person looking down their nose at him and his town.

"It's part of my job to investigate potential investments for my clients, Mr. Miller."

Steve swallowed his smile, his mouth desert-dry. "Yes sir, of course. Can I show you around?"

"Actually, I think I've seen all there is to see." Brighton clipped his words with extra precision and clicked his ballpoint pen. He deposited the pen in the inside pocket of his jacket then pushed his wire-frame glasses up his nose with a well-manicured finger. "Quite honestly, I don't think my clients will be interested. You're aware of the amount of money it will take to renovate this town?"

"Yes sir. I've researched all the possibilities over the past several months. That's why I'd appreciate it if you'd let me show you around. Then we can go back to my office for the proposals."

A cynical twist curled one corner of Brighton's mouth, and he followed with a half-hearted nod. The man's sour expression left no doubt as to what he thought of Miller's Creek.

Steve unfurled the fingers which had bunched into fists. What was it with city people and their uppity ways? An image of Dani's sulky face moved to the front of his memory. He pushed the picture away and began his spiel. "Miller's Creek dates back to the early 1800's. Rumor has it Sam Houston himself traveled through here on a regular basis." He rattled off the speech he'd practiced for weeks. "The town grew by leaps and bounds when the train came through, but in the 1980's the train company canceled the route, and the population dropped. It's getting harder and harder for people to make a living." Steve purposely stopped in front of Granny's Kitchen, where the smell of the café's home-cooked breakfast still lingered.

Brighton's eyes snapped with impatience. "That's the story of thousands of small towns across the country, Mr. Miller. Why would my clients want to invest their money here?"

He squelched the flare of temper that roared inside him and struggled to keep the irritation out of his voice. "The plan is to restore the downtown area and bring in more retail. A few restaurants, antique stores, dress shops. Miller's Creek would make a great tourist attraction, sort of a nostalgic getaway." The disinterest on Brighton's face made his heart sink. This wasn't working the way he'd figured. "The people of Miller's Creek are the salt of the earth, Mr. Brighton. Hard-working folks who want to stay here and raise their families. We offer fresh air, home-grown crops, and a hometown feeling, something I think city folks are hungry for."

The man's eyes steeled and he crossed his arms across his chest. "Us city folks, as you call us, lead very busy lives where we live." His voice dripped indignation. "We have plenty of recreation and culture around us, and we rarely have time to make a visit to a dying back roads town."

Steve clenched his mouth into a smile he didn't feel. Brighton was giving him a city-sized headache. "Sorry if I offended you, sir. That wasn't my intention. We just need someone who's willing to help us get on our feet. Can't afford to increase taxes, these people are barely hanging on as it is."

"Then how will they repay the investors?" Brighton's over-plucked eyebrows appeared over the rim of his glasses. He shook his head. "Look, I appreciate what you're trying to do for this town. I sympathize with your predicament. But I cannot find one thing that I think would interest my clients."

"All I'm asking is for you to give it more consideration. I have proposals in my office. I'd appreciate it if you'd pass them on to your clients."

Brighton's face reddened and his lips clamped into a thin line, but he followed him to City Hall, his black businessman shoes clopping angrily against the sidewalk. He snatched the proposals from his hand with an impatient snort, then pivoted and scurried from the building without a word.

The slamming door sent Steve's heart hurtling to his stomach, where it landed with a fizz.

Wanda peered at him over the reading glasses perched at the end of her long nose. "I think Mr. Big Wig has too much starch in his shorts. If you ask me, he's not the kind of person we want to do business with anyway."

Steve drilled a black look her way, wanting to comment that he hadn't asked her. Instead he reigned in his temper and released his disappointment in a sigh. "Based on how things just went, I don't much think we'll have to worry about it."

This would be the perfect time to implement Plan B. If he had one.

❧6❧

Getting Acquainted

Dani forced open her eyelids and squinted at the sunlight streaming in through the windows. What time was it? She propped herself up on one elbow and labored to open her eyes wide enough to see the clock. 9:54! Her heart skipped a beat, and she bolted upright. That clock had to be wrong. She never slept late. Even on weekends. Come to think of it, she hadn't slept that well in months.

She listened. No traffic sounds. No impatient motorists with car horns blaring. In the tree outside her window, a mockingbird chirped out a song as if there were no tomorrow. Dani snuggled back into the cushioned comfort of her bed and let out a sigh of satisfaction. This she could get used to.

In the soft light of morning she viewed her surroundings. The sun painted the lacy curtains the color of peaches and spread the pattern onto the walls in dapples of light and lace. This room oozed comfort.

Home.

Dani shook herself. This was simply a charming country home in a charming country town. Anyone would feel this way. Outside, in the distance, a rooster crowed. The sound hauled her to a sitting position and plastered a smile across her face. A rooster! A sound she never heard in Dallas. She made a mental note to tell her students.

Dangling her feet over the edge of the bed, she allowed the weight of her legs to carry her to the floor. After a quick stretch, she donned her robe and slippers, peeked out the door, and listened. Good. No male voices in the house.

With Steve's image imprinted on her brain, guilt crept in like a tiger and gnawed at her. Would he forgive her surly behavior from yesterday? Surely he understood it wasn't personal. Just another one of her award-winning days. Maybe she'd have the opportunity to apologize later. An image of his moody expression at last night's dinner leapt to the front of her mind. On second thought, she'd rather run through hot coals. Barefoot.

She descended the stairs and drifted through the house that smelled like fresh-baked sugar cookies. Such a pleasant way to start the day. "Mama Beth?"

"I'm out here." Her aunt's voice sounded from beyond the screen door.

Dani moved to join Aunt Beth on the front porch. "Sorry, I didn't intend to sleep so late."

"Don't apologize. You obviously needed the rest." A kind smile and look of concern rested on the older woman's face.

"Yes, but I didn't come to sleep. I came to spend time with you."

"Want some breakfast?"

"No, thanks. Too close to lunch." She soaked in her surroundings—the porch swing, rose arbors, and picket fence. "I feel like I've gone back in time."

Her aunt's eyes danced. "Would you like the grand tour?"

Dani glanced down at her robe and slippers. "Yes, but should I dress first?"

"Nah." She swished a hand through the air. "Not like anyone will see you on my little country road."

"The neighbors—"

"The Thackers have already left for the morning. Trust me, you're fine."

They ambled down the wooden steps to the cobblestone pathway, and Dani sized up the house. Two-stories, with a tin roof and lacy gingerbread trim. Typical country farmhouse, German influence, most likely built in the late 1800's. Her father would be proud. His training stuck with her, even after all these years. The butter-colored paint with white and black accents made the house an easy sell in a good market. Tall windows stared back, wide-eyed and honest. And the porch issued an invitation to sit and linger, which was exactly what she longed to do. Linger. For the rest of her life.

Sparrows chattered from nearby trees as she followed Mama Beth to the flower beds beside the fence. Colorful blooms stood out in contrast against the white pickets, and a spring breeze started a dance among the flowers, wafting a sweet scent into the morning air. Dani closed her eyes and breathed it in, the familiar ache for home gripping her heart. "Your garden is lovely."

"Thanks. Steve built the fence."

Her curiosity spiked. "Do his parents still live here?"

"Yes, the Miller family operates the area's biggest ranch."

A sudden realization slammed into her. "Miller's Creek is named . . ."

". . . after an ancestor who founded the town," finished her aunt.

A queasy feeling plunked inside. The look on Steve's face when she offered him the money... She moved a hand to her abdomen and forced herself back to the conversation. "But he sees you like a mother?"

Mama Beth chuckled and smiled. "Honey, the whole town sees me that way."

No surprise. Her aunt defined motherhood. Dani sidled up next to her and engulfed her in a hug. "You'd make a wonderful mom. I'm surprised you never married and had a family of your own."

The smile on her aunt's face disappeared behind a curtain of darkness, and she bent low to tug at a weed. "Good gracious, these flower beds need work."

Dani administered a cognitive kick to her backside. When would she learn to keep her mouth shut? Her gaze meandered beyond the fence and across the road, where rolling pasture beckoned and promised peace. She drank it in like a thirsty child. What was happening to her? Was it possible to be seduced by a place?

"Aren't the wild flowers pretty?" Aunt Beth stood at her side. "Now it's the bluebonnets and Indian paintbrush. The buttercups and evening primrose will be next, followed by the wild foxglove and field daisies."

She could only nod, afraid of breaking the spell that had woven itself around her.

"So, you want to see Miller's Creek today?" Mama Beth's voice sounded hopeful.

"I'd love to." She stooped to sniff the fragrant flowers at her feet. "Quite honestly, I didn't know places like this still existed."

"Places like what?"

Like home. "You know, the quaint little country village, like something from a fairy tale."

Her aunt snickered and moved toward the porch. "It's interesting to see Miller's Creek through your eyes. Folks around here think the town is dying."

"Dying?"

"Let's just say the town's not what it used to be. Steve's determined to bring it back. He's meeting with an investor today."

Her interest skyrocketed. "Why?"

Mama Beth followed her up the porch steps. "To get money to renovate downtown Miller's Creek."

"Isn't that a job for the city officials?"

"Well, yes. Steve's the mayor."

A fist of surprise punched her in the gut, and she plopped down in the rocking chair. Ranch owner *and* mayor. Just wonderful. In less than a day's time she'd already alienated the most important person in town.

Steve scratched his head then let his hand drop to the old wooden desk. All morning long he'd racked his brain for another solution to the problem Miller's Creek faced, but nothing measured up to his original plan of finding outside investors. Maybe the answer would come when he wasn't trying so hard to find it.

His focus turned to Dani. Why couldn't he get the city woman out of his mind? Just about the time he had thoughts of her neatly tucked away, she elbowed her way back in. He laced his fingers behind his head and leaned back. Mama Beth mentioned she'd been through rough times, but it just didn't add up. Anyone who dressed like she did couldn't have it too rough. And that rock on her finger could sustain a third world country.

Steve's conscience niggled at him. He shouldn't have been so testy last night, but Mama Beth was gullible and loving, an easy target. She'd worked hard and lived simply to save her nest egg, and he wasn't about to sit back while some long-lost niece took advantage of her kindness.

He hefted a sigh and scooted his chair close to the desk. He'd just returned to work when Wanda poked her head around the door. "You coming out for lunch, or are you going to sit here and sulk?" Her nasal voice sliced the air.

Steve mustered a smile and continued to jot a reminder on a sticky note. "Want to grab a bite at Granny's?"

"Sorry, can't. Got a beauty shop appointment with Jolene."

A shiver raced down his backbone. Jolene Briscoe, the town hairstylist and busybody, married at least four times, now had her sights aimed at him. No thanks. If he needed a trim, he'd drive to Morganville. Besides, what kind of man wanted his hair cut at a place called Country Cutz and Curlz?

Wanda gave him the once-over through narrowed eyes. "If you ask me, you could use a trim yourself. Want me to make you an appointment?"

"No." Definitely not. He rose to his feet and shuffled the papers on his desk. Time for his escape. His lunch buddies might be able to help him come up with a plan for Miller's Creek. "I'm going to meet the old geezers for lunch at Granny's. After that I'll be at the ranch."

The sun on his face refreshed him and made him eager to get to the ranch to spend the rest of the day outside. There was always plenty to do this time of year between plowing, planting, and the calves and colts. Steve whistled as he made the short walk to Granny's Kitchen, operated by elderly identical twin sisters. Opal and Pearl Atwood were now affectionately known as the Grannies since no one in town could tell them apart. He entered the door to the tantalizing smell of southern-fried cooking, his mouth watering, and scanned the crowded room.

Lots of buzz already going on. As the town's only sit-down restaurant, Granny's ranked right behind Country Cutz & Curlz as the best place for gossip. If you didn't count B & B Hardware, that is. He waved, shook hands, and said his "hellos," as he made his way to the usual table at the back.

"Well, look who's here." Coot Sanders' voice blasted like a braying donkey in a tin barn. "The mayor finally arrived so we can ask him about that suit he was walking around town with this morning."

Steve sent him a dark frown. "For your information, I invited Mr. Brighton here to help us find investors." He pulled out a chair and eased onto the seat. "In case you hadn't noticed, things around here are starting to dry up and fall apart." Grabbing one of the fresh tortilla chips from a basket already on the table, he plunged it in the salsa and hoisted it to his mouth, the fresh taste of roasted tomatoes, peppers, and cilantro exploding on his tongue.

"Investors?" Otis Thacker scowled. "We don't need city people getting their sticky fingers all over our town."

Leave it to Otis to be the first naysayer. "Then what're we going to do?" He leaned back for one of the Grannies to pour his coffee, its aroma wafting to his nose.

"Don't know, but we need to solve it from the inside." Otis growled out the words in typical fashion.

J. C., who seldom offered an opinion about anything, spoke up. "Otis is right. The last thing we need is a group of outsiders telling us what to do."

The buzz in the restaurant increased suddenly, and Steve glanced toward the door to see Mama Beth and her niece enter. All decked out in her citified finery, Dani chatted with several people at the front. He gave his head a shake. Someone needed to give that woman lessons on how to dress in Miller's Creek.

Mama Beth made a bee-line for their table, her niece close behind. Dani shook each man's hand, except his. He crossed his arms and moved a finger to rest under his nose as he studied her. She was quite the politician.

"Thanks for helping me yesterday, gentlemen. I appreciate all you did." She handed out one of her brilliant smiles.

The men perked up, all speaking at once. "You're welcome."

"Ah, it was nothing."

"Glad to be of help."

What was wrong with them? Falling all over themselves like a bunch of coon-crazed hound dogs.

"Why don't you ladies join us?" bellowed Coot. He hooked his thumbs under his suspenders while J.C. placed two chairs from a nearby table beside Steve.

Dani settled into the seat next to his and flashed a generous grin. "Hi."

He leaned toward her. "Did you get caught up on your sleep?"

"Yes, thanks. Must be the fresh air."

"Must be." *Just don't get used to it, darlin'.*

"Our mayor was just about to explain why he thinks we need to bring in outside investors to help Miller's Creek." Coot's words echoed off the walls and directed everyone's attention their way.

Steve placed his coffee cup back in the saucer. "Thanks, Coot, but we'll save it for another time."

"Why?" Otis scowled, his sagging jowls reminiscent of a bulldog.

"There are ladies present. I'm sure they'd rather talk about something else."

Mama Beth wrinkled her forehead. "My goodness, Steve. What a chauvinistic thing to say."

"I'd love to hear your ideas." Dani popped a salsa-laden tortilla chip in her mouth with a crunch.

He cleared his throat and tried to ignore her. "I'm not trying to do anything against what the town wants. I just believe finding investors is our only feasible option. That's why I'm planning a town hall meeting. I want everyone's input."

Heads nodded in agreement. He sipped his coffee in quiet victory.

"Why would you even consider bringing in people who are going to want things done their way?" Dani's eyes bored into him. "There are other options you know."

Coffee spewed from his mouth, the rich taste suddenly bitter. Who did she think she was? "Other options?" He reached for a napkin and machine-gunned his words. "Care to elaborate?"

"Have you checked into grants and corporate donations?"

Her lightning-speed response nailed him to the wall. Was she deliberately trying to make him look like a fool? Every person's head rotated back toward him. "I've checked into several alternatives, Mrs. Davis."

"Dani." She spoke the word softly.

"Excuse me?"

"Dani, remember?" Her volume increased.

He glared at her. She'd just undermined his authority in front of influential members of the community. His gaze zipped around the table—all eyes expectantly fixed on him—and he had no witty comeback. Nada. Zippo.

"Corporate donations sound like a great idea to me." J. C. turned toward Dani, and his eyes glimmered with admiration. "You're a very smart young lady."

"Dani has a Business degree." Mama Beth chimed in, her face bright as an Easter sunrise. "She graduated with a double major in Education and Business. With honors."

The old geezers started their chatter again, all directed at Dani, whose cheeks had taken on a powdery pink hue. His blood simmered, but one look from Mama Beth silenced the words that congregated behind his teeth. Somehow he managed to speak with control. "I'd love to hear your ideas sometime, Mrs. Davis."

"Dani."

He forced a smile and nodded in mock compliance. "Dani."

Steve rejoiced when the conversation switched directions, but now everyone focused their attention on Dani, causing his irritation to mount. They bantered with her like they'd known her forever. For Pete's sake, she wasn't that likable!

After lunch she pushed her chair away from the table. "Sorry to break up all the fun, but Aunt Beth promised me a tour of the town." She gathered her things.

He sat up straighter. This little sightseeing expedition should prove interesting. If nothing else, it would be chance to get to know her better and find out what she was up to. Steve moved his chair out beside hers. "Mind if I come along?"

The raucous voices around the table quieted, and wavy lines etched Dani's forehead. "Not at all. I understand you have historic ties to Miller's Creek."

Impressive. The little lady did her homework. Now he just had to figure out why.

He started to stand just as Dani backed toward him. They collided, and she lost her balance. As she descended toward the floor, he grabbed her at the waist and pulled her toward him. She plopped onto his lap, her startled blue eyes and upturned nose inches from his.

"Hey Steve, it's not everyday a pretty girl lands in your lap!" Every head in the restaurant rotated their way as Coot's voice trumpeted. Laughter and cheers broke out.

Heat built under his collar as the scent of her flowery perfume lassoed its way around his head. "You okay?"

Dani nodded and licked her lips. In a second's time she lifted herself from his lap, her hands busy smoothing her skirt, her eyes averted.

He glanced at Mama Beth. Big mistake. An enigmatic smile played on her face, like a mother hen hatching an idea. Steve strode to the counter very much aware of what had just happened. A woman had fallen in his lap all right. But God had overlooked one tiny detail.

She was already married.

∽7∾

Problematic Plans

Dani inhaled the fragrant spring day and waited for Mama Beth while she examined the buildings in downtown Miller's Creek. Years of inspecting properties with her father enabled her to sniff out a good business opportunity, and this was it. The historic structures were two- and three-stories tall, a combination of brick and stone with amazing architectural detail, perfect for loft apartments and commercial space below.

Everything stacked up in favor of a move to Miller's Creek. Her brain whizzed along at rocket speed. She could invest in property, renovate it, and promote the town as a tourist attraction. Some of the older homes would make charming country inns. If she loaded the downtown area with antique shops and boutiques, women would drag their husbands and girlfriends to this place in droves. Her face crinkled into a satisfied grin. A perfect plan. It provided her with work, helped the town, and put her inheritance to good use.

She peered into the café through the plate glass window where Mama Beth and Steve stood, conversing at the checkout counter. What was it about Steve Miller that intrigued her, and more importantly, why? His comments at lunch verified his arrogance. Not exactly an endearing quality. Those cinnamon-colored eyes of his, rimmed by long dark lashes, could only be described one way. Heart-stopping. There was more, something she couldn't put her finger on. Perhaps it was the tender care he lavished on Mama Beth.

Steve held the door open for her aunt as they exited the building, then the three of them strolled down the street while he regaled them with snippets of Miller's Creek history. The longer he talked, the more convinced Dani became. This town fulfilled all her requirements as a place to start over. They rounded a corner, and a view of the town square brought her to a mesmerized standstill, delight bubbling inside. "Oh, how lovely!"

The scene spread out before her, straight from yesteryear. Ancient oak trees encircled a lacy gazebo, its gingerbread trim begging for fresh paint. Park benches stood guard from each corner of the square, one occupied by two men in overalls, and deep in conversation. She imagined the area lit with thousands of flickering Christmas lights, Santa and his elves stationed inside the gazebo, an excited line of children eager to share their dreams.

Steve's deep voice jostled her from her reverie. "You look like you're a million miles away."

Mama Beth spoke and turned their attention her way. "I'm going to park my carcass on this bench." She wheezed out the words, her face strained, her gaze focused on Steve. "Would you mind showing Dani around?"

His eyes latched on to the older woman, and lines of unease stretched across his forehead. "You okay?"

Her aunt held up a hand. "I'm fine. I just need to rest a minute."

"You're sure?"

"Yes, but I want Dani to see the creek."

Steve didn't seem convinced. "Okay. I'll take her. We won't be gone long."

His hesitation triggered uneasy feelings inside her. Did he dislike her that much, or was there something going on she didn't know?

He gripped her elbow and herded her away from the square, her short legs doing double time to keep up. The warmth of his fingers radiated through her skin and unsettled her nerves. Why was he going ninety miles an hour in a strolling speed zone? Something had to be wrong. "Is Mama Beth okay?"

"She hasn't been feeling too great." The stiff set of his jaw accentuated his brusque tone.

Not well? She'd seemed fine at the café. "Well, has she seen a doctor?"

"Yep, they're running tests."

"Tests? What kind of tes—?" His brooding look stopped her short. Never mind. She'd ask Mama Beth later.

Their brisk walk landed them in an undeveloped area, which among the two- and three-story buildings struck her as both out-of-place and charming. Sparsely wooded, it descended to a ravine, where the cheerful gurgle of running water sang out. "May we go over there?"

A slight smile softened the grim line of his lips. "It's just a creek."

No, it was more than just a creek. She envisioned a rustic bridge over the rock-lined water. "You forget I'm from the city." Dani marched on, lured by the musical babble. "If you need to go on, I understand. Don't worry about me. In Miller's Creek there's not much chance of me getting lost."

Instead he fell into step beside her, sending conflicting thoughts through her brain. Part of her wished he'd left her alone to explore, but she also felt oddly comforted by his presence. A structure across the creek caught her attention, and her heart soared. "An old train depot." The words came out in breathy wonder. "It would make a wonderful museum." Though it needed a little TLC, the clapboard siding and decorative wood trim pointed to a time when commerce depended on locomotives. She continued to stare, her mind popping with ideas.

"On the other side of the depot are the original train tracks." He pointed past the building. "We've discussed getting rid of them, but haven't done it yet."

She faced him in protest. "But it's part of the town's history. Why would you do that?"

His eyes, hooded by a squint against the blinding Texas sunlight, studied her like an amoeba under a microscope. She looked away and licked her lips. *Focus, Dani. Think about your plans.*

As if in deliberate opposition to her resolve, he leaned his lanky frame against an oak tree at the creek's edge and crossed his arms. "Tell me more about yourself, Dani. All I know is you're an elementary school teacher here to visit your aunt." His velvety voice made her insides squirm. Why did she suddenly feel like she was on trial?

"What do you want to know?"

He shrugged. "Nothing in particular. What grade do you teach?"

"First." Dani moved down the length of the creek. If he wanted to interrogate her, it would be on her terms, not his. With long strides, his legs took half as many steps as he followed to catch up. Surprisingly he said nothing else, but walked beside her in silence. She sneaked a peek from beneath her lashes. Maybe now would be the best time. "I want to apologize for my behavior yesterday." The words blurted from her mouth. "I'm not normally so short-tempered."

Steve's eyes closed to tiny slits. After several tense seconds, he spoke, his tone even. "Apology accepted. Guess I owe you one, too. I should've gone in with you at B & B. I just wasn't thinking straight."

She toyed with her next words before gathering the strength to say them. "I got the impression you were upset with me."

His brows raised, and then he lowered his head before returning an honest gaze. "I thought you were looking down your nose at Miller's Creek, and it made me mad."

Dani widened her eyes. "I'm sorry I gave you that impression. I love this town." She took in his skeptical expression then wandered closer to the water. "It has so much potential."

"Potential?" His tone darkened.

"Did I say something wrong?" She twisted her head to look at him.

A scowl resided on his face momentarily then disappeared. "Potential makes it sound like Miller's Creek is deficient. I know the town needs work. I just don't like hearing it from an outsider."

An outsider? Is that how he saw her? It sounded so exclusive. Like you had to be a member of the club. "I don't follow you."

He didn't respond right away, as if measuring his words. "I guess it's like your students."

"How so?"

"You're probably more aware of your students' shortcomings than anyone, right?"

"Yes." Was he about to take another swat at her teaching ability?

"Do you like it when another teacher points out one of your students' faults?"

The light in her brain flashed on. "No, I hate it. It makes me feel like a second-rate teacher." She leaned her back against a massive oak tree and rested one foot on the gnarled roots. "When I mentioned potential, I wasn't trying to put down Miller's Creek. I just have an eye for seeing things the way they could be." He twisted his lips to one side but didn't comment. Maybe a friendlier approach would work. "I'd like to know more about the town. Mama Beth told me you're the mayor."

"Yes, I am." He spoke the words in a chilled tone, leaving no doubt this was *his* town. "What do you want to know?"

"I'd love to hear more about your plan."

A smirk curled his lips at the corners. "Funny, I was about to say the same thing to you."

"Huh?"

"Your plan." His voice took on a hard edge. "You come here to visit an aunt you don't even know and start talking about potential like you have some kind of agenda. Sorry if I sound suspicious, but I care about this town and Mama Beth. If we're discussing plans, I think you should tell me yours first."

Her pulse braked to a momentary stop then hammered out a fiery cadence. "Excuse me for trying to express an interest in anything you have to say." She whirled about and marched toward the gazebo, turning her head to call out over her shoulder. "Oh, and you didn't come across as sounding suspicious. Just rude!"

The next day Steve loitered outside Miller's Creek Community Church and searched the crowd. He located Mama Beth and Dani to his left, surrounded by several people. The constant prick at his conscience hadn't subsided since yesterday's run-in with Dani. He'd blown it again. Big time. By now Mama Beth knew all about it, and he dreaded her tongue-lashing.

The two women broke away from the crowd and ambled toward the picnic tables nestled beside the creek amid a tall stand of oaks. This was his best chance to apologize. He fetched his sack lunch from the pickup, and with a few long steps, neared the table where the two picnicked with J. C. and Wanda. As he approached, Mama Beth waved and motioned for him to join them. Her eyes didn't scold like he'd feared, and he blew out a sigh of relief. Dani hadn't told her. The thought yanked at his brain. Why hadn't she mentioned it? It would serve him right for the way he treated her yesterday.

He walked to the end of the table where Dani sat and cleared his throat. "Okay if I sit here?"

"Sure." Her icy tone clipped the word short, and she scooted toward her aunt without a glance his way. Dani placed her lunch bag on the bench next to where he was about to sit. Between them.

His eyebrows raised a notch, and he sat to remove his sandwich from the sack. "Hi, y'all."

"Hey, boss." Wanda gave her typical two-finger mock salute.

J. C. smiled. "Hi, mayor. What's going on?"

He unwrapped his baloney sandwich and took a bite, all the while ogling Dani's piece of juicy fried chicken. It looked delectable, and that smell could make a grown man cry. Why hadn't he remembered to ask Mama Beth to bring some for him? His next thought ushered in a frown. Why hadn't she offered?

The conversation turned to the morning's worship service and the beautiful weather. Everyone joined in except Dani. She consumed her lunch without speaking then stuffed her trash in her lunch sack. "Excuse me."

"No problem." Steve slid down the seat to let her out. As she ambled away, his conscience knifed him again. She had every right to be mad. He watched as she deposited her sack in a trash can and strolled to the creek's edge.

"Dani's such nice girl, Mama Beth." Wanda talked and chewed at the same time. "What does her husband do?"

Mama Beth heaved a heavy sigh. "He did manage her father's company. Now I guess you might say he's out of the picture." She took a bite of chicken and looked away, blinking rapidly.

"Sorry to hear that," said Wanda.

"Don't be. From what Dani told me, it was for the best." Her voice held choked-back tears.

Steve looked toward the creek where Dani stood staring into the water, her shoulders slumped forward. It sounded like she'd had enough trouble without him lousing things up and adding to her burden. He let out an exasperated sigh, slammed his half-eaten sandwich down on the paper sack, and strode after her. Since the sandwich wasn't settling too well, he might as well eat crow. Underneath his boot a twig cracked. She whirled about at the sound, but as soon as she saw him, she flicked a disdainful glance and turned her back.

He gathered his courage. "Dani?"

"Yes?" She faced him, the hurt in her eyes twisting the knife lodged in his gut.

"I'm sorry about yesterday."

No response.

Steve took a shaky breath and let it out in an equally shaky voice. "Seems like every time we meet I need to apologize."

"You noticed." Her sideways look pinned him down. Then in an almost imperceptible move, her lips twitched.

A chuckle bubbled inside, impossible to hold back. "That's okay. Be smart-mouthed. It's what I deserve."

Her face blossomed into a wide grin. "You noticed that, too."

He leaned back his head and gave a belly laugh, glad to finally share a lighthearted moment with her. She joined in with a musical giggle that reminded him of tiny bells.

After the laughter abated, Dani sent him a kind smile. "Don't worry about it. I forgive you."

Her words impacted him with a force he didn't expect. She forgave so readily, unaware of the depths of his suspicion. Again he had the strange sensation her steady blue-eyed gaze sized him up accurately.

Dani tucked a stray curl hair behind her ear. "I know you have doubts about my reasons for being here, and I'm sorry for whatever I've done to give you a bad impression. You asked about my plans—"

"You don't have to explain."

She released a sigh and raised one hand. "I want to clarify things. I appreciate your concern for this town and for Mama Beth. You have every right to be protective. Please believe me when I say I have no plans to take advantage of my aunt or this town." Neither her eyes nor her words faltered.

Steve searched her face. No signs of dishonesty. "I believe you." The words were out of his mouth before he realized it.

The silence between them grew awkward, and she fidgeted. "Well, I think I'll take a walk. See you later."

He longed to tag along, but gut instinct told him no. His gaze followed her a moment, then he glanced toward the picnic table. J. C., Wanda, and Mama Beth leaned in close, their faces animated. Must be a serious discussion.

They continued to chatter as he neared the table, oblivious to his presence. Wanda's nasal voice grew excited. "Well if you ask me..." Her gaze came to rest on him. She sat ramrod straight and clamped her lips shut. When he crossed his arms and sent her a questioning look, she crammed a bite of peach pie in her mouth. The other two turned toward him, slack-jawed, then fumbled with their lunches. Their faces ranged from pale to pink.

Steve shook his head in mock disgust as they avoided his glare. The nosy old busybodies.

❈ 8 ❈

Tough Decisions

Shoving the rest of the clothes in her suitcase, Dani squished them down to tug on the zipper. That suitcase was going to have a blowout if she didn't learn to pack lighter.

"I'm not sure you moving here is a good idea." Mama Beth sat on the bed next to the suitcase, her face kind but sincere.

Dani jerked her head upward. "Why not?"

Her aunt leaned to one side, bringing a hand up to rub her forehead. "Don't get me wrong. I'd love for you to live closer. But all you've ever known is city life. Living in a small town is totally different."

"It can't be that different." She gave the zipper another tug, but it only budged a fraction of an inch.

"Don't be so sure." Mama Beth's face took on a dogged look. "You're used to having everything you want at your fingertips. Entertainment, shopping, even things you buy at a grocery store."

Dani tucked in a piece of stray clothing and inched the suitcase zipper along. "All that has lost its appeal. I want a simpler, slower-paced life."

Her aunt let out a hoot. "It's a simpler way of life all right. Probably too simple for you. And as for being slower-paced, I'm not sure you have the right idea. Life here is busy, but in a different way. It's just the world we live in."

A frustrated sigh puffed out her cheeks. Well, this conversation wasn't turning out the way she'd expected. Moving to Miller's Creek would give her the life she wanted, and in a round-about way would even help the town. Why couldn't her aunt understand? Her shoulders drooped. Maybe Mama Beth didn't want her either.

"This is just a place, like Dallas is a place. Neither one of them is really home. They're temporary dwellings." The older woman's eyes twinkled with life. "One of these days, when the right time comes, I plan on leaving this all behind." She panned a hand around the room.

Dani puckered her forehead. "I thought you liked it here."

"I do. In fact, I love it. There's no place on the planet I'd rather be."

All this talking in circles made her head hurt. She pressed a hand to her temple. "I still don't understand."

Mama Beth mashed down on the final corner of the suitcase and zipped it closed. "As much as I love this place, it doesn't compare to my final home. I'm talking about heaven."

Not that again. She sent her aunt a pointed stare. "I'm glad you have that kind of faith, but don't expect it from me."

"Just keep yourself open to the possibilities." Mama Beth grabbed her hand. "Now back to you moving to Miller's Creek. I'd love to have you, but make sure it's what you're supposed to do. Pray about it first."

Dani pulled her hand away, lugged the bulging suitcase to the floor, and plopped down on the bed beside her aunt, the ancient bed springs whining their complaint. "But I love Miller's Creek. The people here are wonderful."

Mama Beth nodded. "They are wonderful. Some of the best people I know. But they're still just people. They tend to be nosy and suspicious when it comes to outsiders."

"I haven't noticed that at all." Steve's suspicious eyes rose to the front of her memory, but she pushed the image down.

"No, because you're here on a visit. Are you sure you can handle people knowing every move you make?"

"It can't be that bad." She ran her fingers across the bumpy chenille bedspread then looked up at her aunt.

Mama Beth cocked an eyebrow. "Take my word for it. Small town news travels fast, and it's seldom accurate." She rested a hand on Dani's shoulder. "I love you, and I'm glad you came this week. You know you're welcome here anytime, but this isn't something to rush into. Talk it over with Cecille."

Dani's mouth turned down at the corners. Discuss it with her mother?

Only if it snowed in July.

Dani held her skirt down with both hands and glanced at the stormy sky while she accompanied her students to P. E. class. Only a few weeks since she'd left Miller's Creek, the frigid April wind now zipped through the sleeves of her blouse, causing chill bumps to pop up on her flesh. The indecisive Texas weather was a perfect match to her torn thoughts about Miller's Creek.

With a reminder to her class that good behavior during gym would earn them popcorn on Friday, she pivoted and scurried back to the main building. The cold steel handle produced a shiver in her as she yanked on the heavy door to enter the warmth of the red-brick school building. The door closed behind her with a hydraulic hiss and a thump.

Usually she rushed to her classroom, the few minutes of silence and solitude a welcome respite, but today she dawdled. Since Spring Break, everything reeked of loneliness. Even during the busiest times of the day, she found her thoughts turning to Miller's Creek. Was Mama Beth feeling better? Had Steve found a workable solution for the town?

She reluctantly entered the classroom, grabbed a can of air freshener to rid the room of sweaty body smells, and then plodded to the paper-strewn desk to search for her calendar. Four more weeks until the end of school, then she could return to the place that captured her heart. Dani lowered her body to the desk chair, dreaming of long summer days. A country song soundtrack began to play in her mind, and she envisioned herself dressed in her favorite jeans, picking wildflowers from the side of a country road. Friendly banter with her new friends echoed in her thoughts, their smiling faces bright with cheer as they worked together to rebuild the town.

The door opened and Jen poked in her head, her mousy brown hair swinging at her shoulders. "Hey, you avoiding me?"

Her friend's words grated today, but Dani mustered a half-smile. "Sorry. I've been swamped with papers to grade. I can't seem to make my brain focus."

Jen's tawny eyes took on understanding, and she strode toward the desk, one hand on her hip. "You're not still thinking about moving to Miller's Creek, are you?"

Irritation built inside, and her eyes burned. Why couldn't at least one person be on her side? "Yeah." Dani turned her head away, chewing the inside of her cheek, and busied her hands with a stack of papers.

Jen plopped onto a nearby table, her legs swinging. "You just need a break. It happens to me every year at this same time."

She pondered her friend's words. No. One brief two-month break wouldn't mend this brokenness. She needed more. "This is different."

"You're just working too hard." Jen hopped down from the table and approached the desk. "Why don't we catch a movie tonight? Might make you feel better."

"I can't. I promised Mother I'd go to her house for dinner." She twisted her mouth into a cynical grin. "Maybe that's why I'm in such a foul mood today. I dread Mother's reaction when I tell her I'm thinking about moving to Miller's Creek."

"That bad, huh?"

Dani shot her friend a look beneath raised eyebrows. "You know what she's like. That woman can turn a hangnail into an international crisis of epic proportions."

Her friend giggled. "True. I'm glad it's you and not me."

"Sure you don't want to join us?" She shuffled the papers then tapped them against the desk before looking at her friend.

Jen laid one finger against her cheek as if deep in thought. "Gee, I think I have papers to grade. Or was it a root canal?"

She managed a short laugh. "Very funny. I wouldn't want to go with me either."

Her friend checked her watch and hurried to the door. "I expect a full report tomorrow."

The harsh buzz of the school bell sounded, and Dani wandered to the window to watch her students as they lined up. A few minutes more and they'd be inside, clamoring for her attention. She released her exasperation in a soft sigh. Even the job she loved no longer brought joy or satisfaction.

Dani's jaw hinged open as she drove into the circular drive of her mother's large estate in North Dallas later that evening. Something was wrong. The once-sculpted lawn was shaggy and unkempt, and the lush flower beds contained more grass than flowers. What was going on? Mother prided herself on having the best of everything, the best lawn, the best house, the best life.

The best daughter.

She sucked in a deep breath to prepare for the guilt and anger her mother wielded like weapons, weapons that were probably about to be unleashed. Dani forced herself from the car, and trudged to the front door, her legs weighted with lead. She punched the doorbell.

A few seconds later the massive door opened, and her mother, clad in a blue silk pantsuit, placed her perfectly made-up cheek beside Dani's and kissed the air. "Hello, dear, how are you?"

"Fine." Her mother answering the door? Since when? "Where's Bridget?" The house smelled musty and unused.

"She asked for some time off to visit her grandchildren."

Fingers of unease tickled her spine. "And you didn't get a replacement?"

"It just didn't make sense." Her mother's heels tapped along the marble floor and echoed in the expansive foyer. Dani followed, her mind still trying to solve the puzzle.

As they traveled down the corridor, a foul odor wafted from the kitchen. "What died? And the yard's a mess."

"I hired another landscaper, but he quit on me. I haven't had time to hire a new one yet. Let's eat in the kitchen, shall we?"

"In the kitchen?" Cecille Hampton, queen of social graces, wanted to eat in the kitchen?

With dark cherry cabinets, top-of-the-line stainless steel appliances, and recessed lighting, the kitchen reminded her of a photo in a home decor magazine. It stood in sharp contrast to the cozy hominess of Mama Beth's country kitchen. Dani took in the Chinese take-out boxes resting on the chocolate-colored granite countertop. Well, that explained the smell.

"I've been so hungry for Chinese lately." Mother's voice reverberated in the spacious room, and she moved to fill a plate with food from the boxes. "I found this wonderful little place with the best food. You're absolutely going to adore it."

Her stomach lurched. Chinese food? Why couldn't Mother remember she hated Chinese food? She pinched her mouth closed, and following her mother's lead, fixed a plate. Intentionally keeping the helpings small, she seated herself at the island, but one nibble of the rubbery, over-salted noodles brought a grimace she couldn't conceal. With her chopsticks, she rearranged the food on her plate, entertaining thoughts of stopping for a burger and fries on the way home.

The clock on the facing wall ticked down the time while her mother rattled off her social schedule. Fifteen minutes. Thirty. Forty-five. Okay, time's up. Dani cleared her throat. "Guess what? I'm thinking about moving to Miller's Creek when the school year's over." She exhaled the words at a rapid pace then glanced tentatively at her mother.

Mother laid down the chopsticks with unnerving calm, an icy coldness creeping into her cat-like slit eyes. "That's the stupidest idea I've ever heard come out of your mouth, Danielle. Why would you want to live in a backwoods place like Miller's Creek? You don't belong there."

The words knifed into her. Belong? Had she ever belonged? She swallowed against the hurt stuck in her throat, tucked a strand of hair behind her ear, and crossed her legs. "I think it's time for a change. It'll be good for me." She nibbled the edge of her thumbnail, her dangling foot a-dance.

"Stop biting your nails. I used to live there, remember? There's nothing for you there." Mother waved a manicured hand through the air like a television game show model. "This is the life you're used to."

Dani shifted, her breath stuck in her throat. How could she explain her desire to find a place that felt like home? "Mother, you and Father were wonderful to me. You've provided me with so much. More than anyone could ask for . . ." She cringed under her mother's eagle-eyed stare.

"But?" A hard edge lined Mother's tone, and Dani's free ankle danced faster.

"I've never felt like I really belong in this family."

Mother's face paled, her eyes freezing into blue ice.

"I'm sorry, but it's the truth." Dani closed her eyes to shut out her mother's angry face. "I'm thirty-five years old. I want a place that feels like home before it's too late."

"And you think you'll find that in Miller's Creek? What do you suppose are the chances of meeting an available man your age in a small town?"

Steve's face popped into her mind unbidden. "I'm not in the market for a man, Mother. I'm looking for a home. There's a huge difference. Besides, Aunt Beth—"

"You know nothing about your aunt. She's not the angel you think she is." Her mother's eyes morphed from ice to fire. "Richard's been dead a year, and it's time to get over it. Howard Huff would propose in a heartbeat if you'd give him even the slightest bit of encouragement." Her mother's plate scraped against the counter as she yanked it up and stalked to the sink.

So Howard could marry her for her father's company the way Richard had? No thanks. She'd been down that road and had no plans for a return trip. Besides, he was twenty years older and had already been through three other wives. A shaky breath steadied her nerves. No more backing down. Mother needed to know the truth, no matter how painful. She momentarily nourished the anger and bitterness exploding inside her. Then she thought of Mama Beth and her goodness, her way of speaking hard truth with tenderness. "Mother, I love you."

"Then why are you doing this to me?" Mother faced her, her expression tortured. "You know I need you now more than ever."

"I'm not doing this to you. I'm doing it *for* me. I need to make a new life for myself, to be away from the memories."

"You can't leave Dallas. You're my only child." Tears formed in her eyes. "I can't believe you'd choose an aunt you barely know over your own mother."

The guilt-slivered words pierced her heart like always. She shook her head as a weary sigh escaped. "I'm not trying to end our relationship. I want us to work things out."

A relieved smile cascaded over her mother's face. She hurried over and wrapped her arms around Dani. "You had me so scared, darling. I couldn't bear it if you moved away."

Cold crept through her veins. Why didn't she get it? Dani pressed her lips together and extricated herself from her mother's grasp. "I'm still considering a move to Miller's Creek."

Mother's face turned livid except for a white ring around her perfectly applied lipstick. Then she launched into an angry tirade.

Clutching her purse, Dani outdistanced the angry words spewing from her mother's lips, her heart hammering against her ribs as she slammed the front door behind her. How was she supposed to choose between her mother and her dream?

⚘9⚘

Prompted to Pray

Steve planted his fists on his hips and viewed Mama Beth's garden. A nerve pulsated in his clenched jaw. When had she done the weeding? Would that woman never learn to listen to him? The aroma of homemade cookies floated to his nostrils as he stomped up the steps to the front door. "Mama Beth?"

"In here."

The screen door screeched out a welcome, and his boots clomped on the hardwood floors. He found her at the kitchen table, head propped on one hand. "I thought I told you I'd take care of the weeding."

"You did." She gazed at him with droopy eyes.

"Then why'd you do it?"

"I didn't. Dani did."

Her softly-spoken words jabbed his conscience, and Dani's large blue eyes and brilliant smile face flitted to his mind. That image seemed to make its way to his thoughts a lot here lately, and it displeased him to no end. He clamped his lips together and sauntered to the coffee pot to pour the dark brew into his travel mug. The fact that Dani wasn't above getting her fingers dirty somehow impressed him.

"She spent most of her Spring Break out there pulling weeds for me." Mama Beth's voice sounded forlorn, almost homesick.

He made his way back to the table, noted her weary expression, and planted a kiss on her soft curls. If her doctor didn't call soon, he'd make a phone call of his own. "Sorry I overreacted. You okay?"

"I guess so."

Steve blew out a breath and sat, the chair creaking beneath his weight. "Heard from the doctor yet?"

"No, but he's supposed to call sometime today."

He sipped the coffee and peered at her over the top of his cup. Since Dani had left, she'd done nothing but mope. His mug clunked against the wooden tabletop louder than intended. "Why are you so down in the dumps?"

A balking-mule look lurked in her eyes.

"I mean it, Mama Beth. What's going on?"

A compliant sigh whooshed from her. "Okay. I talked to Dani last night." Worried lines inched across her forehead. "I told you she's had a rough year."

"Yes, but you didn't give me any details." The oven timer buzzed, and she started to rise. Steve laid a hand on her arm. "You stay put. I'll get it." He stepped to the stove and removed the cookies. Mmm. Mama Beth's snicker doodles could add five pounds by the smell alone. Hopefully they'd be cool enough to sample before he had to leave.

He returned to his seat. "Okay, finish what you were saying."

"Dani lost her father and husband this past year."

"Lost as in they died?"

"Yes." Her eyes filled with tears and she swallowed. "And that's not the worst of it."

How much worse could it get? It'd be difficult to lose one person you loved. Two was almost unimaginable.

"Right before her husband's car accident, he asked Dani for a divorce. A woman he'd been seeing was killed in the wreck with him."

His stomach churned. Two deaths and a divorce? It sounded too horrible to be true.

"You'd never know what she's been through by looking at her, but she's hurting. I have to find a way to help." Her voice broke.

Indecision battered his insides. Only a calloused heart wouldn't be moved by the tragedy Dani had endured, but what if it wasn't true? If this was a scheme to play on Mama Beth's sympathy, it reeked. He rose to his feet, an odd mixture of guilt and resolve coursing through him. "There's something I need to do. I'll see you in the morning." He kissed her cheek, ignoring her puzzled frown as he exited the room.

An hour later, he fell back against the chair in his home office, staring at the computer, the glow from the screen the only light left in the room. It was all true. Daniel Hampton had died last February. Less than two months later, Richard Davis and Melissa Brown were killed in a car accident. Public records proved Dani's husband had filed for divorce a week before his death.

He rested an elbow on the desk and rubbed a hand across his forehead, his chest crushed beneath a weight of regret. Dani was a hurting soul, but instead of reaching out to her, he'd chosen to believe the worst. *God, forgive me. I judged her based on outward appearances. I assumed she was like Mom.*

Assumed she had an agenda.

Finishing off the last bite of brownie, Dani licked the crumbs from her fingers. While the comfort food hadn't erased the wound she felt from the latest run-in with Mother, at least it tasted heavenly.

She laid her cheek against the cool leather of the sofa in her Dallas townhome. A move to Miller's Creek sounded better with each passing day, but what if Jen was right? What if all she needed was a summer break? It had been a rough couple of years, enough to push anyone over the edge.

Dani grabbed her water bottle and took a swig, her hand shaking. Part of the water sloshed from her mouth, dribbling down her chin, and she swabbed it with her fingers. A rash decision would only lead to regret, but something had to give before she came apart at the seams.

What about spending only the summer in Miller's Creek? The idea tossed in her head. It would provide time away in a relaxing atmosphere, but wouldn't resolve the situation with Mother. She'd still be angry. Dani rolled her neck against the back cushion and stared at the ceiling. How was she supposed to know what to do?

Pray. Mama Beth said to pray. Well, it certainly couldn't hurt.

"God, I don't exactly know how to do this praying thing, but I'll do my best. Surely You understand this problem better than I do, so please help me know what I'm supposed to do." She waited, but nothing seemed different. If anything, the words bounced off the ceiling, leaving the room emptier than ever.

The shrill sound of the ringing phone shattered the silence, and she jumped. She brought a hand to her chest, her pulse sprinting. *Come on, Dani, get a grip.*

The phone shrilled a second time. Probably Mother calling with another guilt trip. She took in a cleansing breath and released it, then made her way to the phone as it rang again. "Hello?"

"Dani?" Mama Beth's voice sounded strained, almost urgent.

"Hi, is everything okay?"

A quiet nothing, then sobs.

Her heart pounding, she collapsed onto the desk chair. "What's wrong?" Her aunt's gut-wrenching cries spread raw terror throughout her body. *God, give me the strength to bear this, whatever it is.*

Several seconds elapsed before her aunt spoke. "I'm sorry. I didn't mean to break down like that."

"It's okay. Just tell me what's wrong."

From the other end came a half-whisper, half-sob. "I have a brain tumor."

∞10∞

Of Pain and Problems

Dani slammed on the brakes and swerved, her heart racing. The car spun around, careening out of control, as the tires squealed against the pavement. She squeezed her eyes shut and tensed in anticipation of the impact and sickening thud. It never came. Instead she came to a jerky stop and pried open her eyes to see the whitetail deer bounding away into darkness. She released a tremulous breath and unpeeled her fingers from the steering wheel, raising a trembling hand to her knotted shoulder muscles.

After several minutes of deep breathing, her pulse slowed, so she eased off the brake, straightened the tires, and resumed her journey to Miller's Creek. It would've been wiser to postpone the trip until tomorrow, but under the circumstances she couldn't. Not when Mama Beth needed her.

As she topped the hill, the streetlights of Miller's Creek came into view, stretched out beneath the star-studded Texas sky. Relief and joy washed over her. Lamps shone in the windows of cottages lining the road, as if to welcome her and light the way home. Her neck tingled. A Presence—a Someone—bigger, stronger, wiser, here with her. Without fully understanding why, she prayed.

God, I'm still trying to figure out who You are and what You want from me. I'm so scared for Mama Beth. I don't deserve Your help, but I'm asking for it all the same.

Her mind quieted and she waited. For what? An answer? Her waiting was replaced by an overwhelming urge to get to Mama Beth.

Dani sped down the darkened road toward the house and whipped the car into the driveway, the tires crunching the gravel. Without stopping for luggage, she opened the gate and sprinted to the front door, the screen door slamming behind her. "Mama Beth?" Panic elevated the pitch of her voice.

Her aunt's figure appeared in the doorway, silhouetted by the kitchen light. "Dani!"

She flew to her aunt's arms, tears already coursing down her cheeks. Had she found her only to lose her again?

Mama Beth rubbed her back and crooned in her ear. "Now, now, don't cry, child. I'm going to be okay." Her aunt smelled of vanilla, the scent of fresh-baked cookies and home.

Dani drew back with a shuddering sigh and swiped at her dampened cheeks. "I'm sorry. I came to comfort you, not the other way around." She sensed Steve's presence and turned to face him. He stood in the doorway, his dark, brooding gaze riveted on her in a way that weakened her knees and sent her nerves scurrying for shelter. "H-hello, Steve." She offered him a tentative smile.

"Hi."

One angst-filled syllable revealed the depth of his sorrow. His troubled eyes searched hers and she allowed it. What did he expect from her?

Mama Beth latched onto her arm. "Come on, you two, let's sit at the table. Dani, would you like some tea?"

"Yes, but I'll get it. You rest." She laid an arm across her aunt's shoulder and attempted to steer her to a chair.

"Nonsense," said Mama Beth, shrugging off her touch. "Steve's already been treating me like a china doll, and here you are doing the same. You'll sit at that table like you're told."

Dani opened her mouth to protest, but one look at her aunt's cemented expression changed her mind. A slight snickering sound drew her eyes to Steve, whose lips twisted in amusement. Her patience snapped as she pulled out a ladder-back chair and plopped into it. "What's so funny?"

"I'm just glad you're the one in trouble this time." His voice was a conspiratorial whisper.

That grin of his made it impossible to think. She bit back a smile then glimpsed Mama Beth headed their direction. "Shhh, she's coming."

"Here you go." Her aunt handed her the cup and positioned a bear-shaped bottle of honey on the table. "I remembered you take your tea with honey."

Dani swallowed against the lump in her throat, touched by her aunt's kindness. Mother couldn't even remember she hated Chinese food. She drizzled the honey into the liquid and stirred the tea, her spoon clinking against the side of the cup. "Okay, tell me exactly what the doctor said."

Mama Beth lowered herself to a chair, her face solemn. "The brain scan they did last week shows a mass. That's what's causing the headaches and dizzy spells."

Her big toe squirmed inside her shoe as she sipped the tea. A frightening question loomed in her mind and caused the honeyed sweetness in her stomach to sour. "Does he know whether . . . ?" The words stuck to the inside of her mouth and refused to budge.

"They won't know if it's malignant until after they operate." Steve's voice cracked.

Mama Beth slapped her fingertips against the table. "Both of you stop it! I'm going to be fine. There's no point in getting all worked up until we know something more definite."

Dani could only stare at her, wide-eyed. "How can you be so calm about this? Don't you . . ." She stopped, unable to put words to her thoughts.

Her aunt leaned close and covered her hand with her own. "I'm going to be okay no matter what happens. God's in control. If He means for me to live, I will. If not, I'm going home."

Home? Not hardly. What her aunt hinted at was death. Death might be a final home to those it swallowed, but to those in its wake it was nothing more than a thief who stole hope and left a big gaping hole. She blinked back tears and found her voice. "Have they set a date for the surgery?"

Steve and Mama Beth shared a look. "Next week in Dallas." Her aunt's voice carried a slight tremor.

The back of Dani's throat cinched. "Why so soon?"

Her aunt's face contorted, but she regained quick control. "They're concerned about the size of the tumor."

The words sucked oxygen from the room and Dani's breath came in gasps. *Air. She needed air.* Her chair scraped against the wooden floor as she pushed away from the table, and words tumbled out between trembling breaths. "I'm going after my things."

Her mind whirled on the trek to the car. This couldn't be happening. Was God going to take Mama Beth from her, too?

She managed to pop open the trunk before hard sobs racked her body and doubled her over. Footsteps crunched in the gravel beside her. Clutching both arms, she straightened, her mouth flooding with salty tears. Through watery eyes she made out a shape. Steve.

Dani cupped her face with the palms of her hands. "I can't lose her, too." The words sounded foreign and distant. As if they came from someone else.

The gap between them closed, and he pulled her to him, her head pressed to his chest as she clung to him and wept. He said nothing, made no sounds, but in his silence she sensed desperate sorrow. Finally her sobs subsided, and her sniffling shudders synchronized with the steady thump of his heart. How she longed to stay in the safe shelter of his strong arms, but she couldn't. Best not to allow herself to even travel that road. She pulled away and used the heels of her hands in a vain attempt to erase the evidence of her grief.

Steve reached into his back pocket and withdrew a folded handkerchief. With a gentle touch he tilted her face toward the moonlight and used the clean cloth to dab her tears. She watched him, enthralled, his jaw fashioned from granite, his mouth unmoving. But his eyes . . .

What was happening? *No!* She refused to let a man side-wind his way into her life again. Had she learned nothing from her empty marriage? Dani tore herself from his grasp and turned to the car trunk to gather her things. Two people caught up in sorrow—that's all this was.

"Can I carry something?" His husky voice disrupted her thoughts.

She handed him her suitcase without looking his way, then grabbed her book bag, slammed the trunk, and headed toward the stone walkway that lead to the house.

He stepped into her path, blocking her way, his eyes questioning. "You okay?"

Okay? After the news about Mama Beth? No, she wasn't okay, but it would be far too easy to get lost in his concern. She shrugged and focused her attention on a wispy cloud that drifted in front of the moon. "I don't know. What about you?"

"I want to be all right for Mama Beth's sake." His strangled words, raw with emotion, drew her gaze to his pain-etched face.

She understood that kind of pain. Had felt its intensity and dealt with it more in the past year than she cared to think about. Without warning something inside shifted, as the stone façade covering her heart cracked a little then burst open wide.

How long had it been since she'd felt anything other than numb, and for someone other than herself? Her long-lost compassion slashed wounds as it twisted through her body, and unbidden emotions surged to the surface. Feelings she wanted to forget.

This was thin ice she trod. *Dangerously thin.*

Steeling her determination, she squelched the feelings and stepped around him to make her way to the porch. As she passed, a single tear slipped down his cheek. Her breath hitched at the electrical jolt searing through her. Flinging her bag to the ground, she used her bare hand to wipe away the tear. Since when had his pain mattered more than her own?

The sorrow in his expression rippled hurt through her chest. Dani pulled her gaze away and stooped to pick up her books. She refused to get caught up in the emotion of a moonlit night. Refused to open her heart any further to a man she barely knew. Refused to let herself care too much.

He placed a hand on her arm, drawing her gaze to the troubled depths of his cinnamon eyes, his touch whispering against her skin. "Mama Beth told me you lost your father and husband last year." His eyes bored into her with an intensity that slashed through the last tenuous threads of her resolve. "I want you to know how sorry I am."

She faced him, grateful he'd been the one to bring it up. Best to explain now, upfront, to make sure he knew where she stood. "Thank you. I know you'll understand that right now I'm an emotional mess. I can't allow myself to—"

"I understand." His voice fell flat and soft and sad.

She ached to know what his tone implied, but it was too late. He'd already turned to go inside.

Two o'clock in the morning, and still no sleep.

Steve shut off the droning noise of the television and stared at the ceiling fan, his mind reeling with the events of the day. Amazing how a mere speck in the vast eternity of time could alter things forever.

Life could be so fickle. One minute you cruised along, able to take the speed bumps in the road, and the next minute you lay flat on your back on hot asphalt wondering what hit you. The news about Mama Beth crushed against him. *Why, God? Why her?* He groaned then wound both hands through his hair, fisting them. *Please let her be okay.*

Steve pulled himself to an upright position and opened the window to let in the fragrant night air and chirp of crickets. The image of Dani's tear-streaked face invaded his mind, and his throat constricted. Something about her sorrow touched him in a way he never expected. Her tears weren't just an act. She truly loved Mama Beth, loved her as much as he did.

Her gut-twisting words echoed in his head. *"I can't lose her, too."* He punched his pillow in frustration, and rolled onto his side, his chest tightening. Poor Dani. One more round of grief to add to her collection. Why had he ever doubted her?

God, forgive me. I have You, but I'm not sure she does. Help me weather this storm in a way that pleases You and helps her.

He puzzled over his feelings. Not since Lauren could he remember feeling this way about a woman, and it made no sense. Dani wasn't the kind of woman he was looking for. Not only was she from the city like his mother, but probably wasn't even a believer. His mind flashed to the scene in the moonlight. What had come over him? Why had he acted so foolishly? He attempted to fit the pieces together, but then remembered her final words.

It really didn't matter what he felt. Dani wasn't the least bit interested.

∞11∞

A Ride to the Ranch

Tears streamed unchecked down Dani's face as she rocked on the porch and stared off into the distance, a half-eaten piece of peanut butter pie on the wicker table beside her. How could God allow this to happen? Mama Beth believed in Him, and had most of her life. Is this how God repaid her faith?

The sound of a diesel engine approaching raised her head, and the gravel popped and crunched as Steve's shiny new Ford truck pulled into the driveway. Just great. She scrambled to wipe away tears, unready to face him, especially with the tell-tale signs of her prolonged crying jag. After last night's scene, she had no choice but to keep a cool distance between them. And he must never know how his kindness affected her.

He sauntered, cowboy-style, onto the porch, his hat pushed back on his head, an apology in his eyes. "Hi, lady."

She returned his greeting then looked away.

"Where's Mama Beth?" Steve reclined his lanky frame against the porch post and crossed his legs, his tone friendly.

"Napping." She forced her gaze on the flower beds, but his scrutiny put her already loaded nerves on high alert.

"She okay?"

Her aunt handled the situation better than anyone, a source of puzzlement to Dani. "You know how she is. She's acting the same as always."

A tender smile touched Steve's face and he shifted. One boot scraped against the wooden floor planks. "That woman's got unshakable faith."

"And for the life of me, I can't understand why!" The words shot out of her mouth as bitterness slithered inside and coiled around her heart. "How can she continue to trust in God when He let this happen?"

A descending whistle sounded from his mouth, his lips puckered. He adjusted his hat and directed his gaze her way. "Feel like going for a ride? Might clear your head."

She hugged her arms to her waist and hunched in the rocker, already feeling guilty about her outburst. So much for playing it cool. The thought of being alone with him made her uncomfortable, but she had to get away, even if only for a few minutes. "I'll be right back." After jotting a quick note to Mama Beth, she hurried out to the truck where Steve waited.

A few minutes later they were on the open road. Dani pressed the button to lower the window, and fresh air whooshed through the opening, tugging her curls from the band that held her hair in a pony tail. She'd have a mess to untangle later, but at this point, she didn't care. Instead she relished the cool wind in her face, blowing away her cares like tufts of silky fiber from a cottonwood tree.

Except for the soft music streaming from the radio, they rode in silence. Steve must have sensed her desire for peace, for he remained quiet. The warmth of the sun loosened her tense muscles, and the fresh air and beauty of the countryside eased her anguish. She closed her eyelids and leaned back. His suggestion to go for a ride had proved to be a good one. Her spirit calmed and righted itself, like a buoy after a storm. Now if she could only make sense of her growing attraction to the man beside her.

She glanced over at him. One elbow rested on the door, and his fingers cupped his chin in a thoughtful pose. His right arm draped the steering wheel. For the first time, she glimpsed the gray circles beneath his eyes. He hadn't slept well either. The realization tugged at her heart. Dani rolled up the window part way to close out the wind noise. "Thank you, Steve. This is just what I needed."

"Me, too." A half-smile curled his lips, his voice kind. "Feeling better?"

"Yes, thanks."

"Want to talk about it?"

Talk about it? Well, that was a first. Had a man ever asked her that question before? And no, she didn't want to talk about it. She couldn't, at least not without losing herself in the process.

Steve cleared his throat. "I'm really sorry for overstepping the boundaries last night. I can't explain what happened. I'm not usually—"

"Please." She held up a hand, the slow heat of embarrassment beginning its ascent from her neck to her face. "You don't have to apologize or explain."

In a move that surprised her, he brought the truck to a complete halt at the side of the road. "Look at me."

She swallowed hard, and tried to steel herself against whatever was about to come.

"Look at me, Dani."

Her chest rose and fell as she turned toward him.

Pure kindness and concern radiated from his features. "We both love Mama Beth, and we're going to be spending a lot of time together over the next few weeks. I can't do this without making things right between us. Besides, that woman has eagle eyes when it comes to this kind of stuff."

Dani nodded. He was right. Mama Beth would notice the strain between them. "Okay."

He glanced away, his jaw flexing. This was as hard for him as it was for her. After what seemed an eternity, he spoke. "I think both our feelings got confused last night because of the fear and concern we have for Mama Beth. That's the only way I know to explain it." His eyes met hers, and her stomach twisted.

This wasn't helping. Not one little bit. If anything it made it worse. She needed to hate him, not like him. Dani struggled for words, hoping she could form a coherent sentence. "I'm sure that's all it was."

"So are we good?"

She bobbed her head, grasping at anything to bring the uncomfortable topic to a close.

He continued to study her for one minute more, then reached up with his fingers and put the truck in gear.

Dani forced her attention from his hands to the wildflowers that dotted the sides of the road and smoothed her mussed curls. "Where are we going?"

"No where in particular. Somewhere you wanted to go?"

Would any place hold the peace she desired? She stared ahead, focused on nothing. "Some place peaceful where I can forget this world and its problems."

"Sounds like heaven to me."

Dani turned her head away. Not the God stuff again. She rubbed her left arm and watched the passing landscape out the side window.

"Best I can do is a place not too far from here." A few minutes later they reached a country lane and Steve put the truck in park to open a gate made from cedar posts and barbed wire. Back in the truck, he inched along the bumpy overgrown path. The wispy leaves from gnarled mesquite trees pirouetted in the spring breeze, while a bull frog croaked in the distance.

The rutted ride bounced her around on the seat. She gripped the arm rest and took in the surroundings. A place to forget the rest of the world existed, beautiful and serene, private and secluded. "This is part of your ranch?"

"Yep, the original homestead. Part of the old chimney is still standing over there." He nodded with his chin toward a pile of stones. "Back then they had to settle close to water. The same creek that runs through town cuts through this corner of the ranch." Steve pointed past a line of live oaks. "We're not far from Mama Beth's. Her house is just on the other side of the creek and across the pasture." The pickup rolled to a stop underneath a gigantic oak.

Dani hopped out of the truck and ambled toward the old oak tree, so large her arms wouldn't fit halfway around. Steve followed. She trailed her fingers over the rough bark and peered up through the tree's sun-dappled branches. "This oak must be hundreds of years old."

"I like to believe my great-great-grandfather saw this tree." A hint of pride played about his lips.

She gauged her emotions. His connection with this place and its past made her envious. What would it feel like to have such a sense of home? A sudden realization hit. He had honored her by sharing this hallowed place—this part of himself—with her.

Dani glanced at him. His broad shoulders slumped forward as if burdened by concern. Concern for Mama Beth for sure, but what else? She mentally retraced their conversation. Had her angry words about God offended him? "I'm sorry for what I said about God earlier. It's just—"

"Don't apologize for being honest. I understand and I think God does, too. He loves us even when we question His goodness."

She let the comment pass, though his words cut into her like a knife. Instead she turned the conversation toward her aunt. "Thanks for taking care of Mama Beth. I can tell how much she means to you."

He squinted across the tree-lined horizon, his eyes shaded by the brim of his cowboy hat. "She's like a mother to me." His voice wavered then evened out, and he pivoted to face her. "I know you love her, too."

More than she ever believed possible. She ducked her head to battle tears, while the dark dirt at her feet coiled its earthy scent to her nose. Unsure of what to do or say, she followed him as he wandered to a grove of trees. Just beyond, the creek gurgled as it snaked along.

She perched on a boulder at the water's edge, and Steve scooted in beside her. His arm accidentally brushed against hers, and she fought the desire to lean against his strength. Instead she rested her back against the sunny warmth of the rock. "You're so lucky to have a place like this. If it belonged to me, I'd build a house near here and use it as a hideaway."

He frowned and tossed a pebble toward the water, where it landed with a *plip*. "Never been a big believer in luck." Another pebble flicked from his hand, followed by another *plip*. "I'm not lucky, I'm blessed."

Blessed? A snarling darkness spun in her brain. She rubbed her forehead then let her hand fall to her lap. "Where does that leave me? Unblessed?"

He looked at her sadly then reached over to tuck an escaped curl behind her ear. "You're blessed too. You just don't know it."

Her insides turned to acid. Yeah, blessed with trouble. "You know nothing about me."

If her scathing remark bothered him, he didn't let it show. "Only what Mama Beth told me. But I know people love you, and that's a blessing."

She stared into the bubbling water and pondered his words. It was true. Her students loved her. Mama Beth loved her. Even Mother loved her, in her own controlling way.

"And God loves you." Though softly spoken, his tone remained steady and even.

Her head snapped around, anger oozing from her like blood from an open wound. "If He loves me, then why have I been to hell and back? Why did He let me develop this relationship with Mama Beth, to find out she's sick and might . . . ?" The question lumped in her throat, and she pinched her lips to battle the rivers of emotion that threatened to spill. *Why, God?*

Steve rested a hand on her bare arm. "I don't have all the answers, but I know He has a reason for everything. Our job isn't to figure out why. Our job is to trust Him."

"Sorry, but I don't have that much faith." She ground out the comment and yanked at her pony tail. Where did faith come from anyway? And how was she supposed to find it?

His arrowed words broke into her thoughts. "You ever stop to think that maybe God brought Mama Beth into your life for her benefit and not yours?"

The question slammed against Dani full-force and her heart dropped to her stomach. Why had she assumed this was about her? The answer came quickly, searing her conscience. Because she was small and selfish, that's why. The thought brought with it illumination. Somewhere along the way she'd let life's tragedies cause her to narrow her focus until it centered on her and her alone. She turned to face him.

He peered at her from under his hat, his rusty brown eyes gentle. "Sorry if that sounded a bit harsh, but sometimes it helps to view things from a different perspective."

How many times had she given her students the same advice? "I always tell my kids to consider other people's feelings. Guess I need to heed my own words."

A wide grin lit his handsome face. "You love teaching, don't you?"

"Is it that obvious?" The shimmer in his eyes made her pulse race, like he understood her better than anyone ever had.

"Every time you mention your kids your face lights up just like Christmas."

Dani rolled her bottom lip between her teeth and lowered her head. His comment pleased her more than she wanted to admit and much more than she wanted him to realize. A shot of fear rumbled through her veins. She was prepared to lose her heart to Mama Beth and Miller's Creek, but not him. Within, part of the carefully constructed wall around her heart crumbled, and she felt powerless to stop it.

A hushed tranquility descended as nightfall drew nearer. Blue jays fussed in a nearby cedar bush, its pungent scent carried on the evening breeze. A mutual understanding, a connection, a bond—she wasn't sure what to call it—rested between them. Its power swelled inside her and rammed against another part of the wall.

Steve rose a few minutes later, extending a hand to help her up. The gentleness of his touch tempted her to toss aside the distance she intended to keep between them. He must have felt it too, because he jerked his hand away quickly and pressed his lips into a firm line. She took one last glance around. The magic of this place was getting to her, somehow weaving a spell, luring her like the ancient sirens of the sea. Steve had already outdistanced her by several steps, so she turned and hurried to catch up with him. They strolled in silence, side by side to the truck, while a sliver of the sun painted streaks of pink and orange on the underside of the clouds.

Later, as they pulled onto the main road, Dani spoke the question that burned in her brain. "How are you so convinced God loves us?"

He smiled and shrugged. "I just am."

Could she trust her thoughts to him? Instinctively, she sensed she could. "I want to believe. But every time I think I'm close, something else happens to make me doubt."

"Are you angry at God?"

An edge of hostility returned. "Don't I have the right to be?" Surely someone as powerful as God could have prevented what she'd endured.

"I can't answer that, but bad things aren't God's fault. It's just a part of the world we live in."

The same answer Mama Beth had given. All the way to the house, his words resounded in her thoughts. As they drove into the driveway, he motioned across the road. "Those trees on the far side of the pasture are the back of the creek. The pasture belongs to the ranch. Feel free to walk there anytime."

"Thank you." She wet her lips. "And thanks for listening. I have a lot I'm trying to figure out right now."

"I know you do." His tender touch on her shoulder spread its warmth through her battered emotions, his voice gentle.

She looked at him. Hopefully the pain in her heart wasn't mirrored in her eyes.

An emotion she couldn't identify flared in his expression, and he wrenched his hand and head away. A moment later, he turned back to her, his face controlled by cool indifference. "We'd better get inside before Mama Beth starts to worry."

Though his indifference stung, she understood. It was for the best.

The aroma of fried chicken met them at the door, inviting them to the kitchen. Mama Beth moved slower than normal, her face a pasty shade of gray. Dani quickly joined her in preparation for the meal, but her tangled thoughts allowed no peace, and tears parked just below the surface. It took every ounce of strength she could muster to maintain her composure, and she struggled to squelch the emotions that lay less than a pinprick away.

At supper she chose to listen to the conversation between Steve and Mama Beth instead of joining in. She watched the two, mesmerized as Steve hovered over her aunt like a guardian angel, bringing her whatever she needed. The tenderness with which he treated her aunt produced a stab of envy. How nice it must be to feel so loved and protected. Dani fiddled with the food on her plate. Tonight even Mama Beth's delicious home-cooked food seemed tasteless.

"Dani." Her aunt's half-shout captured her attention.

She started. "Hmm? I'm sorry. Were you talking to me?"

"I asked if you were okay. You've hardly touched your supper." Mama Beth's eyebrows pulled up in the center.

"I guess I'm just tired." She laid her fork down on her plate, the fatigue from lack of sleep attacking in full force. "If it's okay, I think I'll go to bed early."

Her aunt frowned. "Of course. Is something bothering you?"

The burn in Dani's eyes moved to her throat. "I just have a lot on my mind." She kissed her aunt then stood, careful not to look at Steve. One glimpse of the compassion in his eyes and she'd be lost. She felt his gaze follow her up the stairs.

Several minutes later, she lay in bed listening to the crickets sing and tried to make sense of Steve's words. Whatever it took, she had to move past her selfishness and this overwhelming attraction she felt toward Steve, different from any other feelings she'd known. Friendship, respect, and admiration all rolled into one.

God, help me. I believe you exist. You're in control of everything, even when I don't understand. I want to believe You love me, but I don't know how. Show me. And please make Mama Beth well.

A few minutes later, Dani sank in the soft arms of slumber and dreamed of an ancient oak tree, a gurgling creek, and kind eyes the color of cinnamon.

Steve reclined against the patio chair and fixed his attention on the starry sky that stretched before him like silver glitter sprinkled on black velvet. His thoughts turned to Dani, the pain he'd seen on her face daggering his heart.

He'd never seen a person with their faith so utterly shattered. She needed to know God, to know His peace, to believe He loved her.

Lord, help her to believe. She needs You.

She needs you, too.

He sighed, his heart heavy. *Lord, I don't know how to help.*

Again the voice sounded, the promise he'd heard many times before. ***I am with you.***

Understanding dawned, and he savored the comfort of God's presence. The Lord had created the majesty of the vast expanse before him and He was still involved in His creation. Only an Almighty God could take the threads of their lives and weave them together into such a stunning tapestry. Like the backside of Mama Beth's needlework, the handiwork of heaven sometimes appeared tangled and messy from earth's perspective.

He laid his head back as a laugh of pure joy gurgled from his throat. Now he knew what to tell Dani. God never made mistakes. He made masterpieces. It just took time for a masterpiece to unfold.

෨12ෂ

Waiting

A low murmur of voices hummed inside the Baylor Hospital surgical waiting room where Steve hunkered down in one of the cushioned chairs and observed others awaiting news of their loved ones. How could one room harbor such concern and grief without the walls collapsing beneath the pressure? He scanned the area for any sign of Dani. She'd taken off for another round of nervous pacing half an hour ago and still hadn't returned. Her actions worried him. Refusing breakfast and lunch, her antsy behavior all afternoon revealed how much the ordeal of the past week had affected her.

He made a move to stand and search for her when she thrust a cold can of pop under his nose. "I hope this is okay. I wasn't sure what you liked, so I just guessed."

Steve smiled his gratitude and accepted the can, then popped the lid and poured the cool liquid down his parched throat. He'd promised Mama Beth he'd take care of Dani during the surgery, and here she was taking care of him instead. Something he could easily get used to.

Dani plopped down next to him and slouched in her seat, eyes closed. The vulnerability on her face touched him. He jerked his head away. How in the dickens was he supposed to take care of her and stay disinterested at the same time?

A man's voice called out from the waiting room door. "Dani Davis?"

She jumped from her seat and scurried to the door. With long strides, he arrived right behind her and captured a deep breath to steady his nerves.

Dr. Gray made eye contact while he spoke. "Your aunt made it through surgery just fine. She'll be in recovery for a few hours—"

"And the tumor?" Lines of worry creased the area around her eyes.

The surgeon hesitated, his expression grim. "Larger than expected, but I think we got it. Until we receive the pathology reports, we won't know if it's malignant."

Dani's eyes glazed, and by the look on her ashen face, appeared ready to topple. Steve braced her up with one arm around her shoulders and addressed Dr. Gray. "Do we have time to grab a bite to eat?"

"Certainly." The surgeon nodded with a reassuring smile, his voice friendly.

Her anxious gaze followed the doctor as he hustled away, and she started after him. Steve grabbed her arm and pulled her back. "Sorry Goldilocks, you're coming with me. Dallas is your neck of the woods, and I'm hungry as a bear. Where's a good place to eat?"

She opened her mouth, most likely to protest, but he held a finger to her lips. "Shh. No arguments. You haven't eaten all day." The tactic worked better than expected. She remained quiet all the way to the parking garage.

Steve rubbed his finger against his jeans as they made their way to his F-350 pickup, hoping to erase the feel of her lips, but by the time he'd guided Dani to the passenger side and helped her into the seat, all he'd succeeded in doing was removing a layer of skin. He tried to squelch the anxiety rising inside him. Now for the hard part. Driving in Dallas. Would he never rid himself of the haunting memories? The crunch of metal, the endless spinning and turning, Lauren's screams followed by a deathly silence, the image of her crumpled body. He caught his breath and rubbed the area between his eyes in an attempt to erase the scene from his mind.

"Are you just going to sit there? I thought you wanted food." Dani's voice brought him back to the present.

Steve glanced at her as he started the car. She needed protein and rest, and soon. "Where's a good steakhouse?"

"The West End. It's nearby."

He drove to the parking garage exit and paid the fee, then turned to her as he raised the window. "I'm assuming this place we're going to is west of here?"

Her eyes held questions. "Southwest. Take a right."

Forcing his way into bumper-to-bumper traffic, he proceeded to the light. Dani had zoned out, staring into space as if she were focused on another dimension. "Where to now?"

She heaved herself to an upright position and emitted a sigh. "You need to be in the left turn lane."

"Well, it's too late for that." He viewed the sign that said "Right Lane Must Turn Right" and let out a snort. A little more notice would've been nice.

After inching along and several missed turns, Steve gripped the steering wheel and grit his teeth. "Arrrggh! I hate this!" His voice echoed in the cab, and he shot Dani an apologetic look. "Sorry. I'm not used to this traffic." Hated it would be more accurate.

"Have you never driven in Dallas?" Her tone held disbelief.

"Once a long time ago, and I promised I'd never do it again."

"Bad experience, huh?"

"You might say that." He flipped the blinker to the up position and checked the rear-view mirror for a break in the traffic.

"Car accident?"

Steve glanced at her, her blue eyes revealing a knowing compassion. "Yeah, a friend of mine was killed. I've avoided Dallas ever since."

"Why didn't you say something?" She pointed to a parking lot on the right. "Pull in here and I'll take over."

He let out a relieved breath. She didn't have to ask twice.

A few minutes later, Dani zipped into a parking space at the West End district and handed him the keys. She'd handled the large truck like she'd been driving it her entire life. Pretty heady stuff for a country boy like him. They wended their way along the oak-lined sidewalk toward the restaurant, a rowdy combination of country music and laughter ringing in the air. The whining cry of a siren and the rattle of the DART train sounded in the background. Steve watched in amusement as pigeons bobble-headed away from his boots, but refused to take flight, eager to snare a stray crumb. A mixture of delicious smells drifted past his nose, and his stomach gurgled in anticipation.

After a brief walk, she led them into an upscale steakhouse and secured a comfortable booth. Symbols of Texas decked the walls of the restaurant she'd chosen—windmills, cattle horns, even an old barn front—all things dear to his Texas heart. At first Dani seemed reluctant to talk, but he finally managed to draw her into conversation. By the time their food arrived they'd almost managed to solve the world's problems, at least theoretically.

He sawed off a piece of the juicy steak, popped it in his mouth, and savored the smoky flavor as it rolled down his tongue. One glance across the table caused a grin to spread across his face. Dani crammed in three or four pieces of food at a time, chewed, and followed each bite with a swig of iced tea. For an itty-bitty city gal, she could pack the food away. And fast.

She met his stare. "What?"

"Slow down. We have a few hours, remember?"

Giggling, she laid down her silverware. "Sorry. It's a teacher thing."

"And walking fast. And talking fast."

She held up both hands. "Busted." Her blue eyes flashed merriment in a way he found utterly charming.

"Do you not get very long for lunch?" He relished another bite of the tender T-bone.

"Well, supposedly I have a full thirty minutes, but by the time I take my class to the restroom and cafeteria, get the room set for the next subject, and pick up the kids from lunch, it's more like ten minutes." She rattled out the words, using her hands for emphasis.

Her lunch routine made his hour with Mama Beth or the old geezers sound like a luxury. "Must be rough."

Dani nodded and resumed eating, this time at a slower pace. "Teaching's difficult work, but it also has its rewards."

"Such as?"

Her face lit and revealed the passion she felt for her work. In between bites of food and gestures with her fork, she launched into humorous stories about her kids. Intent on every word, Steve watched her, completely captivated.

". . . anyway, having a child grasp a concept they've struggled with, or present you a flower and say they love you is better than all the gold in the world."

He dropped his gaze, swift shame washing over him. She possessed a beauty beyond mere outward appearance. How could he have been so wrong about her? He raised his head at her sudden silence and noticed tears pooling in her eyes. "You okay?"

"Sorry." Dani waved a hand in front of her face, her tone strangled. "I'm not usually so emotional, just when I'm really, really tired."

"It's okay. No apology needed." Maybe he should change the subject. "Did you have any trouble getting off work for Mama Beth's surgery?"

She didn't answer right away, but chewed her food deliberately and swallowed. Almost as if she wanted to avoid answering. When at last she raised her head to meet his gaze, her eyes glittered with a mixture of conviction and dogged determination. "I've asked for a leave of absence."

"Why?" He frowned and swiped the cloth napkin across his mouth, his tone more demanding than intended.

"To take care of Mama Beth."

"You don't have to do that. There are plenty of people in Miller's Creek willing to help."

"I know I don't have to, but I'm going to. People in Miller's Creek will just have to understand."

A short laugh rushed from his mouth. "You don't know them like I do."

"I'll be the one to take care of her. I'm her family." Her chin hoisted.

Steve checked his anger, too tired to argue that he was family, too, at least in a roundabout way. "Speaking of family, I'm surprised your mom hasn't been to the hospital yet."

A cloud of emotions swirled across her face.

He paused, steak-laden fork suspended in mid-air. "Sorry if I stepped into forbidden territory."

"Nothing my mother does surprises me anymore." She stabbed furiously at her salad, her voice dripping with cynicism.

His eyebrows hitched. He'd struck a sore spot.

❖   ❖   ❖

Later that evening, Steve awakened in Mama Beth's hospital room, the television still set to the same sports channel. Scratching his cheek, he leaned forward and blinked. How long had he been asleep? He rose to his feet, feeling old and creaky, and stumbled to the bed where Dani maintained her silent vigil with drooping eyes. Mama Beth slept, her head wrapped in bandages, gray curls peeking from underneath. The machine on the opposite side of the bed emitted a soft beep, and he monitored the digital read-out. "How is she?"

"About the same." She raised fingers to stifle a yawn, her tone groggy. "Every once in a while she stirs, but then slips back under." Her forehead creased.

"She's going to be okay. For right now, sleep's the best thing for her." He placed a hand on her shoulder, and Dani leaned into his touch. She had to be exhausted.

"I'm so anxious to hear her voice I could scream." Weary concern bathed her face.

Hearing Mama Beth speak would be a relief to both of them. He checked the clock. Midnight? No wonder Dani teetered on the verge of collapse. "Sorry I slept so long."

"Don't be. I'm glad you were able to rest."

"Speaking of rest, you've been running non-stop since they let us in here."

She blasted him with a Mama Beth look. "It's not going to work, so don't even go there. I am *not* budging from this spot."

He let out a soft chuckle. The woman had a stubborn streak as big as Texas. "If you intend to take care of her while she recovers, you'd best take care of yourself."

"But I need to be here when she opens her eyes."

"No, you need to rest. I'll wake you up when she comes to."

Her baby blues held wariness, obviously still not convinced. "Why don't you rest some more first?"

He knuckled her scalp. "You always so hard-headed?"

"You caught me on a good day." She sent him a tired teasing grin. "I'm usually much worse."

"Heaven help us." And he meant it more than she could know. *Careful, Steve. She's already told you how she feels.*

Dani's shoulders sagged, a sign for him to step in. He clutched her arms, pulled her to her feet, and guided her to the recliner. "Get some rest."

"Okay, okay." She sank with another yawn, relaxed into the chair, then bolted upright, holding up a finger. "But first I'm going to check the nurses' station for a blanket."

He gently shoved her back into the chair. "Oh no, you don't. If you get up I'll never get you back down. I'll get the blanket."

When he returned a couple of minutes later, she was already asleep.

His heart fluttered at the sight of her. Long dark lashes rested against gray circles of fatigue, her lips slightly parted in slumber. When had he stopped seeing her as the enemy? He draped her with the soft blanket, careful not to disturb her. Would time mend the broken heart she so carefully shielded, or would the wall built by betrayal continue to hold strong? With an angry mutter, Steve jerked himself to a standing position and raked a hand through his hair. He had to crush these feelings that kept roaring up in him before they destroyed him.

Dani startled awake when the nurse entered the hospital room, then straightened and peered at her aunt. Still asleep. Her eyes traveled to the handsome man at Mama Beth's bedside. Steve dozed, his long legs stretched out straight, his arms folded across his broad chest. A smirk worked onto her face. All he needed was a cowboy hat perched over his lowered head to complete the scene.

After disentangling her feet from the blanket, she tiptoed to the nurse. "Is she doing okay?"

"It's too soon to say, but her vitals look good. The doctor gave orders to reduce the morphine, so today she'll be more alert." The nurse smiled and wrote something on a chart.

Dani gazed at her aunt, and a surge of protectiveness blazed to life. It didn't matter what anyone else said or thought. She would move to Miller's Creek to care for Mama Beth and start her new life. It was her decision, and she didn't need anyone else's permission. A soft snore from Steve caught her attention and weakened her resolve. But how could she keep her heart protected?

The nurse turned toward the door. "The doctor will be in later. The cafeteria's serving breakfast if you and your husband are hungry."

"Oh, but he's . . ." It was too late to explain.

The door clicked behind the nurse and Steve roused to a sitting position. "I was just resting my eyes."

She crossed her arms and sent him a pseudo stern look. "Mm-hmm. Some watchdog you are."

His blurry-eyed boyish grin accelerated her pulse to race car speed. "Sorry, didn't mean to fall asleep."

"No problem."

Steve unfolded himself from the chair and moved closer to Mama Beth. The tender light displayed on his face shot a searing ache through her chest. He lifted his gaze. "Did you sleep well?"

His husky murmur and stubbled jaw reduced her insides to mush, and she quickly shifted her attention to the floor. She needed breakfast. Now.

Within a few minutes they entered the cafeteria on a mission to find coffee. The shared breakfast turned out to be both enjoyable and rejuvenating, with better-than-average cafeteria fare, and stimulating conversation punctuated with frequent laughter. On the walk back to the room, a realization dawned. She felt so at home in his presence, and the friendship developing between them felt . . . right.

He held open the door to Mama Beth's room. "After you, sweet lady."

She returned his grin then immediately stiffened at the sight of her mother, garbed in an Armani suit and perched in the chair next to Mama Beth's bed. No doubt Mother's attire was intended not only to impress, but to overpower. She stepped over to her mother and bent low to give her a hug. "Thanks for coming."

Her mother's face was a wooden mask.

"Steve, I'd like you to meet my mother, Cecille Hampton. Mother, this is Steve Miller."

He leaned forward and offered his hand. "Nice to meet you, ma'am."

"And you." Mother's face assumed a curious demeanor. "You must be Bo Miller's son. You look very much like him."

"Yes ma'am."

She swiveled toward Dani. "How is Beth?"

"The surgery went well, but that's all we know at this point. The doctor will be in later."

Mother's gaze traveled to Mama Beth's face. Dani longed to crawl inside her mother's brain, to know what she was thinking, to figure out a way to mend the fracture between them. An uncomfortable tension pervaded the room like steam in a heated kettle. Finally Mother stood and broke the silence. "Well, I'll go now. I just wanted to stop by to see how you were." Mother gave a pointed stare.

She'd stopped to see her, not Mama Beth. Dani lowered her head, humiliated by her mother's indifference and unconcern.

With a rustle of silk, Mother glided to the door then turned. "Danielle, may I speak with you privately before I go?"

More of a command than a question. "Of course. Excuse us, Steve."

They stepped into the hallway, the cloying scent of her mother's perfume trailing behind and mixing with the antiseptic smells of the hospital. "I apologize for my behavior the last time we were together." Her voice was cold and void of emotion. "I was distressed and responded accordingly. Please forgive me."

Her apology pealed like a broken bell. "It's okay. Sorry if I upset you. It wasn't my intention."

Mother reached into her purse and produced the car keys while she spoke. "I've made my wishes concerning Beth and Miller's Creek perfectly clear, Danielle. I understand your concern for her during this time, but once this is over I fully expect you to consider my position."

Dani chewed the inside of her cheek, dreading what would come next. Life was about to become even more unpleasant.

"Well?" Her mother's lips pinched together.

She straightened her spine. "I'm moving to Miller's Creek."

White-hot anger crawled into Mother's eyes, and her face paled.

"I'm sorry, but she has no one else."

"May I remind you that I don't either?. What about your job?" The venomous words erupted from her mouth.

"I'll make one last visit to my students, but I'm taking a leave of absence for the rest of the year."

"I see." Her eyes diminished to pencil-thin lines. "Well, you've made your decision. Don't say I didn't warn you." She pivoted and stormed away.

Dani fisted her hands, her stomach churning. Why did this have to be so difficult? "Mother, let's talk through this." Her voice reverberated in the empty hallway. "Please don't leave angry."

The only response was the furious click of her mother's designer heels against the tile floor.

∞13∞

Out on the Town

Dani stared in the mirror at the bubblegum-popping hairdresser behind her and inhaled the combined odors of nail polish, hair spray, and permanent solution. Something told her this wasn't going to be the pampering session she'd envisioned.

"So tell me, hon, what kinda look ya goin' for?" Jolene Briscoe, sporting a rhinestone-studded hair clamp and a pronounced country drawl, lifted curly strands of Dani's blond hair and let them fall to her shoulders.

"Um, look?"

"Yeah, I could give ya some really swanky layers and put a streak-a black down one side. It's the latest fad." She blustered out the words as if Dani were across the room, blew a big bubble, and let it pop. Then she sucked in the pieces between her dark maroon lips and started smacking again.

"A-actually, I just need the ends trimmed up a little." She raised a trembling thumb and index finger to show how little.

Jolene clicked her scissors by Dani's left ear and looked disgruntled. "Well, what's the fun in that?"

Maybe she should have settled for a walk as a way to get out of the house. Had Mama Beth not commented on how long her hair was getting, she probably wouldn't be here now.

The hairdresser huffed out her disappointment. "Okay. Let's move ya to the sink."

Not knowing what to say, she nodded and followed her to the back. Once in the vinyl recliner, Jolene slapped a towel around her neck and lowered the chair without warning, leaving Dani in a prone position staring at the longest, mascara-clumped eyelashes she'd ever seen. The woman launched into an incessant monologue while she shampooed her hair, the water scalding hot. Each time she came up for a breath, Dani attempted to speak, but Jolene barreled right back into her monologue again. All she could do was chomp down on her bottom lip and make a concentrated effort not to scream out in pain.

Ten minutes later, she found herself once more in front of the mirror, this time with Jolene snipping away while she continued to chatter. "So, I hear you're from Dallas?"

"Yes."

"Married?"

Why did everyone always want to know her marital status? "Not anymore."

The hairdresser patted her shoulder. "Me either, hon. My first husband was as lazy as the summer days are long. Husband number two was mighty fine to look at, but I don't think that man had a brain in his head. Husbands three and four both had rovin' eyes, if ya know what I mean." She reloaded her lungs without missing a beat. "Now I got my eye on a rugged cowboy that knows how to treat a lady right."

Dani eyed the growing pile of hair on the floor with dismay. "Um, that's nice."

"Can you guess who?" Jolene stopped snipping and rested her fist on Dani's head, the scissors still open. The hairdresser's eyes rounded with anticipation, and she hoisted her penciled-in eyebrows. "It's someone ya know."

"I've been inside taking care of Mama Beth. I don't get out much."

Jolene glowered when she didn't wager a guess and gave her a stinging slap on the back. "Oh, ya silly goose, it's the mayor."

"Steve?"

The hairdresser let out a blustery laugh. "Yep. Don't cha think he's handsome? Now I know he's always a-stoppin' by Mama Beth's, so ya put in a good word for me, hear? And let me know if someone tries to steal 'im away." She placed her heavily made-up face next to Dani's, the scissors resting on the opposite shoulder, uncomfortably close to her left ear. "I don't take kindly to 'nother woman hoofing it in my territory if ya know what I mean."

Her hair chopped way too short, Dani gulped and jotted a mental note to steer clear of Steve. And Jolene Briscoe's scissors.

"For goodness sake, why'd you let her cut your hair so short?" Mama Beth eyed her now shoulder-length hair.

"'Cause I couldn't get a word in with a pry bar. I'm just glad I still have my ears." Dani grimaced remembering the scene, then turned her attention back to her aunt, who wore an amused smirk. "Are you sure you feel up to the town hall meeting?" She studied Mama Beth. Every day showed marked improvement, but she still tired easily as a result of the radiation treatments.

"I'm going even if I have to drive myself!" Her aunt's sharpened voice and bulldog jaw left no room for rebuttal.

Dani skewed her lips to one side. They were both testy. Three weeks of constant contact in a confined space would have the same effect on Santa Claus and Mother Teresa. She released a slow breath and gathered the supper dishes from the table, the smell of burnt mac and cheese lingering. No wonder Mama Beth hadn't eaten much and Steve had stopped showing up for meals.

"I'm sorry, I don't mean to sound so cross." Her aunt's voice quivered and tears puddled in her eyes.

After depositing the dishes in the sink, Dani returned to the table. "Hey, it's okay." She knelt beside her aunt and placed a hand on her shoulder to offer comfort. "I know you're ready to get out of the house."

Mama Beth nodded and blinked back more tears. "I feel like I could scratch someone's eyes out. Please don't think I'm always like this."

She patted her aunt's trembling hand. "I don't. This is all because of what you're going through, first the tumor and surgery, now the recovery and radiation. You've been through a lot, so take it easy on yourself." Everything would be a lot less stressful if Steve weren't so pigheaded. No amount of pleading could change his mind. He refused to budge from his insistence that Mama Beth stay home and rest.

"This could've been so much worse." Mama Beth choked back more tears. "But I didn't expect it to be so hard emotionally. I think getting out of the house will do us both good, don't you?" Her voice lowered to a mournful plea.

Dani took in her aunt's hopeful expression. Steve would be beyond livid if she went against his wishes, but if he could see Mama Beth on the verge of tears surely he'd soften and give in.

"You're such a sweetheart to put up with me." Her aunt reached for a hug. "I want you to know how much I appreciate all you've done."

She returned her aunt's embrace and offered a reassuring smile. "Let me take care of these supper dishes, and then we'll see how you're feeling."

As she rinsed the plates and put them in the dishwasher, her thoughts returned to Steve. How many times had they quarreled over what was best for Mama Beth? More than she could count. A tired sigh escaped. The week at the hospital had cemented their friendship, but he'd changed—and not for the better—once they'd come home to Miller's Creek.

Scenes and conversations from the last three weeks jumbled in her mind as she tried to decipher his behavior. She'd often glanced up to find him watching her, an unreadable expression on his face. Sometimes he was talkative and friendly; other times he seemed distant and withdrawn, almost as if he resented her presence. The queasy feeling in her stomach flared and launched a slow burn through her chest. *Stop over-analyzing things, Dani. Let it go before you give yourself an ulcer.*

She turned her mind to the upcoming move. A few more weeks and Mama Beth would be allowed to drive. Then what? Mother had made her feelings about the matter perfectly clear. Could she handle it if Mama Beth and Steve disapproved as well?

Dani slammed the door to the dishwasher and punched the button. The sound of spraying water joined the motor's hum. She glanced at her aunt, whose desire to escape the confines of the house still flickered in her expression. It wouldn't hurt to give the outing a try. If Mama Beth got tired they could always come home. Recuperation involved more than just physical rest, and her aunt needed time away. They both did.

She pushed her lips into a firm set. No matter how much she treasured Steve's friendship, she would no longer allow him to dictate her movements.

Steve scanned the crowded gymnasium, tired but pleased at the turnout for the first town hall meeting. The rows of chairs he'd spent the afternoon setting up were almost full, and the crowd numbers provided further proof his strategy would work. He rubbed a hand across his face in an attempt to erase his fatigue. Once the townspeople approved his plan, he'd catch a few days' rest. The four or five hours of sleep a night he'd allowed himself over the past few weeks had worn him to a frazzle. Between the proposal, town hall meeting, and wrestling with Dani over the best way to care for Mama Beth, he was beyond exhausted.

Jolene Briscoe pranced in the side door in a sparkly outfit that demanded attention. Uh-oh, the hairdresser with hooks was headed his way. She proceeded toward him, hips in full swing, so he swerved to the other side of the room to greet folks and shake their hands, only stopping long enough to talk about the weather or ask about their kids. Once he'd made the rounds, he hustled to the podium to call the meeting to order.

He opened his mouth to speak just as Mama Beth and Dani entered the back door. The blood in his veins frosted over, and his mouth clamped shut. Bringing Mama Beth out in this heat? Had Dani gone completely nuts? They'd butted heads on more than one occasion here of late, but this time she'd gone too far. And why had she cut her hair? He nailed her with a glare.

She raised her chin and slung back a defiant look before helping Mama Beth to her seat. A ripple of movement and conversation erupted as people stood to allow them to pass. Dani chattered away like a mockingbird, like she'd known these people her entire life. Couldn't she see it was time for the meeting to start? He harrumphed loudly to get her attention. Her smile vanished, and she slumped in her chair, drilling him with a black look.

"We're about to get started, so y'all find your seats please." Most of the babble and moving around ceased. "Thank y'all for coming out for our town hall meeting. As you know, I've been working on a project to help Miller's Creek. I've spent weeks researching ways to bring the town back to what it used to be. There's no question it's going to take money and lots of it. So after studying the options, I think our best choice is to find investors—"

"What investors?" One of the Grannies rose to her feet.

A rumble of displeasure surged through the room.

"Big-city suits." Otis Thacker's eyeballs bulged as he groused the words, once more cementing his reputation as the town grouch and naysayer.

Steve waited for the words that always followed, the words Otis was known for. The crotchety old man didn't let him down. "We've never done it that way before, and I don't think we need to start now." He shook a crooked finger Steve's direction. "We don't want a bunch of outsiders calling the shots!"

The rumble grew louder and people shifted in their folding chairs, setting off a cacophony of noise that echoed in the large room. They turned left and right to speak to those nearby. Some even pressed their lips together, shaking their heads and sending him dark looks, obviously questioning his ability as mayor.

He pasted on a smile he didn't feel and attempted to laugh off the comment, raising one hand in the air. "Now Otis, don't get your dander up. They're not going to call the shots."

A few snickers and comments filtered in from the crowd.

Otis rotated in his chair in answer to those who laughed. "Well, I'd sure want to have a say in how things were run if it were my money."

Steve's blood rolled into a slow simmer. He'd put too much work into this plan to let Otis rip it to shreds. "Then what do you suggest, Otis? All the downtown buildings need major work. Unless they're repaired, we can't expect to attract businesses. If anyone has a better idea I'd sure like to hear it." He forced the words through an ever-tightening jaw.

The crowd noise escalated to a roar, and several stood to congregate in the back, their arms crossed. Now what? His brain fished for ideas, but nothing took a bite. The ruckus died down and stares fixed on him.

Out of the corner of his eyes, he saw Dani lean toward Mama Beth and whisper something in her ear. The older woman nodded and rose to her feet. "Some of y'all have met my niece,

Dani. She just mentioned something that I think bears repeating."

The people around them motioned for Dani to stand. She hesitated for a moment then gave in. What in the Sam Hill was she doing? He plastered on a scowl in warning, but he should've known better. Instead of conceding, her shoulders squared. "In my opinion, Miller's Creek has everything it needs to rebuild."

He let out a derisive laugh that sounded through the microphone. First an expert on how to care for Mama Beth, and now a town improvement guru? The color rose in her face, but she didn't back down. Steve sent her a look designed to put her in her place. "Well no offense, but you don't live here. How could you possibly know what we need?"

Dani's expression cooled. "You're not giving this town or its people the credit they deserve." On each word her voice strengthened. Like the calm before a storm, the mob ceased to move, latching on to her every word.

Steve cocked his head to one side, his frustration and fatigue giving way to mockery. "Well, this is quite a change from the opinion you expressed your first day here. Perhaps you'd like to expound on our inadequate schools and our antiquated way of life?"

Her mouth hinged open momentarily, but then her voice rose above the sudden crowd noise. "Having never visited your schools, I'm sure I couldn't offer an opinion other than to say the kids in this town are the best-behaved and most respectful children I've ever met. To me that speaks highly of your schools. As for the antiquated way of life you mentioned, I'm not sure I know what you mean, unless you're referring to your conversational skills."

His blood exploded into a full-blown boil, sending heat up his neck and onto his face. The crowd "ooh"-ed then settled into silent anticipation.

Dani's face blanched. "As I already mentioned, Miller's Creek has what it needs." She gazed around the room, her words unfaltering. "Yourselves."

He considered her comment. Sure, manpower was important, but how could they manage without financial resources? J. C. shuffled to his feet amidst the murmuring. His old geezer buddy would set things straight. "J. C.?"

"I'd like to hear more of what Miss Dani has to say."

Steve battled to keep his expression calm and tone even. "Mrs. Davis, we'd like to hear more. Preferably specifics."

"Thank you." She lifted her nose and head as she answered him, then turned and beamed at J. C. "I've experienced firsthand how you all band together and help each other. If you combine your skills, I'm sure you can rebuild this town. It will require extra work and commitment, but I know you can do it."

"What about supplies?" hollered Otis.

"Donations." Her comeback was quick. "Ask building supply stores to donate materials or money in exchange for free advertising at town events and in the town newspaper."

Heads nodded in agreement, and Steve felt his jaw go slack. The people were actually buying into this harebrained idea. The plan might have some merit, but it wouldn't be enough without money to back it up.

Dani continued. "Some of you have probably considered starting a business."

Otis sneered. "Yeah, but common sense kept us from it. What good is a business without customers?"

A smattering of laughter trickled from the group, but they quieted and stilled to hear more. Dani spoke with resolve. "Why not host special events to attract potential customers? Advertise in other towns and nearby cities."

From the front row his sister Trish popped to her feet. "What kind of events?"

Steve scowled. Her too? What about *his* plan?

Dani's eyes sparkled. "A tour of historic homes at Christmas, or—"

"Or a country festival," chimed someone from the left. A soft whir of discussion started, and people twisted and leaned this way and that, their faces animated.

"We could advertise our annual rodeo and host a parade." Clay Barnes, his best friend and ranch foreman, winked at Steve from the front row with a good-natured grin. Some friend. The crowd noise grew louder, and people stood to call out to others on the other side of the room.

Like a bad case of poison ivy, chatter and movement escalated across the gymnasium and erupted in complete chaos. Dani and Mama Beth rose to their feet in the midst of the mayhem and moved toward the door. The sinking feeling in his stomach dumped a sour taste on his tongue. In a few short minutes, that woman had singlehandedly managed to destroy months of his hard work.

ℭℛ14ℬ℘

An Invitation Home

S teve stared through the door window into the Sunday school classroom where Mama Beth perched in her rocking chair, reading to the kids. There was no stopping her since Dani had chosen to ignore his warning. Last night's outing to the town hall meeting had given Mama Beth a taste of freedom that would refuse to be reined in. Now back at work in Sunday school, next the daycare. He shook his head in disgust.

One classroom away from where he stood, the door flew open, and kids scrambled down the hall to find their parents, their joyful chatter trailing behind. Steve flattened himself against the wall to let them pass, then moved back to watch Mama Beth through the door window. He must admit she did look better. As she read to the kids, the happy light in her eyes brought sweet memories flooding over him. She'd impacted hundreds of lives by her witness and ministry to children, his included.

His gaze traveled to Dani, and he blew out a frustrated breath. Thanks to her the whole town was in an uproar to overhaul Miller's Creek. At the meeting last night, they'd approved her plan. His phone had jangled all night long, and she was to blame. Now, overdressed as usual, she lounged in the floor with the Humphrey girl in her lap. A tender smile played on Dani's face as she held the girl close. A boy snuggled to her side and she placed an arm around him. The kids obviously adored her.

At the town hall meeting she hadn't backed down, even in the face of his anger, and it somehow impressed him. A sudden awareness hit, and he rubbed his chin in surprise. Him and his stupid pride. Dani had only been trying to help. Though he still wasn't convinced her plan would provide the funding they needed, at least people were excited about the project. That was an answer to prayer in itself.

Inside the classroom the story ended. Mama Beth lowered her head to pray, and the sight brought on another onslaught of memories. He offered up his own prayer of gratitude. *Thank You, Lord, that she's better.*

The kids exited in a more orderly fashion than the other class, and he entered the room behind them. Mama Beth spied him first. "Good morning, Steve."

"Morning, Mama Beth. Dani."

"Morning." Dani turned away, her tone chilled.

Steve raised his eyebrows and looked at Mama Beth. She shot him the you-got-yourself-in-this-mess glare and busied herself with straightening the room. Why was he always the one who had to apologize? He took a few tentative steps toward Dani while his brain scrambled for the right words. "Dani, y'all left before the vote last night, but I wanted you to know that we approved your plan."

She whirled toward him, her face beaming and eyes wide. "Really?"

He nodded, lowered his head, and pressed his lips together. "And . . ." Words eluded him. This should be easier by now, not harder.

"And?" Dani tilted her head, a teasing smile on her lips.

A chuckle gurgled from his throat. "And I apologize for—"

"Apology accepted."

He sent her a grateful grin. Better treatment than he deserved.

She laid a hand on his arm. "So tell me what happened." Her smile and eyes grew bigger, like a kid at an amusement park.

"Well, we've set up committees—advertising, funding, needs assessment, and so on—to get the ball rolling. My phone's been ringing off the hook. I don't think I've ever seen people in this town so excited."

Dani clasped her hands together in front of her. "That's wonderful."

The pretty glow on her face made it hard to concentrate, so he shifted his gaze to the floor. "I'd like to sit down and discuss this with you sometime, if you're willing."

Mama Beth ambled over. "It's not like you don't know where we live. So if we can, let's cut this conversation short. I could use both of your help to straighten this room before the service starts."

Sharing a conspiratorial smile with Dani, he followed Mama Beth's command. Several minutes later they strolled to the sanctuary. Once inside, Steve stepped over for Mama Beth to follow Dani into the pew, but she pushed him in ahead of her. Great. More fodder for the town grapevine.

He glanced at Dani, busy smoothing her skirt. Oh well, let 'em talk.

Dani studied the program the usher had given her. A beautiful teenager, identified in the bulletin as Graciela Soldano, stepped to the microphone, her shimmering black hair pulled back with barrettes on each side. She nodded to the music minister, and he began to strum the guitar strings. The woman's pure voice split the silence and echoed throughout the sanctuary.

The beauty of the music lulled her into a trance-like state, and as the girl reached the chorus, Dani's heart climbed to her throat.

> *"The home that you are longing for is right*
>> *before your eyes.*
> *Set your heart on Jesus, He will lead you to*
>> *the prize.*
> *Heaven is waiting for the faithful and the few.*
> *His arms are open wide; He is waiting there*
>> *for you.*
> *This road leads home, where the Father waits*
>> *for you.*
> *This road leads home, have the faith to see it*
>> *through.*
> *You will find hope and peace when you fall*
>> *down on your knees.*
> *The Father waits for you; this road leads home."*

The song ended and the congregation erupted with applause. Dani pulled a tissue from her purse and wiped tears from her eyes, the longing for home stronger than ever. She hated that she felt so emotional today, but she knew why.

Her birthday.

It wasn't as if her parents had ever made a big deal out of it, so she shouldn't feel disappointed that no one remembered. Besides, she was too old for birthday parties anyway.

The man Mama Beth called Brother Mac moved to the pulpit. Not what she expected. No bouffant hairdo or ten-pound Bible. No red angry face and raised voice. He seemed . . . well, normal. Not like her mother's description of preachers. She couldn't help but notice how the people around her listened, intent on his words. Church wasn't a place she'd have chosen on her own, but if it made Mama Beth happy, she'd make the best of the situation and try to learn something new.

Brother Mac finished a joke and laughter rang out, then his tone and expression grew more serious. "Let's open God's Word to John 14, as we continue our study of making Christ our home, just like Grace sang about."

God's Word? She'd never thought of the Bible in those terms. Dani fumbled with the Bible Mama Beth loaned her. The sound of turning pages whispered across the room. Where was John 14? She thumbed through the onion-skin pages, feeling more out of the loop than ever. What was she doing here? Mother was right. She didn't belong. Her clothes were too fancy, she didn't know any of the songs, and now she couldn't find the verse. Dani scooted the Bible to one side, hoping Steve wouldn't notice her confusion. Too late. He reached across, the light scent of his cologne teasing her nose, and with the flip of a few pages located the passage.

She attempted to discern his motives. No gloating, just a friendly smile.

Brother Mac continued. "Let's bow for prayer. Dear Lord, help us forget about everything else and concentrate on You and Your Word. Thanks for being our abiding place, our home. In Jesus' name, Amen."

Dani straightened, confusion tearing through her brain. How could a person be a home?

"Our key verse today is verse twenty-three. *'If anyone loves me, he will obey My teaching. My Father will love him, and We will come to him and make Our home with him.'*" He placed his Bible on the pulpit, his eyes lit from within, his tone one of conviction. "Hear me, folks. This earth isn't your home. That pile of wood and bricks and stone you make mortgage payments on each month isn't your home. Even your precious family isn't your home. No place on this planet will ever be home."

She shifted in her seat, her pulse quickening. Then why had she moved here? Why had she given up all she'd ever known in hope of belonging to someone, somewhere?

"Look with me at the first few verses of chapter fourteen. Remember this is the message Jesus shared with His disciples right before He was crucified. He says: *'Do not let your hearts be troubled. Trust in God; trust also in Me. In My Father's house...'*"

Tuning him out, she thought about the words he'd just spoken. Her heart *was* troubled. According to what he'd just said, the way to cure a troubled heart was to trust in God. But how was she supposed to trust Him when He'd allowed so much pain in her life?

She shifted her attention back to the words as he read. *"'... so how can we know the way?' Jesus answered, 'I am the way and the truth and the life. No one comes to the Father except through Me.'"*

The words sounded . . . so final.

Brother Mac removed his glasses, folded them, and looked across the congregation, sincerity etched on his face. "God has prepared a place—a home—for those who love Him. One day, at a time only God knows, Jesus will come back and take us home. No earthly place will ever satisfy our souls. Only Christ can fill that spot in your heart. He wants to make your heart His home."

The lump in her throat thickened making it difficult to breathe. Notes sounded from the piano and people rose to their feet and began to sing. *"Come home, come home, ye who are weary come home ..."* Dani's chest tightened. All this singing and talk about home only underscored what she already knew. Her life was empty. And now they were trying to tell her that home was God? Questions tangled in her head as she gripped the back of the pew, her knuckles white.

A part of her was missing, leaving in its place a gaping hole. She knew that much. The part she'd searched for her entire life, the part that had brought her to Miller's Creek. But was God the answer?

After what seemed like an eternity the song ended and church dismissed, her heart brick-heavy. She gathered her belongings with trembling hands.

"You okay?" Steve grabbed one arm, drawing her gaze to his.

"Yeah." She lowered her head and moved out of the pew. It wouldn't do for him to see the tears lodged behind her eyes.

"Why don't you come over for lunch, Steve?"

Dani jerked her head up at Mama Beth's question. Why today? She needed time alone, time to process all that had just transpired.

Steve nodded. "Thanks for the invite. I think I'll take you up on that, so I can talk to Dani about the renovation plan. I'll meet y'all there."

Within a few minutes, they all congregated in the kitchen. Mama Beth wrapped an apron around her waist. "Dani, why don't you go up and get comfortable. Steve can help me get lunch started."

"Okay. It'll just take me a second."

After changing into a t-shirt and pair of jeans, she hurried down the stairs, the dialogue between the other two immediately halting. She studied their faces. Why did she get the distinct impression she'd been the topic of conversation?

Mama Beth stirred a pot on the stove, while Steve pulled plates from the cabinet and headed to the table. "Dani, do you mind me picking your brain for the renovation project?"

"Pick away. What do you want to know?"

"For starters, I want to know the best way to approach businesses for donations."

A car door slammed outside and Mama Beth snapped her head to attention. "Did y'all hear someone pull into the driveway?"

Dani and Steve both shook their heads. A second car door slammed, and a car horn blasted. They moved to the front door in time to see a red Volkswagen speed off down the road.

"What in the world is going on?" Mama Beth swung open the screen door, and Steve and Dani followed her into the front yard.

On the opposite side of the road the tall grass stirred, followed by a tiny mew. Dani rushed out the front gate. A baby kitten! She knelt and scooped it into her hand, so small it fit perfectly into one palm. Mama Beth and Steve joined her.

"Well, my goodness, that cat can't be more than a few weeks old. Did they drop off a mama cat, too?" Mama Beth peered around Dani.

"I don't think so. What do we do?" She met Steve's gentle gaze.

"I'm not sure it will make it without the mother, Dani." His words came out soft and concerned, and he reached to take the kitten from her. "A baby girl. Probably the runt of the litter. She looks healthy enough, but she needs a mama."

Dani reclaimed the kitten. "Well, we've got to do something. We can't just leave this poor baby out here to die." She turned toward Mama Beth. "Can I keep her? I promise to take care of her."

"Good heavens, how are you going to have the time to take care of a baby kitten? Have you even had a pet before?"

She shook her head. "No, Mother and Father wouldn't let me." She knew her voice sounded desperate and whiny, but this cat needed her. Mama Beth's hardened face didn't offer much hope, so she turned to Steve.

His eyes softened. "Y'all go back in and get lunch finished. Let me make a quick phone call."

As they trekked toward the house, Mama Beth eyed the kitten with disdain. "I can't believe I'm going to let you keep that thing in my house. I'd suggest you not get too attached. There's every chance in the world that cat won't last a week." She bustled up the porch steps. "You stay out here. I'll call you when lunch is ready. Maybe by then, I'll figure out something for you to keep that cat in."

"Thank you, Mama Beth."

Her aunt swiveled, and a soft smile touched her face. "You're welcome."

Dani stepped around the corner to the side porch and positioned herself on the swing, cooing to the kitten. She studied the small creature, pristine white except for black spots, and a wave of compassion rolled over her. "I know exactly how you feel, kitty." Abandoned and unwanted. "It hurts when no one wants you, but you're going to make it. I promise to take good care of you. I don't know much about being a mama, but I'll do the best I can."

In her peripheral vision she glimpsed movement, and twisted her head to see Steve standing nearby, his cell phone to his ear. How had he come up on the porch without her hearing him? And how much had he heard?

A strange expression flitted across his face as he eyed her and the kitten. "Hey Doc, I'm at Mama Beth's, and we found an abandoned kitten, probably only two weeks old. Do you have anything we could feed it? You do? Good. I'll be out later to get it." He stopped talking, his profile one of concentration as he listened.

Her heart filled to overflowing. How considerate of him to make this effort for the kitten and for her. She puzzled once more over the incongruity in his behavior. One day he made her madder than a mother bear ready to take a swipe at his head, and the next he pulled something like this.

"That'll be great. I'll be waiting. Thanks." Steve flipped the phone shut and smiled, his eyes crinkling at the corners.

"Well, what did he say?"

"Doc has a powdered milk formula made especially for abandoned kittens and puppies. He was already on his way into town, so he's going to swing by the clinic then come by here to drop some off."

She raised the kitten close to her face. "Did you hear that, little bit of kitty? We're going to get you some food here shortly." The kitten blinked as if she understood every word.

Steve lounged next to her on the swing and reached for the kitten, enclosing her hands in his before she released the small animal. He sat the kitten on his chest, and she clawed her way to his shoulder. "I think you just came up with a great name for this cat."

Dani moved her head to one side. "What's that?"

"Little Bit."

"Lunch is ready!" Mama Beth called out the words from inside the house.

Steve handed the kitten back to her with a grin. "The general's calling."

She cradled Little Bit in the crook of her arm as they made their way into the house.

"Happy Birthday!" Her aunt's face shone as they entered the kitchen.

A birthday cake aglow with candles sat on the table. The moisture in Dani's eyes made the flickering light glow especially bright. Someone had remembered after all. "When did you have time to make a cake?"

A proud gleam covered Mama Beth's face. "Early this morning while you were still asleep."

Dani passed the cat off to Steve then enveloped her aunt in a hug. "This is the sweetest thing anyone has ever done for me, Mama Beth. Thank you. How'd you know today was my birthday?"

Her aunt pulled back, a quizzical look on her face. "Well, shouldn't I know my own niece's birthday?"

"Of course, I just didn't know if anyone would remember." Mother always thought of it a few days late, like an unnecessary addendum to her social calendar. Would she remember this year, or was she intentionally punishing her for moving to Miller's Creek?

Steve leaned close, stroking the cat's head. "Happy birthday."

Surprising heat rushed to her cheeks, and she ducked her head. "Thanks."

Mama Beth snatched a package from the table. "Blow out the candles so you can open your presents."

Dani obliged while the other two sang. When she raised her eyes to their smiling faces, she had to blink back the sudden sting of tears. Mama Beth handed her a gift.

"You didn't have to get me a present."

"I most certainly did. Go ahead. Open it."

She moved to the window seat and ripped into the package, glancing up at the other two with excitement. Steve put the kitten down on the table and plunked down beside her as she uncovered a Bible with her name engraved in gold. She stiffened, unsure of what to say. "Thanks Mama Beth. It's beautiful."

"I wrote you a note on the inside cover. Open it."

Dani followed her invitation and read out loud. *"To Dani, with all my love. This book will help you find what you're seeking. I love you. Mama Beth."* She choked out the words then turned a watery gaze to her aunt. "I don't know what to say. Thank you just doesn't seem like enough."

Her aunt stooped to give her a quick hug. "It's more than enough. Here's another present." She handed Dani a larger box. "This one is from Steve."

She turned a questioning gaze toward him. He'd bought her a gift? Why? And when had he found the time with his hectic schedule?

"Mama Beth helped with the size. Hope you like it."

The older woman rested a hand on his shoulder. "Steve picked up the Bible for me since I couldn't get out of the house."

Dani thought back to other birthdays. Never had she been made to feel so special, and from two people she'd only known a few weeks.

"Well, don't just sit there. Open it." Mama Beth's voice took on impatience.

She tore through the paper and opened the box, immediate laughter spilling from her throat. "I love it! My first country clothes." She held up the denim overalls.

"It's about time." Steve grinned and winked.

Dani remembered his comment about her clothing on the ride into Miller's Creek and returned a sheepish grin before looking at Mama Beth.

Her face had taken on an enigmatic sheen, but then she seemed to snap out of it and clasped her hands together. "Well, why don't we fix our dinner plates so we can cut into the cake?"

Steve's laughter ripped the air. "Too late."

They turned to look in the direction of his gaze and Mama Beth raised both hands to let out a "Hyeah!"

Unfazed, Little Bit continued her stance in the middle of the cake, licking chocolate frosting from her mouth and nose.

෴15෴

Mamas and Marigolds

Steve strode across the yard to his parents' house early one morning spurred on by guilt. He'd delayed this visit far too long. In the weeks following the town hall meeting, his life had accelerated from fast to super-sonic-speed, and it was all he could do to keep up. He clamped his lips. Dani's idea for Miller's Creek had taken root like an invasive weed. Even the old geezers had formed a construction team, their constant questions and ideas driving him nuts. He was ready to inform them they could paint the whole town purple with pink polka dots for all he cared.

To make matters worse, not an hour went by when he didn't think of Dani. Her tireless efforts on the behalf of Mama Beth and the town evoked a stronger reaction in him than anticipated, and he had to make a concentrated effort to stay away. If the truth be told, only two things held him back. Her earlier request for nothing but friendship, and more importantly, the fact that she still hadn't professed faith in God. A heavy sigh poured out of him. Life would be a lot easier when she moved back to Dallas. Out of sight, out of mind, right?

He paused in front of the main house and brought a hand up to shield his eyes from the morning sun. To call the massive structure a farmhouse or even a ranch house was an understatement. More like a Southern mansion. If his mother's goal had been to impress, she'd succeeded. Mom insisted on having this house built, a tribute to her Southern roots, and they'd moved from the family home in town, the house Mama Beth now owned. He turned his head to view the ancient live oaks which shaded the large circular drive, then trudged up the steps that led to the front door.

Steve entered the two-story foyer, complete with marble floors and an over-sized crystal chandelier. His boots thudded against the floor and echoed in the spacious room. Bypassing the grandiose staircase, he strode down the hall, his thoughts on his mother. The seven years of her illness seemed like a lifetime. He drew in a deep breath to prepare himself for what lay ahead then stopped outside the open door. Dad was stationed on one side of the hospital bed and a nurse on the other.

"Come on, honey, let's try another bite." Bo Miller held a spoon in his large hand, his voice pleading.

"Don't want it." His mother turned her head away, her lips pinched.

"But you've hardly eaten a bite. Please try. For me?"

Mom blurted out a string of expletives that would've once embarrassed her Southern sensibilities. Dad lowered the spoon and his head. His big shoulders sagged.

Steve breathed a quick prayer for help then rapped on the door frame. Dad looked up with weary eyes. "Come on in, Son. Maybe you'll have better luck than I am."

He smiled at his father and the nurse as he approached the bed, his heart stone-heavy, the scent of fresh flowers mingling with medicinal smells. How much longer could they endure seeing her like this? "Hi, Mom."

"Who are you?" Her blank stare and derisive tone pierced his heart.

"I'm Steve, your son. Remember?"

"I don't have a son. Get out of my house."

He fixed his gaze on Dad, uncertain of what to do.

His father motioned toward the door with a jerk of his head. "I'll join you in a minute. Go ahead and step out."

Steve shuffled to the hallway, unable to halt the sudden rush of tears. He released a ragged breath then pushed down the bitter taste in his mouth. Footsteps sounded on the stone floors, and he swiped at his wet cheeks. Dad didn't need any more grief.

Strong arms encircled him. "It's okay to cry, Son."

Steve hugged him back and swallowed against the pain in his throat. "I know. I just don't want to burden you with my grief. You've got enough to deal with."

His father pulled away. "You're not burdening me." Dad sniffed and pulled a handkerchief from his pocket. "It helps to have someone understand what I'm going through. She doesn't know me half the time." He stuffed the cloth in his back pocket and pointed a gnarled finger at him. "If I ever see you trying to hide your crying from me again, I'll take you to the wood shed."

Steve smiled through a mist of tears. "I'll remember that."

"You have time to sit and visit?"

He didn't, but he'd make time.

They traveled to the terrace, canopied by live oak trees, and sat on the wooden patio chairs. "Son, I appreciate all you've done for the ranch these past few years. I couldn't have made it without you." Dad's voice quivered.

"And I couldn't have done it without Clay." Steve leaned forward and rested his elbows on his knees, his gaze trained on a trail of ants. "Without his help as ranch foreman, there's no way I could serve as mayor." He struggled to find a topic to take Dad's mind off his problems. "You should see downtown."

"So I've heard. Sounds like Beth's niece had a good idea."

Was it a good idea? On one hand, it had created a new spark of life in Miller's Creek, and for that he was grateful. But how could they keep going with a shortage of funds? His plan would've corrected that issue. "Yeah, but we need more money.

The donation from HomeAcres Building Supply is only going to stretch so far."

His father stared toward the fields, a vacant look in his eyes.

Steve patted him on the back. "You okay?"

Dad shook his head and let out a shuddering breath. "Your mama's going down in a hurry. The doctor thinks in a few months she'll be gone."

The words knotted his stomach. How much more could Dad endure? The illness had taken its toll. His shoulders were more stooped, hair more gray, face awash with fatigue. Steve patted his father's arm. "I'm worried about you."

The big man's eyes watered. "It's just so hard to see her like this. Only God's grace gets me through each day." He rubbed his chin and blinked away tears. "How's Beth doing?"

"Doing well. A little tired from the radiation, but her prognosis is good."

A tender look crossed his face. "Glad to hear it. Now tell me about this niece of hers."

Steve clenched his jaw. Should he start with her bullheadedness or the big blue eyes that sometimes kept him awake at night?

Dani gave a happy sigh and inhaled the flower-scented air. What was there about a beautiful June day that made you feel like a kid? In some ways she'd never really had a childhood, but nothing stopped her now. She tilted her face and spun around, arms flung to the side in joyous abandon.

When she stopped, the landscape continued to spin for a few seconds. Her head finally cleared, and she viewed her recent work in Mama Beth's garden. Knowing she'd planted and nourished these small pieces of life brought satisfaction. Like the flowers she'd planted this morning, she was a transplant, but the move had gifted her with the home she'd always longed for and a chance to start her life anew.

She watched as Little Bit busied herself chasing a grasshopper then looked up as another car drove by at a crawl, the old women inside craning their necks to stare as they passed. Her happy mood spiraled to the ground and crashed. The one thing she didn't like about life in Miller's Creek. Nosy people. A scowl planted itself on her face as they continued to stare. "Take a picture. It'll last longer."

The screen door slammed. Mama Beth stood on the porch with a glass of fresh-squeezed lemonade which she raised toward Dani. "I brought you some lemonade. How's the gardening going?"

"Good. I still have more to plant, but I don't mind. I'm having a wonderful time." She ambled to the porch for a drink, studying the woman who'd become such a vital part of her life. Every day she looked better. "Thanks, Mama Beth."

A slow smile spread across her aunt's features.

Dani cocked an eyebrow. "Why are you looking at me like that?" She guzzled the tangy lemonade, quenching her thirst.

"It still takes me by surprise when you call me Mama Beth, but I like it." Her voice lilted like that of a happy child.

She gave her a hug. How she loved this woman! "The longer I'm around you, the more you feel like my Mama."

A dark frown altered her aunt's face. "Have you talked to Cecille lately?"

Well, that was a great way to ruin the day. "I've tried, but she's still mad." The hum of another slow-moving vehicle caught her attention. "What is it with these people? They've been driving by all morning, gawking like I was an animal at the zoo."

Her aunt laughed. "Don't be too hard on them. They're just curious."

"That's no excuse. Haven't they ever heard of privacy?"

An I-told-you-so look replaced Mama Beth's smile. "I tried to tell you that life in a small town would be different."

"And I expected it to be, but I didn't expect this."

Otis Thacker, the next-door neighbor, appeared at the fence, his hands on his hips.

Dani blew a puff of air between her lips. Not him again. "Snoopy neighbor alert."

"Morning, Otis! How are you?" Mama Beth called out and waved an arm in the air.

"Fine." He glowered as he took in her gardening work on the side of the yard that edged his own. "That niece of yours planted cannas over here."

She grimaced. Now he was going to tell her what to plant and where to plant it? In her own yard?

Mama Beth placed an arm around Dani's shoulder. "I told her to plant what she wanted. I can't work the garden this year, so I've turned it over to her. She's done a marvelous job, hasn't she?"

"Well, I'd thank you to have her move 'em somewhere else. They'll get so tall they'll block the morning sun from my tomatoes."

Gladys Thacker joined her husband at the fence. "How much longer is Cecille's girl going to be here anyway?"

How rude! It wasn't like she was holding all-night parties and disturbing the peace. Dani crossed her arms and shifted her feet. "My name's Dani, you old snoop." She kept her voice lowered, but her temper continued its ascent.

Mama Beth giggled then spoke to Gladys. "Just 'til I get better."

Dani stretched her lips into a tight line. Could she ever convince her aunt that a permanent move was for the best? Since the gentle nudges didn't appear to be working, maybe she needed a shove. "I'm actually thinking about moving to Miller's Creek," she shouted to Gladys.

Her aunt's eyebrows shot up her forehead.

"Why would you want to do that for?" Gladys Thacker's scratchy voice split the air.

"So all you busybodies can stick your nose in my business." The words ripped from her mouth before she could stop them, and she popped a hand over her loose lips.

Mama Beth's mouth flew open and consternation sparked in her eyes. "Dani!"

Immediate remorse washed over her. She turned to apologize, but the Thackers stormed away from the fence, their heads wagging. Okay, maybe she'd carried this childhood thing a little too far.

Later that day Dani finished planting the last flat of marigolds in the side yard, brushed her hands on her new denim overalls, and tightened the bandana she'd tied around her hair to keep it out of her face. She looked and felt like a bona fide country girl. A smile spread her lips out wide.

With a happy hum she picked up the aluminum watering can and moved over to the marigolds, their pungent scent filling the air. She knelt to give them a drink. The hum turned into a happy tune that burst from her lips. *"The farmer in the dell, the farmer in the dell, hi-ho the derry-o, the farmer in the—"*

"Be careful you don't drown those plants."

Heat scurried to her cheeks, and she jerked her head around to see Steve standing near the corner of the house. She jumped to her feet, her gardening clogs slipping on the saturated ground, and landed in the middle of the marigolds. On her backside.

Steve doubled over with loud guffaws, tears rolling down his face.

She sent him a daggered glare. It wasn't that funny.

He caught his breath and wiped his face. "Sorry I laughed, but that's the funniest thing I've seen in a long time." He ambled toward her to offer a hand, his face still creased with laughter. "You all right?"

Okay, cowboy, payback time. She bent toward her ankle, careful to keep her face hidden. "I don't know. I think I may have sprained something."

He squatted down next to her, his face full of concern.

Opportunity pounded on the door. She grabbed a handful of mud and plopped it on top of his unsuspecting head. Dark streams of goo trickled down his face. That would teach him to laugh at her. She dissolved into a fit of the giggles. "Sorry I'm laughing," she mimicked in a singsong fashion, "but that's the funniest thing I've seen in a long time."

The look in his eyes . . . no! "Oh no, you don't!" She sprang to her feet and bolted for the front yard. A wad of muck made contact between her shoulder blades, and she let out a scream.

Dani turned to see Steve make a fist in the air and bring his elbow down in a motion of victory. "Yes!" He beamed a triumphant gloat.

This fight wasn't over. Not by a long shot. She bent down to pick up mud balls to chunk at him and he returned the favor. One of his tosses pelted her in the face and deposited grit in her mouth.

The back door slammed. "What's wrong?" Mama Beth flew through the gate, panic in her voice.

They both froze in their spots, the look on Steve's face like that of a naughty schoolboy caught in the act.

Mama Beth's tongue clicked louder than Dani had ever heard. "Good gracious! Just look at the two of you." Then she spied the yard. "And look at my garden!"

She thought fast. "Steve started it." While Mama Beth ogled the muddy mess, Dani turned to Steve and stuck out her tongue. She wasn't about to take the blame for something he initiated.

Less than a second later a clump of mud landed on her head and oozed down toward her ear. Oh, he was going to pay for that. Mama Beth had seen it, and based on her expression, he was in big time trouble.

"Why, Steve Miller, I ought to box your ears." Mama Beth accentuated his name with an indignant tone. Her lips pinched together then twitched.

She could play this to the hilt. Dani feigned a pout and hung her head, but gave him a sideways glance.

Steve chuckled under his breath. "Okay, I give. You win."

"No, I win again. And you know what that makes you." She used her thumb and index finger to make an L then mouthed the word, "Loser."

His mouth swung half open then clamped shut again.

Mama Beth, still clicking her tongue, turned to go in the house. "Make sure you both clean off before you take one step in this house. I just cleaned the floors, and I won't stand for you tracking mud in."

"Yes ma'am," Steve said dutifully.

Dani glanced down at the mud-caked overalls. How in the world would she ever get it all off? She reached down and began swiping at the spots. "Just look at my new overalls. I'll never get them clean."

"Here maybe this will help."

She glanced up just as Steve twisted the nozzle of the water hose, a defiant grin bigger than Texas stretched across his good-looking face.

☙16❧

From Despair, Hope

Steve stared at the living room clock and grimaced, raking fingers through his hair. Almost midnight, and the numbers looked as bleak as when he'd started. This is what he deserved for giving in to Dani's plan too soon. The donation from the lumber company had dwindled to nothing. More projects than money, but what else was new? Last night he'd spent several hours pouring over the ranch accounts. The cost of feed had gone up again. They'd have to do really well at the bull sale in the fall and probably sell off a few cows in order to have a profitable year.

He laced his fingers behind his head and released a weary sigh. Burning the candle at both ends was burning him out. Scooting his chair closer to the desk, he laid his head atop folded arms and allowed his eyes to close. He'd just rest a few minutes before he ran the figures one last time.

The next thing he knew, the morning sun shone through the study window hitting him right in the face. He groggily lifted his head, wincing at the crick in his neck. One glance at the clock told him what he'd already suspected. He was late, and on Sunday of all days. Mama Beth and Dani had probably eaten breakfast, but there would still be coffee. It took every ounce of strength he could muster to stand and drag to the shower.

Pounding water on his neck muscles relieved some of the pain, but did nothing to alleviate his sour mood. Even reading his Bible took great effort, and his prayers seemed to dissipate in air above his head. *Lord, I don't know what's wrong, except I'm exhausted. The people will be so disappointed if we get part way through this and have to quit. I can't let them down. Show me what I need to do.*

A half hour later, Steve traipsed through the front gate at Mama Beth's. She sat, dressed for church, rocking away on her front porch, no doubt waiting for Dani. He shoved down his despair and plastered on a smile. No need to worry her with his problems. Her eyes narrowed before he made it to the top step. "What's wrong?"

He shook his head. "Nothing. Why do you ask?"

"Well, those saddle bags you have under your eyes for one thing. Now quit stalling and tell me what's wrong."

"Did I ever tell you that you're the most obstinate old woman I've ever met?" he groused as he stepped past her.

Mama Beth laughed and slapped her knee. "You got that right. Now sit down and tell me all about it."

He plunked down in the other rocker, unable to stop the short smile that turned his lips up at the corners. How was it she always knew what he was feeling? Ten minutes later, he finished his spiel about the financial difficulties of the town and ranch, all that still needed to be done for the town fix-up, and how tired he was from trying to take care of it all. He faced her, certain she would sympathize with his plight.

"Are you through venting?" she asked.

He chuckled. "Yes ma'am."

"Okay, then I want you to listen real hard to what I'm about to say. And I can almost guarantee you're not going to like it."

His smile faded and he pursed his lips. What had he gotten himself into?

She leaned toward him, forcing eye contact. "First of all, you need to climb out of that pity party you've gotten yourself into. And don't bother sending out invitations, 'cause no one will want to come."

Steve glanced down, eager to take a break from her hawk-eyed stare. Mama Beth had him pegged. He *was* feeling sorry for himself.

"Number two, I heard plenty of things about what's wrong in your life, but didn't hear one thing about what's right. If you only look at the bad, that's all you're going to see. Number three, have you prayed about it?"

Okay, now she was getting a little personal. His ire quickened. "Yes, as a matter of fact, I have."

Mama Beth raised both eyebrows. "Then why'd you come crying to me? God's already got it under control."

Steve laughed out loud. No other tongue lashing except Mama Beth's made him feel better instead of worse. He leaned over and planted a kiss on her cheek. "Not only are you the most obstinate old woman I've ever met, you're also the wisest."

Her blue eyes glinted. "You got that right."

"So you're the woman who's managed to snag my brother." The slender brunette with twinkling eyes extended a hand toward Dani while people spilled from the open church doors into the noonday heat.

Huh? Had she missed something? Unsure of how to respond she took the woman's outstretched hand.

The lady smiled. "I'm Trish James, Steve's sister. My husband's the town vet."

"Nice to meet you. What did you mean about snagging your brother?"

"The latest news on the grapevine is that you've hooked and reeled in my brother." Trish's look and tone teased her.

Her cheeks flooded with heat. Dani glanced up at Steve, his mouth set in a thin line. "Not true. I don't fish." She tempered the comment with a polite smile.

Trish burst out laughing. "Good for you. I love this big nut like crazy," she said, placing an arm around Steve, "but I pity the poor woman who finally lands him."

A full-blown smile bloomed on Dani's face. Already she liked this woman. Potential friend material. Now that Mama Beth was better, it was time to step up her original plan to establish a business and move on with her life. And that included making new friends.

A boy about the age of five sprinted toward them, screeched to a stop at Trish's side, and squinted up at her. "Jimmy invited me to his house. Can I go? He said we could play video games and go swimming—"

"Wait a minute." Trish held up one finger. "Aren't you forgetting something?"

The sandy-haired boy pursed his lips in a thoughtful pose. "What?"

"You're grounded, young man."

"Aw, Mom, please, just this once?" Trish arched an eyebrow at her son, and the boy's expression revealed that the message had been received. "Yes ma'am." His tone deflated, and a disappointed pout turned down the corners of his mouth.

"Go let Jimmy's mom know you can't come today, then find Daddy and tell him Mama said it's time to leave." She tousled his hair.

Steve stepped forward. "But not until you give Uncle Steve a hug."

"And a schlerbert." The boy latched hold of Steve's leg and scaled him like a tree.

Dani took in the scene with skyrocketed interest. What a wonderful father he would make. She shook herself. Where had *that* come from? She made a concerted effort to appear disinterested, but her eyes were drawn to the scene.

The boy placed his lips against Steve's cheek and blew. The blatting sound that ensued brought forth a boyish chortle. Steve grinned and winked at her. "Now that was a mighty fine schlerbert. Bo, can you say hello to Dani?"

"Danny?" He made a face and tucked in his chin. "Danny's a boy's name."

"Not all the time." She giggled and offered him her hand.

He gave it several hardy shakes. "Hi, girl named Dani." Everyone laughed and Steve set him down, his legs in motion before they ever touched the ground. "Dad's never going to believe this. A girl named Dani." He raced away at full speed, the adult's laughter following him.

Trish patted Mama Beth's shoulder. "How are you feeling?"

"Wonderful. Dani's taken such good care of me." She sent Dani a smile that melted her heart.

"Good, 'cause if you feel up to it, I'd like to have y'all over for lunch. I fixed a brisket."

"Sounds like a great idea to me." Mama Beth sent Dani a questioning glance.

Dani nodded her agreement as two men sauntered up with little Bo. The man with a handlebar moustache and cowboy hat anchored himself behind Trish, most likely her husband, the vet. The older man offered his hand to Dani, his eyes wide. "My goodness, if you're not the spitting image of your aunt. I'm Bo Miller, Steve's dad."

Mama Beth's face seemed to pale in the bright sunlight. "Nice to meet you, Mr. Miller, I'm Dani." She looked at Mama Beth, who had taken a step backwards.

"Please call me Bo. Makes me feel old to be called Mr. Miller."

Her gaze shifted to the boy then back to the older man. "So I take it your grandson is named after you?"

Little Bo tugged on her fingers. She bent toward him and he whispered. "He's big Bo and I'm little Bo." His thumb punched his chest.

Dani's breath hitched, but she hid it with a forced smile. How long would this ache for a child haunt her? "Oh, I see." She eyed big Bo. "What are you going to do when he gets big?"

The older man laughed. "I haven't thought that far ahead. I'm just glad they call me big Bo instead of old Bo." He wheezed into another round of laughter.

Minutes later the group dispersed to their separate vehicles for the ride out to the ranch. Dani settled into the backseat of Steve's pickup next to Mama Beth, and big Bo rode in the front. Classical music streamed from the radio, reminding her of their drive in the country. Steve had listened to the same type of music then. Not the usual musical fare for cowboys, but as she was quickly learning, nothing about Steve Miller was typical.

He pulled into the driveway of a limestone ranch house a few minutes later. Surrounded by live oak trees, the house appeared to have shot up from the Texas soil the way peanuts and cotton did. For some unexplained reason, this kind of life appealed to her on many levels. To wake up each day surrounded by family, knowing you belonged to a place the way the Millers did must bring such joy. Steve opened the door to help her from the vehicle, and Bo did the same for Mama Beth. The pickup doors slammed, but Dani hesitated for a moment to take in the peaceful surroundings. What would it be like to live in a place like this?

Steve started toward the door then stopped to wait for her. "Coming?"

She took one last glance around and joined him. They entered the house to the smoky smell of barbecued brisket. Trish bustled about the kitchen taking care of many tasks, so Dani moved to join her. "Lunch smells amazing. Is there anything I can do to help?"

"Thanks." She smiled and pointed with her head. "The glasses are in that cabinet. We need seven."

Soon lunch preparations were completed and they gathered at the table, Dani positioned between big Bo and Steve. Doc James spoke, his handlebar moustache dancing on his face. "Shall we ask the blessing?"

They joined hands around the table, and Steve took her hand in his, her pulse curiously accelerating. At the end of the prayer, he smiled and gave her hand a gentle squeeze. Her heart skidded to an almost-stop. Why was she reacting like a love-sick school girl? She gulped and focused on her plate, convinced her cheeks had colored to cardinal red.

The tender brisket melted in her mouth as she bit into it, and unleashed jealousy nibbled at her insides. Why couldn't she have this kind of life? And why was it everyone knew how to cook except her? Her specialty thus far was burnt mac and cheese.

Conversation and laughter flowed throughout the meal, the round of smiling faces setting off a throb in Dani's heart. This was the life she longed for. Life with a family and a home. She lowered her head and fingered the napkin in her lap. *Get over it, Dani.* It would never happen now. She'd already closed the door on marriage, that chapter in her life over. The sooner she came to grips with it the better.

After lunch the older Bo sought out her company, seemingly eager for conversation. They moved to the tree-lined patio which was surprisingly cool for the heat of the day. Nearby a mockingbird belted out his repertoire. "So tell me, Miss Dani, how do you like living in Miller's Creek so far?"

"I love it, but compared to what I'm used to ... well, let's just say it's a big change." She recalled the flurry of by-passers the day before, certain she could never grow accustomed to the lack of privacy. Steve stepped out, spied them and sauntered over, swiveling a chair around and straddling it to rest his arms on the back. She sensed his gaze on her, but avoided looking at him directly.

"Stick around here long enough and you won't be able to leave." Bo waggled his eyebrows then turned to look at the horses grazing in the pasture, their soft whinnies and snorts combining with the whispered breezes.

"Mama Beth's already taught her how to garden." Steve's comment forced her attention, and he gave her a wink. She returned his lazy grin, remembering the mud fight.

"Not a bit surprised." The older man chuckled. "Watch out, or next she'll have you working that daycare of hers."

She smiled. Bo knew her aunt well, another fringe benefit of living in a small town. "Actually she's already scheduled me to start at the daycare this week. One of the workers is going on vacation. But I'm happy to help. I love kids."

"Dani's a teacher." Steve shifted the position of his feet then lowered his head, his eyebrows scrunched into wiggly lines.

"Really? Any chance you'll sign on in Miller's Creek?"

"Well—"

Steve interrupted. "She's only here for the summer."

Dani rolled her lips under. Might as well get it out and over with. "Actually, I've decided to move to Miller's Creek on a permanent basis." She shot out the words then focused on Steve's reaction. Shock. Quick control. A hint of aggravation?

The older man spoke. "Well, I'm glad to hear it. Let me be the first to officially welcome you."

"Thanks." Dani sent him an appreciative smile then glanced at Steve's profile, his lips set in concrete.

Bo leaned toward her. "By the way, I like your ideas for Miller's Creek. I hear you encouraged the people to do the work themselves. Steve tells me the whole town has come together for this project."

"I'm sure it's because of Steve's input, not mine." She cringed remembering the town hall meeting and her rude comments. "He's the one who organized everything."

The conversation grew quiet, but not uncomfortable, and her gaze wandered to the horses. "It's so beautiful and peaceful here. I'm sure it's wonderful to wake up to this every morning."

"Do you ride?" Bo rested one elbow on the arm of his chair.

She gave her head a quick shake. "No, but I've always wanted to."

"Steve would be happy to teach you, wouldn't you, Steve?"

"Sure." His tone remained non-committal.

Bo rose to his feet with a yawn. "I'm going in for more tea and a nap. Y'all need anything?" He ambled toward the house.

"Nope." Steve's voice sounded tight.

"No, thanks." She watched the older man shuffle away then studied Steve's expression. He could switch moods faster than any person she knew. It's a wonder he didn't have permanent whiplash. "I was downtown earlier this week, helping J.C. with some painting. Things seem to be progressing well."

He shrugged, still not meeting her gaze. "I guess."

"What do you mean?"

"Well, the people are still gung-ho, but we're out of supplies and money."

She frowned. Already? "Have you tried going back to the companies—?"

"Yep, they're not giving us anymore."

Her heart skipped a beat. "So what are you going to do?"

"Good question." Steve's face hardened as he stared across the field, his eyes cloudy and dark.

Later that evening Dani retired to her room, her thoughts troubled. All afternoon Steve's downcast face had stuck with her, the problem gnawing at her brain. As she readied herself for bed, the hint of an idea exploded into a plan without warning. It formed so fast she scrambled for pen and paper. An hour and a half later, hands cramping, she leaned against the iron bed headboard and reviewed her notes. Yes, this plan just might work.

Her neck tingled with the prospect, but not without some trepidation. The idea plopped her in the crossroads, and once she chose a path, she couldn't—no, she wouldn't—turn back. She'd never intentionally hurt these people by pulling out after offering them hope. But was this the best way? Could she commit to this plan with all her heart?

She switched off the light and lay in the stillness, listening to the crickets and bull frogs compete for solos in the nocturnal symphony. The idea might prove to be the perfect solution, but it would also be costly. Her original plan to use the inheritance to build a business would have to be sacrificed. Was she crazy for even considering this idea? What if she needed the money later? She marveled at the change in her thinking. Had Miller's Creek bewitched her, or was this something bigger?

It felt so right. More right than anything had felt in a long time. She rolled to her side and snuggled her nose into the pillow. With a sense of peace and contentment she couldn't understand or explain, she drifted off to sleep.

The next morning after Mama Beth left for her ladies' Bible study coffee klatch, Dani munched on a sausage biscuit and punched the speed dial on her cell phone.

"Dani! How are you?" Andy Tyler's friendly voice brought a grin to her face.

They spent the next few minutes catching up then she moved to the matter at hand. "I called because I need your expert legal advice."

"Anything for you, pretty lady. What can I help you with?"

She explained the situation and her plan.

"Are you sure about this?" He sounded skeptical.

Was she doing the right thing? She took a deep breath, the aroma of breakfast still in the air. "Yes. I'm sure."

"Okay." Something about his tone hinted at disapproval. "When do you want to get started on this plan of yours?"

"Yesterday."

He laughed. "That figures. You haven't changed a bit."

After saying goodbye, she clicked the phone shut. Doubt immediately jabbed her, and she chewed the inside of her cheek. Was she making a huge mistake? She heaved a sigh and shoved the thought away. The wheel had already been set in motion. A slow smile inched across her face. Wouldn't Steve be surprised?

·17·

The New Man in Town

Steve crammed the last bite of stale doughnut in his mouth and pressed the stack of papers against his chest. He hated to even entertain the thought, but maybe he should consider buying a brief case. A mental image of his normal attire of boots, jeans, and hat flashed into his mind. Somehow a brief case didn't quite fit his image. The wind gusted and threatened to pull the papers from his grasp, so he hugged them closer to his body and trudged toward City Hall. The attempt to locate more funding for the town had doubled the paperwork, and the daily shuffle verged on scary. What if he lost something important?

He entered the building to pounding hammers, the buzz of power saws, and the smell of fresh paint. The old geezers had spent the past week sprucing up the interior of City Hall and now worked upstairs renovating the upper floors. With an attractive shade of beige on the walls, the refinished wood floors, and donated furniture, the place was actually starting to look like an office.

Wanda glanced up from her new desk as he blew in the door. "If you ask me you could use a briefcase."

Her way of stating the obvious scraped against his nerves like sandpaper. He hid his exasperation and attempted to sound pleasant. "You're right. What's your schedule like today?"

She peered at him over the top of her glasses, and he braced himself for a lecture. "Well, besides answering the phone that's been ringing off the hook, posting water bill payments, listening to that racket upstairs, and answering questions for every Tom, Dick, and Harry who comes through that door, not a thing. Why, what d'ya want?"

He grimaced under her blast then offered a sheepish grin. "Could you help me organize these into folders?"

Wanda glared at him for a long minute, then shook her head and marched around the desk to take the papers, her expression dark. "I don't get paid enough."

Steve held his tongue, the phone ringing just as he transferred the papers to her arms. He made the mistake of making eye contact.

"Don't look at me. I've got my hands full. You'll have to get it yourself." Her tone bristled.

He snapped the phone to his ear. "City Hall, Steve Miller speaking."

"Mr. Miller, glad I caught you. This is Andy Tyler with Tyler and Coleman Law Firm in Dallas."

A lawyer from Dallas? "Yes, what can I do for you, Mr. Tyler?"

"I understand your town's in the middle of a renovation project."

Goose bumps tickled his spine. Had Brighton come through after all this time? He leaned his weight against Wanda's desk. "Yes sir."

"I'm calling regarding a foundation that's been created to assist Miller's Creek with funding."

Cotton formed in his mouth and his ears roared. Had he heard the man right? He glanced up to see Wanda's interested stare and upturned ear. "Can you hold just a minute while I transfer this call to my office?" The words came out as a croak. Steve punched the hold button, laid down the phone, and ignored Wanda's glower as he headed to the privacy of his office. If he wanted the rest of the town to know about this phone call, he'd tell them himself. The office door clicked behind him, and he picked up the phone. "I'm back, Mr. Tyler. Can you give me more details?"

"Actually, I'd like to schedule a time to visit with you in person. Would that be all right?"

All right? Did kids like candy? "Sure."

"Friday morning at ten okay for you?"

"That'll be great." He provided the man with directions then dropped into his chair. What had just happened? A sudden smile erupted on his face and he squashed the temptation to let out a cowboy yee-haw. The meeting with Mr. Big Wig Brighton had finally paid off. Miller's Creek had an investor. Wouldn't Dani be surprised?

Like gathering storm clouds, he remembered the townspeople's opposition to outside investors. How would they react when they heard the news? He pushed the question away. After the visit with Mr. Tyler, he'd mention it to the people of Miller's Creek. Then he'd break out in a sweat.

Andy Tyler wasn't what Steve expected. He'd imagined someone along the lines of Mr. Brighton, but not this personable man close to his own age. With sand-colored hair and a bright smile that seemed permanently etched on his face, he looked more like a movie star than a lawyer. And better yet he wasn't wearing a suit.

"Nice to meet you in person, Mr. Tyler." Steve shook his hand and motioned for him to take a seat.

"Call me Andy." He glanced around the room. "Nice office you got here."

Steve folded himself into the desk chair and swiveled to face the attorney. "Thanks. Some friends of mine surprised me earlier this week. Apparently I was close to the top of the renovation list and didn't know it."

Andy laughed. "Your friends must think highly of you."

"I don't know about that, but I think highly of them."

"Spoken like a true leader." The man scrutinized him with lips pursed and eyes narrowed.

What was he after? Steve intentionally kept his face blank. "I'd like to hear more about this foundation you mentioned."

The man nodded and shifted to business-mode. "Okay. The foundation's been organized so the city and individuals can apply for funding of improvement projects."

He thought over the attorney's words, wanting to believe, but unable to shake his cautious nature. What if the money came from an illegal source? "Where's the money coming from?"

"My client wishes to remain anonymous. I'll be your contact in all business matters."

The news sent unease skittering across his scalp. "That didn't really answer my question."

Andy cleared his throat. "Sorry, but I'm bound by contract not to divulge my client's identity. I assure you the money is from a legitimate source, if that's your concern."

Was this guy honest or just speaking legalese? He brought a hand up to rub his chin. "You have a way to verify that it's legitimate and legal?"

"Of course."

Steve pondered the information then gave Tyler a hard look. "I must admit this all sounds too good to be true."

"I'm sure it does, but it's the truth." Andy maintained eye contact, the mark of an honest man.

Steve leaned forward, propped his elbows on the desk, and steepled his fingers. "I'm going to be upfront with you, Mr. Tyler. This idea won't fly if your client's going to call the shots."

Andy's brows darted upward. "What do you mean?"

"I'm the boss of this operation, not your client." Sweat trickled down Steve's back, but he forced himself to remain still. What if Tyler rescinded the offer?

The man eyed him a moment then spoke. "That's understandable. The only thing my client will determine is who gets the money." He removed a file from his briefcase, laid it on the desk, and pushed it toward him. "For the purpose of protecting our resources, the recipients will be required to send in progress reports and financial records."

He perused the file. "I'll want another attorney to check this. Do you mind me asking how much is available?"

"At least ten million dollars."

Steve's heart skipped a beat. His jaw hinged open and he shifted in his seat, leaning across the desk toward Andy. "I'm sorry. I don't think I heard you correctly."

The attorney chuckled. "You heard me, all right. Ten million dollars."

He exhaled a long puff of air between his lips in an attempt to slow his pulse, which had taken off like race horses at an opened gate.

Andy continued. "My client reserves the right to pull funding at any time, but we'll protect your interests by stating in a contractual agreement that no project will be left without enough funding to see it through to completion."

His mind whirled. They wouldn't come close to spending ten million dollars.

The lawyer laced his fingers in front of him and let his elbows rest against the arms of the chair. "The foundation will fund improvements to the downtown area as well as private homes. Money will also be available for advertising and other promotional expenses."

The funding covered more than renovations to downtown? There'd be enough money to bring in businesses and customers—a dream come true—no, a prayer answered. He fell back in his chair and let out a low whistle. "Why does your client want to be anonymous?"

"I'm not at liberty to say, but I assure you my client strongly believes in this town and what it can become."

"This person has visited Miller's Creek?"

"Yes."

Steve mulled over this last piece of information. He couldn't sneeze without someone in Miller's Creek calling to say "Bless you." Whoever this anonymous person was, they knew how to be discreet. Brighton must've found an interested investor. Or maybe Brighton *was* the investor.

Andy lifted one corner of his mouth. "Trying to figure out who my client is won't help. If I were you I'd just accept the offer and move ahead with your plans."

Would it be that easy? With the town so opposed to an outside investor, he somehow doubted it.

Queasiness roller-coasted in Dani's stomach and catapulted a vile taste onto her tongue. When Mama Beth mentioned who she'd invited to lunch, Dani had launched into a full-blown panic attack. Now she paced from the kitchen to the front window, then back to the kitchen again.

The crunch of truck tires on the gravel driveway drew her to the living room window like a magnet. Could she make this work? She emitted a slow breath to still her racing heart and returned to the kitchen where her aunt pulled homemade dinner rolls from the oven. Normally the aroma of fresh-baked bread made Dani salivate, but today she pressed a hand to her stomach. "They're here."

"Well, don't just stand there. Let 'em in." Mama Beth dumped steaming baby carrots into a brown earthenware bowl.

Dani scurried to the front, her heart knocking against her ribs. Steve held the screen door for Andy and motioned for him to enter, but barely glanced at her. She frowned. Why did he look so uncomfortable? The news should have him dancing a jig.

"Mr. Tyler, this is Mrs. Davis. She's the niece of the lady I told you about."

Mrs. Davis? When had he stopped calling her Dani? And did he still only see her as Mama Beth's niece? She extended a hand with a warning smile. "Please call me Dani."

Andy, a teasing gleam in his eye, seized her hand and held it longer than necessary. His conspiratorial wink sent panic hurtling through her body. Didn't he realize how serious this was? She ignored him and led the way to the kitchen.

Mama Beth bustled toward them wiping her hands on her apron, her voice welcoming. "You must be Mr. Tyler."

"Yes, and you're Miss Adams." Andy took her hand in his. "The food smells awesome."

Her aunt's face lit. Leave it to Andy to win her over. It wouldn't be long before every female in town lined up for a glimpse of his golden curls, dark lashes, and sea-green eyes.

After the blessing Andy initiated conversation while the bowls of food made their way around the table. "This is a magnificent house, Miss Adams. Have you lived here all your life?"

Mama Beth clanked a serving spoon against the bowl of mashed potatoes and shook her head. "I've lived in Miller's Creek all my life, but I've lived in this house about thirty years."

"My grandfather built this house." Steve joined the conversation, his tone and expression still somber. "It stayed in our family 'til we moved to the ranch. That's when Mama Beth bought it."

This house once belonged to the Millers? Dani mentally filed the new information.

Mama Beth passed the mashed potatoes to Steve, but focused her attention on Andy. "Where are you from?"

"Dallas."

"Really? That's where Dani used to live."

Dani choked on a carrot and reached for her water. *Stay calm!* She darted a peek at each of their faces then took a slow breath. No one seemed to have noticed her nervousness ... except maybe Steve.

Andy continued to cut his pork chop, but glanced at her while he carved the juicy meat. "Miller's Creek must be quite a change from the Big D."

She shot him a look of appreciation. "Definitely, but I still love it." Steve's eyes narrowed slightly. With a bite of her hot roll she lowered her gaze. Was he opposed to her living here, or did he already suspect her role in all this? Dani turned to Andy again, but looked past him at Steve. "So what brings you to Miller's Creek, Mr. Tyler?"

Various emotions flitted across Steve's face. Relief. Joy. Indecision. Worry. Why? "Andy has a client that wants to invest in Miller's Creek. They've set up a foundation so people can apply for funding." His voice was tight, like a kite string in a gust of wind.

Mama Beth clapped and produced a broad smile. "I told you God would work this out."

"Yes, you did." Steve's expression and tone momentarily softened, but as soon as his attention shifted back to Dani, he frowned.

Why was he acting so weird? Had she done something to offend him?

Several minutes later, Andy pushed his plate away and rubbed a hand over his belly. "That was the best home-cooked meal I've had in a long time, Miss Adams. I appreciate you having me over for lunch."

"Glad you enjoyed it. I guess your work will be bringing you back here from time to time." Her aunt sipped her sweet iced tea.

"Yes, in fact, I need to talk with my client about leasing an office in one of the buildings downtown."

Dani struggled to keep the smirk off her face at Andy's sly hint. Her smile disappeared as quickly as it had come. How could they handle private business in a town with such nosy people? She lifted her head to find Steve staring at her, his eyebrows joined in the middle.

Mama Beth's chair scraped against the hardwood floors as she scooted her chair from the table and grabbed Andy's plate. "Well, if you ever need a place to stay, you're always welcome at Mama Beth's Bed and Breakfast."

Andy gave a good-natured laugh. "I may have to take you up on that." He stood and shifted to the window. "Mind if I look around your garden?"

She jumped at the chance to speak with Andy alone and vaulted to her feet. "I'll show Mr. Tyler around if you'd like me to." The words tumbled from her mouth.

"That's very thoughtful of you, sweetie. Steve can help me clean up."

The glare on Steve's face propelled paranoia through her insides. Was he just being his usual moody self, or was his behavior based on suspicion?

৫১৮৯৩

Secrets Kept

Elbows propped on the kitchen table, Dani rested her head in her hands and waited for the caffeine from her third cup of coffee to kick in. A yawn crept out. How had she maneuvered herself into this mess? She'd labored on a to-do list until the wee hours of the morning. Now it lay hidden beneath her pillow with no way to make it happen, at least not without arousing suspicion. How could she steal away from Mama Beth long enough to phone Andy?

Her aunt wandered in from the living room. "You look bushed."

"That bad, huh? I didn't sleep well last night." She sipped from her cup then grimaced—nothing like strong coffee to make your tongue grow fur.

Mama Beth pinned her with a quizzical look. "The Holy Grounds coffee klatch is meeting today. Want to come?"

She brightened. The opportunity she hoped for had just landed in her lap. "No thanks, I'll hang here or get out and drive around Miller's Creek."

A half hour later her aunt left with a promise to return after lunch, so Dani dragged herself up the stairs for the list. The first order of business: to call Andy. She punched speed dial while she descended the stairs, then plunked the list down on the table and stared out the window at the drought-wilted flowers. Their drooping petals mirrored her energy level. Zapped.

"I was starting to think you weren't going to call." Andy's cheery voice rang out on the other end.

If he knew how punchy she felt, he'd be a little more careful about irritating her frayed nerves with his over-exuberance. "Sorry. Lack of privacy is a bigger issue than I expected. How are the plans going on that end?"

"Great. We've received several applications, and I think I located an office space."

"Good. Where?"

"Steve suggested an office at City Hall. There's even an apartment on an upper floor that I can rent. A little antiquated, but it will do."

She tensed. Wasn't City Hall a little too ... public? "I don't think that's such a good idea. We should find you a different building where I can come and go without Steve's knowledge."

"You don't need to worry about Steve. Trust me. He's completely focused on this project. Besides, it makes sense for me to be near his office for the application process."

A niggle in her brain tapped out a warning, but she flicked it away. Andy was right. She was worrying for no reason.

He rattled on. "Before I forget, I located the owner of the property you're interested in buying. A Mr. Bo Miller. Any kin to Steve?"

Her heart fluttered. The Millers? Would they approve of her plan for the land? "His dad, but I had no idea the property belonged to them."

A buzz of voices filtered through the phone, and then Andy came back on the line. "Listen, can I call you back? I've got something I need to tend to here."

"Sure." The words were out of her mouth, and the conversation closed, before she realized her error. What if he called back while Mama Beth was home? Well, she couldn't worry about it at the moment. There was too much to do. Dani checked her call to Andy off the list and studied item number two. She'd rather have her toenails removed with pliers. And no anesthetic. Howard Huff wouldn't take kindly to her news, but she couldn't let him stand in the way of her plans.

The current president of the company her father once owned wore his sneaky-snake reputation like the Congressional Medal of Honor, but the time had come to let him know who was boss. Dani eyed the clock and released a heavy breath. If she didn't get a move on, there wouldn't be enough time to visit Trish and big Bo before Mama Beth returned. Plus, she'd promised the old geezers she'd help clean out a couple of the buildings downtown, and she still needed to feed and bathe Little Bit. She pressed the phone key pad with a clenched jaw, while the furry kitten batted at her shoestring.

"Hampton Enterprises."

"This is Dani Hampton-Davis. Mr. Huff, please."

"Please hold."

The canned music furthered her aggravation until she imagined Howard on the other end sweating bullets. She forced down a smirk. All work and no sleep made her snarly.

"Dani, how are you?" Howard's syrupy-sweet voice oozed through the phone. "Haven't seen you—"

"Since Richard's funeral." She sounded intentionally blunt, already tired of his phony baloney. "I wanted to let you know I've reached a decision on what we discussed earlier."

"Yes." He dragged the word out into three sticky syllables.

"I've decided not to sell the company."

Silence, then his once-sugary words turned surly. "But we agreed. You have no desire to run the company."

Fiery heat blazed through her. He'd picked the wrong day to argue. "You mean I *had* no desire to run the company—past tense. I've changed my mind."

"I see." He clipped the words then cleared his throat, his tone taking on a whine. "Can't we work something out? I can—"

Her patience snapped. "I need a construction crew for an out-of-town site, and I need it by next week."

He let out a disgusted snort. "That's not possible. Our crews are booked for at least a month."

The previous heat morphed to icy steel in her veins. "Then hire another crew. Of course I'll do it myself if you're not able to handle it."

"I'll take care of it. Just let me know the details." The phone clicked in her ear.

A shuddering breath stooped her shoulders. Why had she lost her temper? Now Howard would be out for blood. She definitely smelled trouble, but it didn't start with a T.

Half a million dollars? Steve snapped his head to attention and stared at his dad. Maybe he'd misunderstood.

On the terrace behind the main ranch house, Dad clunked down his cup on the teak table and repeated the information. "The man said he wanted the land on both sides of the creek, plus the train yard and depot, and he'd pay half a million dollars."

What man, and why so much? He ran a hand across his mouth. "I have plans for that property. Did he leave his name?"

"I wrote it down somewhere. Want me to find it?"

Steve shook his head. "I'll get it later." He had too much to do to stay longer. He rose from the slatted chair and stretched, his muscles achy from lack of sleep.

"Sure is dry." His father peered out at the fields where round bales of hay had been placed to provide food for the horses.

"And hot." He sniffed the dusty air. Another scorcher on the way. The temperature was already in the eighties at seven in the morning with the two hottest months of the year still ahead. The grass had long since withered to a crunchy brown. They needed rain, and soon.

"So, people are on board with this foundation idea?" His father clasped his hands in front and leaned forward, elbows resting on his knees.

"Most of 'em." Otis Thacker's grousing comments shoved their way into his mind, and he breathed out in exasperation. "I hate to cut this short, Dad, but I should probably head into town."

His father sat back in the chair to peer up at him. "But you just got here. I hoped you'd stay long enough to chat a while and visit your mama."

A lump of guilt clogged his throat. Not today. He couldn't take her wordless blank stares anymore. With the toe of his boot, he kicked at a pebble. "Sorry, Dad, but I've got lots of work to do."

His father pushed himself to a standing position, his eyes sad and droopy. "I understand." They ambled toward Steve's pickup, parked beneath a clump of live oaks. Dad reached over and patted his shoulder. "You're doing a great job as mayor, Son. I'm proud of you."

"Thanks, but I can't take credit. I'm still dumbfounded at how it all happened."

"Dani certainly seems impressed."

He frowned. Dani? Impressed with him? Since when? "You've seen her?"

"She comes out to visit Trish and the kids and stops by from time to time. She's real good with Evelyn."

Dani had visited his parents? Emotions he couldn't decipher stabbed at him. Anger? Guilt? Gratitude? He was so tired, he wasn't sure how he felt.

They reached the truck. "Think I should accept the offer on the land?" His father's low words interrupted his confused thoughts.

Steve paused beside the truck. The ranch had suffered a rough year financially, but should they sell land that had been in their family for over a hundred years? He massaged his neck and released a breath through his nose. How could he make these spur-of-the-moment decisions with no time to think? He gave a reluctant nod and climbed into the truck. "Half a million dollars is a lot of money. At that price, I don't see how we can say no."

Dad pushed the pickup door shut. "Okay. I'll call the guy and tell him we'll sell."

On the ride into town, his mind churned with thoughts of Dani. The coffee he'd downed in place of breakfast curdled in his stomach, and a nasty taste made its way to his mouth. At last week's lunch she seemed to have formed an instant connection with Tyler, and it bothered him to no end—like he'd missed something—like there was more to this story than Dani had mentioned.

Steve glanced at his watch. Work called, but it would have to wait until he put the pieces of this puzzle together. He steered a path toward Mama Beth's house, and minutes later let himself in the front door and strode to the kitchen.

"Andy, no one else can know." Dani started as he entered the room, her eyes and mouth widening. In less than a heartbeat her voice took on instant cheer. "Thanks for calling. Good to talk to you. Bye-bye."

A stone of suspicion sank in his gut. What was between her and Andy that no one else could know? And why did he get the impression she'd known the man for longer than a few days?

"Hey, Steve." Dani leaned down to pick up the kitten. Still unsteady on its feet, it's white round tummy dragged the floor when it toddled around. She'd done a good job of caring for the cuddly critter. Holding Little Bit up to her face, she landed a smooch on the kitten's pink nose. "There's my cute baby. Come to Mama." Her voice took on the sound of a mother crooning to a infant.

He scowled at the conflicting emotions rolling inside him. One minute she had him doubting her every move and the next admiring her mothering skills.

Dani turned toward him. "If you're here to see Mama Beth, she's at her Bible study."

"Actually, I came for a cup of coffee. Mind if I pour myself a cup?"

She hesitated briefly then nodded. "Sure, go right ahead. Hope you like it chunky."

"That strong, huh?" Steve sauntered to the coffee pot and filled his travel mug. Her expression told him she didn't want him to stay, but why? Well, too bad. He was here for answers and answers he'd get. "I couldn't help but hear you talking on the phone when I came in. Were you talking to Andy Tyler?"

Bright red blotches appeared on her cheeks. "Um, yeah."

He pulled out a chair and sat across the table from her, his eyes glued to her face. "What is it that no one else can know?"

She swallowed. Hard. "Sorry, I don't know what you're talking about."

"I thought I heard you say that no one else could know."

Dani tucked her top lip between her teeth, shifted her weight, and lowered her eyes. "I don't remember."

He scrutinized her face. She *did* remember, but she wasn't going to share it with him. Maybe he'd have more success with a different tactic. He took a swig of coffee. "You two seemed to have hit it off pretty quickly."

"I guess so." She busied her hands playing with the kitten, who chewed on her pinkie finger. "This baby's hungry again." Without even a glance his direction, she rose to her feet and moved to the cabinets. A minute later she returned with a saucer of the pet formula and an eyedropper. Soon the kitten greedily sucked down several droppers full of liquid, her eyes closing in slumber.

Steve watched with interest as Dani gently brought the black and white fur ball to her chest and moved to the pet pillow in the corner of the dining room. Anyone with that much compassion couldn't be planning something underhanded. Could she?

She returned to her seat, took a sip of coffee, and looked him straight in the eye. "Andy and I have a lot in common. We both grew up in Dallas. It's only natural that I would hit it off with him, don't you think?"

"Guess so." Why did he feel so . . . disappointed? The answer hit him like a wrecking ball. He cared about her and had hoped that one day circumstances would allow them to move their relationship to a different level. The thought added another weight, and his shoulders slumped. "Well, I guess I'd better get going." He pushed himself away from the table and stood.

She rose to her feet. "How are things going downtown?"

"Great. So fast I can barely keep up actually."

"But that's a good problem, right?" She seemed eager to know his answer.

He nodded. "Yeah, it is. I can always sleep after the renovation's complete."

Her musical laughter echoed off the walls as she escorted him to the front door. "I totally understand the lack of sleep thing."

Steve took in the dark circles beneath her eyes. Why was she tired? Maybe it had to do with the kitten. He checked his watch, not wanting to leave, but knowing he had no choice. "Well, I'll see you later."

"Maybe so. I promised J. C. I'd help him and the old geezers clean out a couple of buildings."

He took notice of the news. It wouldn't hurt to be on hand while she was downtown. Just to keep an eye on things. "I'll try to drop by and help. What time will you be there?"

She glanced at the clock, the same expression on her face as when he'd invited himself to stay for a cup of coffee. "Hmmm, I don't really know. I've got a couple of other errands to run first."

He wasn't letting her off the hook that easy. "Like what? We could meet for lunch and then get to work on that cleaning project."

"I already have lunch plans, but thanks anyway. I'm eating at the ranch."

Suspicions surged to the surface like bits of ocean debris after a hurricane. Why did she spend more time at the ranch than he did?

❦19❦

Torn

Dani peeked furtively between the mini-blinds of the daycare office window. Good. No one should walk in on her unannounced like Steve and Mama Beth always did. The kids and workers congregated on the playground and would remain there until the heat forced them inside. Cell phone to her ear, she faced the door. Andy answered on the second ring.

"It's me, Andy. Sorry I hung up on you earlier, but this time it was Mama Beth who walked in on our conversation." She hated keeping secrets from her aunt—hated the sneaking around—but it was the only way. Dani nibbled her thumbnail. Father and Mother had utilized their wealth to purchase people's admiration and friendship. In a word, to manipulate, and she refused to follow their example. From her front-row perspective, she'd seen enough of their grand-standing to leave a permanent sour taste in her mouth.

Muffled voices sounded over the phone before Andy spoke. "No problem. Listen, we have a couple of law students clerking for us this summer, and they can handle a lot of my work load here. That will allow me to spend a few days a week in Miller's Creek to keep up with this paperwork."

"Okay."

"Just okay? I was hoping you missed me more than that." His words took on a mock tone of hurt.

Her spine stiffened. Was he serious? She cleared her throat. "I'm sorry. What were you saying?"

Andy's voice flattened. "Never mind, I'll see you on Friday."

Friday? She eyed the applications she'd just approved. They needed to be processed now. "Okay, but I'm going to fax some approved applications for you to forward to Steve."

After goodbyes were said, she flipped her phone shut and powered up the fax machine. While it hummed and zipped, her thoughts returned to the conversation with Andy. Surely he wasn't interested in her as more than just a good friend. Anything else would be awkward.

Laying the next application on the machine, she closed the lid and punched the button. Steve made life awkward enough. His latest behavior had her bamboozled. At first he seemed overly eager to be around her, but not in a good way, almost as if he didn't trust her. Here lately he'd been distant and aloof, and his visits to the house timed for when she was gone.

Dani released a heavy sigh. The renovation would be through in a few months. Then hopefully she and Steve could resume their original camaraderie. She missed their friendly banter. She missed him. The realization rattled her. Maybe it was a good thing that the renovation project kept them both busy.

Once she finished the paperwork, she stuffed the requests for funding into her bag, peered out the window, and smiled. Now she could do what she'd been itching to do all day—spend time with the kids.

The shaded canopy of pecan trees behind her aunt's daycare provided the perfect location for children to play during the heat of summer. She breathed deep of the morning air. This place was an anchor of sanity in her chaotic life.

Her gaze traveled the playground, pain coursing through her. She squeezed her eyes shut. Having a child of her own would never happen, just an old dream that wasn't meant to be.

Moisture gathered in her eyes, but seeing Little Bo brought a frown. He straddled the sand box wall in front of her, tears streaming down his round cheeks. She hurried to him, intentionally slowing her pace as she approached. "Hi. Can I sit here?"

He hoisted one shoulder, then sniffled and wiped his face against his shirt.

Dani perched on the big timbers surrounding the sand pit, dug one hand in the sand, and allowed it to sift between her fingers. Little Bo's light brown eyes focused on the movement, and he joined her. "You want to tell me what's wrong?" She took care to keep her tone non-confrontational.

He didn't answer.

Maybe a back door approach would work better. "Seen any movies lately?"

Another shrug.

"I heard about a good kid's movie showing in Morganville. Maybe we can go sometime."

Again no response. Okay, she was running out of ideas here. She brightened at the next thought. This would work. "Your mom told me you got a new horse."

Bingo! A big grin that reminded her of Steve spread across his face. "Yeah, I named him Domino, 'cause he has spots all over him!"

She laughed out loud at his enthusiasm, but the ache in her heart for a child of her own returned with a stabbing intensity. What would it be like to cradle a child of her own in her arms, to watch him take his first steps, to hear him call her Mama?

❖   ❖   ❖

Steve eyed the encroaching pile of paper stacked on his desk. At first he'd been able to keep up with the requests for funding and had thrown himself into the work, mainly as a distraction to keep his mind off Dani. But over the past three days the workload had tripled, with more and more people adding their applications to the pile. Would the mysterious donor be put off by all these requests? He shook the thought off like a dog after a swim. As if he didn't already have enough to worry about. Why add more?

He circled his head to relieve the tension in his shoulders and neck, every creak and pop a reminder of age. In addition to the paperwork, his personal responsibilities mounted. Mom's health declined more everyday. Part of him wanted to pray for her suffering to end, but that kind of prayer seemed almost impossible. How could you pray for something when it meant loss for you and those you loved?

Dani had been so good to visit his parents, and though he didn't understand her motives, he was grateful. He clasped his hands behind his neck and stretched out straight in the chair. The image of her happy face at church yesterday floated to his mind. Country life certainly agreed with her. She'd changed somehow, as if her sorrow had been gently erased and replaced with joy. Was it because of God or Andy? The thought of losing her thrust ice through his veins, and he immediately chastised himself. You couldn't lose something that wasn't yours.

His office phone buzzed. He punched the speaker button and leaned forward to hear Wanda's nasally voice. "Trish on line one."

He smiled, clicked to the other line, and brought the phone to his ear. "Hey, Sis."

"How much do you love your little sister?"

A chuckle erupted. "Okay, what do you want?"

"I'm doing some shopping in Morganville and running a wee bit behind." From her pleading tone he could visualize her puppy-dog eyes. "I called Doc, but he's snowed under. And I think Dani must already be at the daycare. Can you pick up Little Bo for me? I promised him I'd be there before lunch."

Steve viewed his own snowy mountain of paperwork and raised his eyebrows. "Sure, why not?" Besides, if Dani was at the daycare . . .

"I owe you, big brother."

"Yep, but I can be bought for the right price."

Her throaty laughter made him grin. "Okay, I'll bake you a batch of caramel brownies. How's that?"

"Perfect."

He hung up, gathered the papers, and stood, suddenly overjoyed at the prospect of spending time with his nephew. Or could it be the chance to see Dani? The walk into the open sunshine planted a sense of freedom within him, like a kid on the first day of summer vacation. A ton of work screamed for his attention, but he shut it out and continued to walk away. He needed this. He'd swing by the daycare to get Bo, treat him to an ice cream, then dash to the lake for a picnic, boat ride, and afternoon swim.

A short two blocks' drive placed him at the country blue bungalow now converted into Just for Kids daycare. Mama Beth kept the place looking like a storybook cottage, with white shutters and planter boxes loaded with flowers. The carefree laughter of children at play brought a grin to his face and sent him in the direction of the playground. A little girl pointed him to the sandbox, where Bo sat deep in conversation with Dani as they built a sandcastle.

His heart skipped a beat, and he puzzled over why the scene evoked such a strong reaction. Steve pressed his lips together. Probably best if he didn't think too long on that question. He sauntered toward them, neither one noticing him until he spoke. "Is this a private conversation or can anyone join?"

"Uncle Steve!" Bo yelled out his words, then jumped up and engulfed him in a hug that knocked the air from his lungs.

"Hmph." Steve brought a hand to his abdomen with a soft chuckle. "Hey, Tiger, how are you?" He tousled his nephew's hair.

Bo's eyes twinkled. "Good. I was telling Dani about Domino."

"You were?"

"Yep. Why are you here?" Bo squinted up at him and pooched out his lips.

"Well, your mom's shopping—"

His nephew rolled his eyes. "Girls!"

Dani's laughter pealed like ringing bells. "Hey watch it, bud. I'm a girl." She reached over and tickled his belly.

Bo giggled and ducked behind him. Steve grabbed him by the arms and swung him around in a semi-circle. "Why don't you play with your friends for a few more minutes, and then we'll leave."

"Roger, over and out." Off like a streak, he made car sounds with his lips while he sprinted toward his friends.

Dani's yearning gaze followed Bo until he disappeared in a crowd of kids. She turned a smiling face to him, and he caught his breath. Could she hear his heart jack-hammering against his shirt? "Looks like y'all were having a serious conversation."

A slight frown creased her forehead. "I think he must've had a disagreement with one of his friends. He was sitting here by himself and crying, but once I mentioned his horse all was forgotten."

Steve shifted his weight and searched for words, but none came. He hated this tongue-tied feeling. The light scent of her perfume drifted past his nose, and beads of sweat broke out under his collar.

Dani squinted toward a group of kids standing nearby. "One of the things I love most about kids is they're so forgiving. One minute they're hurt and upset, and the next back to being best buddies."

The light shining in her eyes sent his heart back into jackhammer mode. She'd make a great mother. He swallowed, trying to wash away the cotton that formed in his mouth.

Her expression darkened as she faced him, her words hesitant. "Speaking of forgiving, I want you to know I'm sorry if I did something to upset you."

"Me? Upset?" He sat down beside her.

"A couple of weeks ago when you brought Andy over you seemed upset. And a few times since then I felt it again. I thought maybe I'd offended you in some way."

A pang jabbed him in the ribs. He'd been a jerk, and she was the one apologizing. "I wasn't upset at you. I have a lot on my mind right now."

"Is that why we haven't seen much of you lately?"

Her scrutiny made him squirm like a kid caught with his hand in the cookie jar. He nodded. The renovation, the ranch, his mother, they'd all been his excuse. But if the truth be told, he'd avoided her because of the instant attachment she and Andy had formed. It hurt to admit he was attracted to a woman who didn't return his feelings.

She chewed her lower lip and surveyed the playground, the morning sun coloring her face a golden hue. "I saw your Mom and Dad earlier."

"Yeah, Dad mentioned you'd stopped by."

"He seems so lonely." The outer corners of her eyes and mouth sank.

The punch to his gut hit its target. Except for five-minute rushed conversations, he'd been too busy to do anything about Dad's loneliness. He let out a deep breath. "So Little Bo told you about Domino?"

Dani's lips curved into a smile. "He's so excited about that horse. Can't say I blame him." Her eyes took on a distant look. "I remember wanting a horse when I was his age. Probably wouldn't have gone over well with the neighborhood's homeowner association in North Dallas."

Steve smiled with her, but could think of nothing to say in response. Her childhood seemed somehow lacking. Each moment grew more uncomfortable as he struggled to find words. Nothing. He rose to his feet, hat in hand, and stared at the dusty toes of his boots. "Well, guess I'd better go. See you later."

A small crinkle appeared between her brows. "Oh, okay. Bye."

When he left with Bo two minutes later, Dani still crouched in the same spot, her chin propped on one fist, in her eyes a longing. He paused hoping to catch her attention, but she never glanced his way.

Later that evening, with Little Bo safely deposited at home, he wandered to the wooden fence encircling the horse paddock. The horses grazed in the hush of evening, the tips of the trees golden in the ebbing daylight.

His nephew's pinto pony reminded him of the earlier conversation with Dani, and he emitted a heavy sigh. Good grief, he was thirty-eight years old. Why was it so hard to ask her for a date? Surely she'd agree to at least a movie. His lips pursed. No, he wanted more. He wanted conversation so they could get to know each other. So he could find out where she stood with God. But how? He shook himself and peered at Domino, a smile broadening on his face.

He had his answer.

❧20❧

Seeking

Dani reached for the pink Ropers she'd found at a consignment shop last weekend in Morganville and tugged them on, then inspected her reflection in the mirror. Combined with the vintage jeans, she looked the part of a country girl. What happened to the overdressed woman from six weeks ago? She brought a hand to her cheek, not quite sure she recognized herself. When had the sadness disappeared, and why? The answer came at once.

After years of searching, she'd finally found a place to call home. Like her blue jeans and boots, this new life in Miller's Creek somehow fit. Steve, Mama Beth, the whole crew, they'd become her new family, and she didn't want to consider how empty her life would be without them. She snatched her cowboy hat from the antique rack next to the vanity and shoved it on her head. The creek and a beautiful morning beckoned, and she had no time to waste.

She clomped down the stairs to the kitchen, and Mama Beth looked up, a big grin spreading across her face. "You look like you've lived here your whole life."

"Interesting you should say that." Dani hustled to the cabinet, grabbed a breakfast bar, and peeled back the wrapper. "I was just thinking how it feels like I've lived here a lot longer than six weeks." Like her life in Dallas belonged to a different person.

A happy smile adorned on her aunt's face as she rose from the table. "I'm glad you like it here. For a while I wondered if you'd be able to adapt to small-town life."

She thought back to her first weeks in Miller's Creek with the nosy neighbors and her confused feelings about Steve. Well, at least the nosy neighbor part was over. "I wasn't sure about that myself, but things seem to have quieted down, especially with the neighbors." Thank goodness. She bit into the chocolate oat bar and stepped to the fridge to pour a glass of milk.

Mama Beth laughed. "If you can win over the Thackers, you can win over anyone."

Dani followed her aunt to the front porch. The screen door screeched its familiar song, and a squirrel fussed at the interruption from the leafy branches of the red oak. Her aunt plopped into the rocking chair. "What's on your agenda today?"

Oh, what she'd give to have no agenda. "I thought I'd walk to the creek while it's still cool. What about you?"

"I promised Gladys I'd go to Morganville, so I'm glad you have something to do."

Her mind traveled to the stack of papers in her room. She had plenty to do all right. Monitoring the expense reports had become an ever-increasing chore. At least Andy was in town now to give her a hand. After a quick hike, she'd take advantage of Mama Beth's absence to catch up on business. She finished breakfast and hugged her aunt, then headed out the gate, over the barbed-wire fence, and across the pasture.

Once in the wide-open field, a comfortable peace settled on her like a bed sheet straight from the clothesline. The warmth from the sun's rays kissed her bare arms, and joy played its song in her heart. Could life be any sweeter?

An overnight rain shower had left behind its musty scent, and she drank in a deep breath. How long had it been since she'd allowed herself the luxury of a few stolen moments? Five minutes later Dani reached the happy burble of the creek, hungry for the cool shade of the trees. With a twist of her head, she viewed her shoulders, already tinged with pink. A sleeved shirt would've been a wiser choice. She settled onto a boulder near the creek and allowed the gentle trickle to lull her into a relaxed state.

Peace. Why had she discovered it in Miller's Creek of all places? She mulled over the question. It had to be God. His presence seemed to surround her, but was it because He was so real to Mama Beth and Steve?

Horse hooves pounded behind her, and she jerked her head around. Steve sat atop a large reddish-brown horse and led a smaller spotted one. She jumped to her feet and smoothed her hair, then tucked her hands in her hip pockets, her heart thudding with excitement. Why? It had to be the horses. Steve was just a friend of the family—nothing more, nothing else—ever.

The horses slowed to a stop, and Steve pushed his hat back, an interested grin on his handsome face. "Well don't you look like a country gal?" His gaze swept over her with an intensity that launched a burn in her cheeks.

Snap out of it, Dani. "Do you always take a spare horse when you're out riding?"

He chuckled, his cheeks dimpling. "Only when I'm looking for company."

Her skin tingled. He was looking for her? "How'd you know where to find me?"

"Mama Beth." Steve adjusted his weight and rested his wrists on the knot of leather at the front of the saddle. "You like it here at the creek?"

She bobbed her head. "Love it. Thanks for letting me come here."

"You're welcome." He swung his frame off the horse in one swift movement.

"Dani, I'd like you to meet Domino." Steve pulled the reins, and the second horse stepped closer, his hooves making a hollow clopping sound against the river rock.

The spotted horse pricked his ears and dipped his head, his soft chocolate-drop eyes focused on her. "The Domino? How'd you steal him away from Little Bo?"

"Wasn't easy, but when I told him who was going to ride him, he gave his consent." His lazy perusal made her breath catch. "Seems you've charmed even the youngest member of the Miller clan."

Dani lowered her gaze, her pulse thumping in her throat. How was she supposed to respond to that? She inched closer to Domino, rubbed between his eyes, and murmured soothing tones. He nuzzled up to her, his velvety nose inches from her shoulder.

Steve's face loomed close, his eyelids half-closed. "See, Domino likes you, too."

The words came out low and soft, and her heart headed into a gallop. Okay, a little too close for comfort. She backed away, wiping sweaty palms against her jeans. "Are we going to stand here talking, or can I ride him?"

He didn't answer. Instead his hooded eyes searched hers.

"What do I do first?" She gulped out the words.

His lazy grin sent sparks along her backbone. "Well, the first step is getting you on the horse. You can crawl up yourself or I can lift you, whichever you prefer."

She swallowed against the dryness in her mouth. "I think I can handle it."

He gripped her elbow and guided her to the left side of the horse. "Grab a hold of the saddle horn and reins with both hands."

"Um, is the saddle horn that little knobby thingy sticking up in front?"

Steve's smile inched into a chuckle that ended in a laugh. "Yeah. That little knobby thingy is the saddle horn. Grab hold of it." He handed her the reins. "Now put your left foot in the stirrup and pull yourself up."

After two tries she finally managed to land her foot in the stirrup. It would've been nice to know that riding a horse entailed lifting your leg higher than your belly button. With one foot on the ground, she scanned the height of the horse and skewed her lips. This horse looked so much smaller a few minutes ago. She took a deep breath. *Come on, Dani, you can do this.* Pushing off with her right leg, she used her arms to hoist herself onto the horse. Now towering over Steve from Domino's back, she let out a crow. "I did it! Wow! Am I ready to go?"

"Whoa there, girl." He held up both hands. "Give me a sec to adjust the stirrups."

Steve's strong fingers moved her left leg out of the way, shortened the leather strap, and set her foot back in place. While he made his way to the other side, she pulled her right foot away, one less thing for him to have to do.

He raised the stirrup on the right side, then guided her foot into it, patted her leg, and peered up at her. "How does that feel?"

Dani checked her feet in the stirrups, ignoring her racing heart. "Good."

Steve mounted his horse and gave her a grin. "Ready?"

She nodded. "I think so."

"Just give him a gentle nudge with your heels."

Dani followed his instructions, and the powerful beast shifted beneath her in a steady rhythm. Her spirit soared. She flashed a grateful smile Steve's way, but it immediately faded. Head lowered, his eyes focused on the ground, and his lips pressed together in a determined line.

❖ ❖ ❖

Dani wasn't as much of a city gal as he'd first thought. She'd taken to horseback riding like a bird dog to water. Steve angled his head to look at her then quickly looked away. He wasn't prepared for what being around her did to him.

He steered the horses close to the creek, then through pastures interspersed with live oak, mesquite, and cedar. Dani rode beside him without speaking, but other sounds filled the silence—the breeze in the trees, the steady clop of hooves on the soil, and Domino's and Biscuit's gentle snorts.

She wore a contented smile, but squinted against the brightness of the climbing sun. "Does all this belong to your family?"

"Yes."

Dani brought one hand to lower her hat against the glare. "Pretty impressive."

"Thanks. The land's been in my family a long time."

"I can tell it's special to you." She flashed him a sweet smile and sent his pulse into overdrive.

Special didn't begin to explain his feelings for this place. The land was as much a part of him as breathing. "Yep, it's home."

The smile on Dani's face disappeared, and her eyes took on a distant look. "Must be nice to have such a connection to a place." She spoke in a sad little voice.

"Don't you feel the same way about Dallas?"

"No. I like Dallas, but even after growing up there, it never felt like home."

Biscuit's sweaty horse smell reached his nose as he tried to wrap his brain around her comment. How could you live some place your entire life and it not be home? Then again, he'd never be able to see the city as home either.

Dani's heavy sigh turned his head toward her. "I guess that's why I've enjoyed this summer so much. Miller's Creek feels like home."

The waters of his mind muddied as old feelings battled with new. Her thinking of Miller's Creek as home bothered him at one time, but not anymore. But exactly how did he feel? He pondered the question until the right answer came. "I'm glad you like it here."

She studied him for a long minute then glanced away. "I just can't figure out why being here makes me feel this way."

"Mama Beth probably has a lot to do with it."

A smile softened her mouth. "There's definitely a closeness to her I can't explain. I guess that's what home is. Your family." She spoke with hesitation.

"Mama Beth would say—"

Dani cut him short with a laugh, finishing the familiar words. "—our only home is heaven." Her words sounded cynical.

Did she doubt heaven's reality? "What do you think?"

"About heaven?" The inside corners of her eyebrows raised, and her lips tightened. "I don't know. Maybe that it sounds too good to be true."

His heart skipped a beat. *Lord, help me know how to help her.* He tugged Biscuit's reins and stopped beneath a large oak tree situated about five yards from the creek. "How 'bout some lunch?"

Her eyes widened. "You brought food?"

"Yep. Perfect day for a picnic, don't you think?"

Dani nodded, but her expression clouded.

He dismounted, opened the saddle bag, and glanced up at her. "You all right?"

The strain on her face vanished, replaced by a smile. "Yes, but, um, how do I get down?"

A wicked idea popped in his head. This should be interesting. He gave a noncommittal shrug. "Figure it out for yourself."

Her eyes narrowed then took on a gleam. "Okay." She dropped the reins to the ground and swung her right leg over Domino's ears to perch sideways on the saddle.

Good grief! If the horses spooked she'd be thrown and trampled. He raised both hands skyward and hurried to her. "I was only joking. Here let me help you." She slid into his arms, her fingers against his chest, and he froze.

Her eyelids fluttered, and she cleared her throat. "You can let me go now."

"Oh, sorry." He stepped away as heat steamed his face.

Dani dusted off her palms with a slapping sound. "Now where's that food? I'm starving."

They rested in the cool shade of an oak grove and feasted on the fried chicken and potato salad he'd picked up at Granny's, then washed it down with cold cans of pop while the grasshoppers and locusts cranked out their raspy song. During lunch she seemed reticent, so he took advantage of the time to study her.

How had he misjudged her so? She wasn't the ditzy blond or snooty city woman he'd first imagined. He blew a puff of air from his mouth and rested his elbows on his knees. Truth be told, he liked her. A lot. For the first time in forever, he was interested in a female, but her comment about heaven proved she wasn't yet a believer. Besides that, the timing was all wrong. With Mom's illness and his work for Miller's Creek, he didn't have time to breathe much less pursue a relationship. And she'd always be a city woman, no matter how she dressed. It was much too soon to tell if she could truly adapt to country living, so why had he jumped at this idea of taking her for a ride without giving it more thought?

Dani stared into the distance, her lips pursed. Without explanation, she stood and moved closer to the creek.

His eyebrows knit in concern. He couldn't let his feelings rush ahead of his brain. She needed time to figure things out, time to grow in her understanding of God and her relationship to Him. The last thing she needed was pressure from any guy. He gathered the sack of trash and started toward Biscuit, when she called out.

"Steve."

"Yeah." He stuffed the sack into the saddle bag.

"There's a rattlesnake by my foot."

He jerked his head up, his heart pounding. She was frozen in place. "Are you sure?"

"Pretty sure." Her voice sounded calm, calmer than he felt.

"Don't move."

"Wasn't planning on it."

With slow moves, Steve inched toward her, his heart pumping double-time. Not one, but two diamond backs slithered in the dirt at her feet. He glanced up at her. "You doing okay?"

"Yes."

"Just wait them out."

"Them?" Her eyes widened, but she didn't move.

"There are two. Must be a nest nearby."

A minute later the snakes were gone, and Steve hurried to her side, afraid she'd collapse. "Are you gonna be all right?"

Dani arched an eyebrow like he'd gone nuts. "Of course, what did you expect?"

He released a short laugh and scratched his cheek. "I guess I thought that since you were from the city—"

"—that I'd fall apart?" She snorted. "You don't know me very well, do you? I've been through much more than having a couple of rattlesnakes at my feet. The human version is much worse."

Dani moved toward Domino, a frown carving lines on her face. "Can I ask you a question?"

"Sure."

"How can you be so certain about your belief in God?" Her troubled blue eyes focused on him.

He sucked in a deep breath, the scent of the rich dirt filling his nostrils. *Lord, give me the words to bring her closer to You.* "It's more than something I believe—it's something I know. I feel Him. I know He's real."

She nodded, but didn't speak.

His heart fell to the ground. Why couldn't he explain in a way she could comprehend? He transferred a hand to his neck to swipe away the moisture from the heat of the day. "They call it faith for a reason, you know."

"Yeah." She pointed to a road barely visible in the thick underbrush. "Where does that road lead?"

"Home."

Without another word, she mounted Domino as if she'd done it all her life and prodded the horse in the direction of the road.

His head slumped forward. Her way of saying their time together was over.

෬21ຉ

A Star-Spangled Rodeo

Man, it didn't get any better than this! Steve eyed downtown Miller's Creek, where red, white, and blue banners adorned every building and anything else that stood still long enough to be decorated. Every day revealed more of the town he remembered from childhood. Though scaffolding still spidered along the sides of many buildings, his heart swelled at glimpses of the town's former glory.

"Hey, Mayor!" Coot's voice boomed from across Main Street. "Looking good, ain't it?"

"Hey, yourself, Coot. Sure is." He waved to Coot and the other old geezers then scurried on down the street. Flags popped in the breeze and flew from the old-timey street lamps purchased with foundation money. There were people everywhere. They'd shown up for the Fourth of July parade and now swarmed the town like a bunch of bees to check out the progress. Did the anonymous donor know how much their generosity meant to the town and its people? How much it meant to him? And would any of it have happened without Dani's ability to rally the town's support?

He whistled as he made his way to the creek, his favorite part of the re-do. When he and Dad had agreed to sell the property, he'd never dreamed the new owner's plans would line up so closely with his own. Miracle of miracles, Miller's Creek now had a city park, providing further proof that God worked in amazing ways.

At the first sight of bulldozers and cranes, he'd feared for the large oak trees that lined the creek like ancient sentinels, but his fears were unfounded. The new owner knew exactly what to do, and not one of the trees had been removed. To make things even better, the new owner had turned over most of the creative control to the city, and he'd been able to oversee most of the construction himself. He breathed a quick prayer of thanks, with a reminder that he needed to fear less and trust more.

Pausing at the corner of Main Street and Creekside Road, he looked across the park and allowed the sight to sink in. Stone and cedar shelters with picnic tables and barbecue pits had been erected along the creek, and in the center of the park, a large, well-lit pavilion. Now the area would be used for everything from birthday parties to family reunions. Already the place was full of happy faces and the laughter of kids as they romped on the state-of-the-art playground.

His cell phone vibrated in its holster at his waist. While he reached for it, his gaze traveled to the nostalgic foot bridge which joined the park to the old train depot on the other side of the creek. The new owner was responsible for that addition. Whoever it was, they definitely had an eye for detail.

He punched the talk button. "Hello?"

"We sure could use your help at the ranch." Trish sounded huffy.

Steve took in the depot's new paint job and laughed at his sister. "Why? It couldn't be too busy out there yet. Everyone's still in town." The annual Miller family barbecue usually meant extra work for everyone, but they'd hired an event planner this year to make things easier.

"We've had a crisis." She launched into a panicked tirade. "The caterers got here late. We spent so much time getting them situated that we don't have all the chairs set up."

Well, so much for easier. He let out a weary breath and brought a hand to his neck. "Okay, I'll get there as soon as I can."

Several minutes later he pulled onto the ranch road. Cars lined both sides, and based on the amount of traffic, he was too late. The crowds had already arrived, and Trish would be ready to strangle him. He parked and climbed from the truck, the smell of mesquite-smoked barbecue provoking hunger pangs in his belly. Conversation and laughter rang through the summer heat, and Trish hurried toward him, her head lowered. He gulped and prepared himself for her ire.

"Sorry you rushed out here for nothing." She smiled up at him and gave him a hug.

He lifted a brow. "What about the chairs?"

"While I was on the phone, Dani organized a crew and took care of it."

Dani was here? "That's good." He scratched his cheek and feigned a look of nonchalance. "Did you, uh . . . happen to see where Dani went?"

"Last time I saw her she was headed inside." A devilish grin came on his sister's face. "Why do you ask?"

"No particular reason."

She said nothing, but shot him an I-don't-believe-you look before heading back to the crowd with a wave of her hand.

Steve hurried toward the house. Here lately, he could never catch Dani without Andy at her side. This might be his chance. Even if he couldn't find her, he'd stop in for a quick visit with Dad. Animated voices caught his attention as he neared the living room. He stopped outside the entry. Dani perched next to Dad while he told a story Steve had heard a million times. Her face glowed with a smile, and her giggle mingled with his dad's hearty guffaws. A lump of unexpected emotion rose in his throat. How long had it been since he'd heard his father laugh?

Dad motioned him into the room. "Come on in, Son. I was just telling Dani how you broke your arm jumping out of the swing at school."

Her smiling face tipped toward him. "Afraid the teacher was going to catch you, weren't you?"

"As a matter of fact, I was." Now another teacher had caught him. Was she totally oblivious to the effect she had on him?

Dani rose to her feet and stooped to hug his dad. "Sorry, Bo, but I need to go. I left Mama Beth eating with the Thackers. She's probably wondering where I went."

Go? But he'd just found her.

She turned to face him. "Guess I'll see you at the rodeo later?"

He'd better stick his foot in this open door while he had the chance. "Sure, why don't I pick you up and we can go together?"

Dani nodded, but her smile dissipated. "Okay. What time?"

"I'll be there at 6:30. Ever been to a rodeo?"

"Nope, this will be another first." An awkward silence ensued. Moving toward the doorway, she gave a whisper of a smile and dipped her head shyly. "See you later." The sound of her retreating steps ricocheted off the marble floors.

When he turned to face Dad, his father's eyes skewered him. "You'd better not let that sweet woman out of your sight. Some other feller will snatch her up before you can blink twice."

He thought back to last Sunday when Andy had accompanied her to church. It could very well be too late.

Later that day Dani planted herself in front of the over-stuffed closet, hands on hips. What should she wear to the rodeo? Mama Beth would know. She scuttled down the stairs and into the kitchen, the air filled with the aroma of fresh peaches.

Her aunt hummed at the kitchen island while she diced the fruit into small slices for jelly. Dani sidled up to her and popped a juicy chunk of peach in her mouth, its tangy sweetness rushing onto her tongue. "Any idea what should I wear to the rodeo?"

The humming and dicing stopped, and Mama Beth faced her with raised eyebrows. "You going alone?"

Oh great. The last thing she needed was for her aunt to read something into this that wasn't there. She took a deep breath and tried to sound disinterested. "No, Steve said he'd take me ... as a friend." It was best to add that last part to clarify.

Mama Beth dried her hands on her apron, her tone suddenly all business. "Let's go upstairs and look through your closet."

After a few minutes of digging, her aunt heaved an exasperated sigh. "Dani Davis, you're never going to wear half of these clothes in Miller's Creek!"

"Too fancy?"

"I'll say. We've got to get to Morganville and buy you some regular people clothes."

Well, that didn't help her tonight. "Will my jeans and pink boots work?"

Her aunt let out a snort. "You talking about those raggedy things you bought at that consignment shop? No, you need something nicer." Mama Beth nailed her with an indecipherable look then swiveled back to the closet. She selected a blue and white sundress. "Maybe if you wear this with sandals, it won't seem too dressy."

An hour later Dani stood in front of the mirror, one hand to her churning stomach. This was *not* the message she wanted to send. The pictures she'd seen of rodeos showed people in jeans, boots, and cowboy hats, not flowery dresses.

She descended the stairs to find Steve and Mama Beth at the table. Her aunt's eyes misted over, and a smile curved her lips. "Oh, Dani, you look so pretty."

Pretty? She flitted a hand to her burning face. "I'm overdressed. I'll go put on my je—"

"Please don't." Dani froze at Steve's soft words. "You look beautiful just like you are."

Dressed in cream-colored jeans and a white shirt that set off his dark complexion, Steve rose and came toward her with a lanky-legged saunter. Her heart skidded to a stop. Cowboy clothes had never looked so good. She lowered her gaze at the encouraging smile he sent to bolster her confidence. Maybe the dress would be okay after all.

Senses overloaded, Dani had tried all night to take it in—the roar of the crowd and the blaring speakers, the ten-gallon hats and swaggers of bowlegged cowboys, their over-sized belt buckles a-glare in the bright lights.

The scent of Steve's cologne floated past her nose, and she raised her gaze to look at him, his dimpled grin fluttering her heart. He gripped her hand as they pushed through the crowd on their way back to the bleachers, but only managed two steps when someone else stopped him to chat, like he was some kind of celebrity. He took it in stride, smiled, laughed, and shook their hands, completely in his element.

Dani glanced at the other women around her, dressed in dark and carefully starched jeans, and then took in her flowered dress, confirming her original suspicions. More than just a fish out of water, she was a circus pony in a barn full of thoroughbreds.

Once back in the stands, she overcame her initial reserve and joined in with the rest of the crowd in what they called hooting and hollering. Steve raised his voice against the crowd noise. "Having a good time?"

She nodded and wrinkled her nose. "Well, except for that." Dani pinched her nose between her thumb and forefinger and pointed to the holding stall.

He leaned his head back and belted out a laugh. "Why darlin', that's Texas gold." He leaned closer to make himself heard. "What's your favorite thing so far?"

Dani thought about the question. "I can't decide. I liked the barrel racers, but I absolutely love the clowns."

Steve smiled, and with a light touch to her waist, turned her toward the arena. From their vantage point in the bleachers, she peered down into a stall, where a cowboy straddled the meanest looking bull she'd ever seen.

She tapped on his arm to get his attention. "What's he doing?"

"That's the bull rope. It gives the rider something to hang on to."

Attaching yourself to something so enormous and ferocious seemed rather . . . well, unintelligent.

He must have sensed her apprehension, because he squeezed her arm. "Don't worry. He knows what he's doing."

Her hands fisted into tight balls, and her stomach changed to pure acid. Why would anyone do something so idiotic? The cowboy astride the bull gave a single nod, and the chute opened. A whirling mass of muscle writhed into the arena, the roars of the crowd deafening. The bull's hind legs shot into the air time after time, while the cowboy bounced like a ball on a string. Without warning, the bull and rider separated, and the cowboy landed in a crumpled heap at the bull's stomping feet. Dani flinched and covered her eyes with both hands. *Please God, don't let him be trampled.*

Steve spoke into her ear, his arm cinched firmly around her shoulders. "You okay?"

She peeked at him between fingers. "Did he get hurt?"

"Nope. He's walking away. See?"

Dani forced her eyes toward the arena, released the breath she'd been holding, and pressed a hand to her churning stomach. Everything started to spin, but she didn't want to make a fuss.

She looked up to see Steve's concerned eyes focused on her face. "I think it's time to take you home."

"I'm okay."

"Yeah right, that's why your face is whiter than my shirt."

He grabbed her hand as they descended the bleachers and didn't release it when they reached the parking lot. "Feeling better?"

"Yes, thanks. I think I must have overheated. Well, that, and over-reacted. I'm sorry, if you want to watch the rest . . ."

Steve came to a standstill in the middle of the dusty field-turned-parking-lot, the crowd buzzing in the distance. He brought a hand to her face, and her heart galloped as his eyes probed hers. The light from the rodeo grounds captured the angles of his face and emphasized his pulsing jaw. Her heartbeat escalated to a rapid thud, leaving her powerless.

"Hi, you two."

Blinking hard, she let out a shaky breath. It took her a second to pull her attention away from Steve's brooding face. Andy. He'd come along at just the right time. "Hi, Andy." She pulled her hand from Steve's grasp.

Andy peered first at Steve, then her, his eyes full of questions. "Wasn't the rodeo great?"

A nervous giggle sputtered from her mouth like some giddy schoolgirl. "Loved it."

"You look particularly beautiful tonight, my lady." Andy smiled at her funny—not funny ha-ha—but funny peculiar.

Heat crept up her neck. "Th-thanks." Steve's solemn expression rattled her. He looked ready to pound something. Or somebody.

Andy faced him. "Guess this rodeo stuff must not be a big deal to an old-timer like you."

"Work going okay?" Steve's voice was tinged with ice.

"As a matter of fact it is." Andy's eyes narrowed, and his demeanor became all business. "I'll bring more applications by your office first thing Monday."

"Good." Steve brusquely clipped the word.

She studied them both, locked in some kind of alpha male face-off. "I hate to break up good conversation, guys, but if I don't get home soon, Mama Beth will worry."

Andy took the cue. Only offering Steve a nod, he looked directly at her. "See you around, Dani."

Steve's eyes and mouth tightened. He didn't speak, but latched onto her elbow and guided her to his pickup. Angry? Check. At her? The verdict was still out. Except for his music, the ride home was silent. Dani puzzled over the tense minutes of animosity between the two men. Something was amiss. Now she just needed to figure out why. They soon reached the house, and Steve came around to open her door.

Her mind went on overload as they made their way to the front porch. This was worse than a high school date. What should she say? I had a nice time? No, that sounded like she was fishing for more.

He broke the silence as they reached the front door. "Hope you had a good time."

"I did."

"Me, too." He stepped toward her, his face shadowed in the darkness of the porch.

Her pulse ca-thumped in her throat. She wasn't ready for this, but the last thing she wanted was to hurt his feelings.

He cleared his throat and shifted from one foot to the other. "There's, uh . . . a theatre in Morganville that plays old movies."

"There is?" She choked on the words. *Good one, Dani. So original.*

A muscle in his jaw flexed and echoed the tempo of her heartbeat. "Would you like to go tomorrow night?"

"Sure." What was she thinking? She had to stop this, this whatever-it-was, before it went any further.

Then the moment was over. Steve held open the screen door, waited for her to enter, and followed her into the house.

Mama Beth perched in her chair with her crochet, her gaze flitting to the clock when they entered. "You two sure are back early." Her voice was laced with disappointment.

❧22❧

Double Trouble

"I know this is awkward because of our business relationship, but I'd be a fool not to tell you know how I feel." Her attorney's hopeful green eyes searched hers, a trace of a smile on his lips.

Air rushed from Dani's lungs, his confession hitting like an unexpected slap in the face. She wiggled in her seat and scrambled for words. "I-I don't know what to say."

He raised his gaze to the ceiling of the diner and groaned. "Didn't you know how I felt about you in college?"

"I saw us as good friends. I had no idea . . ." Dani stared at her hands and twisted them. Any girl would consider herself lucky to have a man like Andy admit his feelings. She sucked in a deep breath and tried to gather her thoughts, then raised her eyes to his. "I'm very flattered."

Andy's boyish grin faded. "But?"

"But nothing. I'm just not ready. After what happened with Richard—"

"Richard didn't deserve you. If I'd known he was in the picture the summer I finished my classes, I'd have dropped everything." His eyes didn't blink.

What was she supposed to say? Thanks? Sorry I didn't call?

He grimaced and ran a hand over his lips. "Well, this is embarrassing. I guess I should've kept my mouth shut."

Dani's head throbbed, pounding behind her eyes. What was the best way to handle this? Her mind still reeled from all that transpired last night at the rodeo. How had she ended up in this mess, not just with one man, but two?

"Is there something going on between you and Steve?" His jaw visibly tightened.

She lowered her head. The question she'd wrestled with all night. Hadn't her pain-filled marriage to Richard been enough to teach her a lesson? She massaged her temple. This had to be stopped before it escalated out of control. Determination welled inside, and she raised her spine ramrod straight. "Right now I'm not ready for a relationship with anyone. Not you. Not Steve Miller." Her words sounded harsh, but it was truth. She couldn't trust her heart to a man ever again.

"I understand." A sad smile rested on Andy's face, and he reached across the table to take her hand, his tone soft and gentle. "I hope some day you'll be ready. I plan on being around when that day comes."

She couldn't return his smile. Refused. To offer false hope was cruel.

He stroked her fingers, but she felt nothing. Not like with Steve, whose tender touch reduced her insides to molten wax. "I don't want things to be weird between us, Andy. Your friendship means too much."

"Ouch. I get the message." He dropped her hand. "In other words, back to business."

She nodded. "Right."

They spent the rest of their meeting time reviewing applications and filtering through spending records. Her eyelids drooped. She needed sleep, and lots of it. A quick peek at her watch revealed the elapsed time. Two o'clock in the afternoon already? This renovation was turning out to be more tedious and time consuming than she could've ever imagined. A yawn worked its way from her mouth.

"Prince Charming must've kept you out late last night." Andy's wry smile and insinuation set her nerves on edge.

"No, he didn't. I was home early." She sipped her hazelnut coffee and averted her eyes. Surely he got the message from her peevish tone. She glanced up and caught his pained expression.

Ugh. Why was she being so snarky? Maybe a little humor would help lighten the mood. She lifted her nose and feigned a snooty voice. "My golden coach didn't even come close to reverting to a pumpkin."

Andy's smile disappeared quickly. "You look exhausted. I'll put the rest of these in an envelope for you to sign later. Let's get you home."

Dani didn't argue. She had no intention of telling him she needed all the rest she could get before her date with Steve tonight. Setting two men straight in one day was hard work, especially when she was so confused about one of them.

Steve had been a goner from the minute he'd first laid eyes on Dani in her blue and white dress. He put his F-350 pickup in gear and eased out of the driveway on his way to Mama Beth's. If he'd known in advance how beautiful she was going to look last night, he could've prepared himself. He gave his head a shake. Not true. Nothing could've prepared him.

He allowed images of Dani to play in his mind like a slide show—her musical laughter at the antics of the rodeo clowns, her cheers of encouragement for the barrel racers, the horrified look on her face during the bull ride—but especially how she'd looked in the parking lot, with the lights from the rodeo illuminating her clear blue eyes. His pulse quickened. For one all-too-brief moment, no one else existed and time had ceased. If Andy hadn't come on the scene, he would've kissed her.

Steve drew in a breath. *Lord, I don't understand everything that's going on here, so I'm leaving this in Your hands. Dani's hurting and needs answers. Keep me out of Your way, and help her to know You. Whatever happens tonight, I accept as Your will and Your plan.*

When he pulled into Mama Beth's driveway a few minutes later, the familiar peace that always followed his prayers settled over him like a warm quilt on a cold night. The light scent of honeysuckle scented the air, and the locusts and dove sang their evening songs. Steve whispered a prayer of gratitude and strode up the steps to where Mama Beth rocked on the front porch.

She wore a knowing smile. "Well, aren't you handsome?"

"Thanks." He leaned down and kissed her cheek. "How you feeling?"

"Better everyday. Especially now that the radiation treatments are finished and the doctor says I'm good to go." She cocked her head, a gleam in her eyes. "And how are you?"

Steve couldn't halt the chuckle that rose in his chest. She knew him too well. He tried to keep the grin off his face, but it didn't work. "Never been better."

Her smile broadened. "Glad to hear it. I'll go get Dani."

While she shuffled into the house, Steve surveyed the area. Cottage-style gardening according to Mama Beth. Blooms of various sizes, shapes, and colors packed every square inch, with tomato plants and their cages inserted as space allowed. The tasty vine-ripened tomatoes would hopefully land some of Mama Beth's homemade salsa in his pantry.

Dani had been the one to plant, weed, and water this year. He brought a hand to his face, surprised at the torrential feelings rushing through him. Every day revealed more about her that he admired. As if he needed anything else.

The screen door squeaked, and he turned his head. Dani stepped onto the porch dressed in an elegant cream-colored pantsuit. Her hair was swept away from her face to reveal tiny pearl earrings. A teardrop pearl suspended from a dainty gold chain at the hollow of her neck. Air bottle-necked in his throat. Mercy, he was in big trouble. "You look stunning." He hated that his voice quaked.

She lowered her gaze. "Thank you."

Was she being coy? He didn't know, nor did he care. "You ready?"

"Yes." She turned to kiss Mama Beth. "Don't wait up. I don't want you overtiring yourself."

Steve offered Dani his elbow and winked at a teary-eyed Mama Beth while they headed down the porch steps. He helped Dani into the passenger side. Not only did she look beautiful, she smelled beautiful. Like roses and sunshine.

He hurried to the driver's side, a spring in his step. The sun, just beginning to set, perched like a giant orange on the horizon. A contented sigh whooshed from his mouth as he turned the key and peered at Dani, struggling to comprehend how he'd managed her company for the entire evening.

After a few minutes, it became all too obvious from Dani's quiet and withdrawn behavior that she was bothered about something. Maybe he could put the twinkle back into those baby blue eyes of hers by pouring on the cowboy charm. He whistled a cheery tune, lowered the volume on the stereo, and turned to her. "You okay?"

"Yes. Why?" The frown on her forehead told a different story.

"You're so quiet. You haven't said more than two words since we left Miller's Creek."

"Sorry." Her lips jutted out and she folded her arms across her chest.

Someone didn't get their afternoon nap. Did he dare take the risk of pushing her into a better mood? "Okay, make that three."

"What?"

"Four."

Her lips said nothing, but her expression screamed what-are-you-talking-about?

"Words. Now you've said a total of four. Some kind of Guinness Book of World Records thing going on here?" He shot her his best playful grin.

Her lips locked together, and judging by the set of her jaw, she'd thrown away the key. He couldn't just give up. "You know I'm going to keep pestering you until you talk, don't you?"

She glared at him then turned her head away.

"Ve have vays to make you talk."

Her head rotated back toward him, and he waggled his eyebrows. She raised her gaze to the ceiling and blew exasperation between her lips. What was the old saying? Desperate times call for desperate measures. He grabbed her hand and brought it to his lips, planting a whispered kiss on her knuckles.

One corner of her lip quivered then turned up, pulling the rest of her mouth with it. "Okay, okay, I give."

He chuckled. "Good for you. We're making progress. You just doubled your word count."

Dani burst into a gurgling laugh so contagious he couldn't help joining her. Her smiling face lightened his heart. Before he realized it, he brought his hand to her face and allowed a finger to brush her cheek. "Now that's more like it."

A few minutes later he glanced over. Her look was that of a lost and bewildered child, cloudy and full of turmoil. He gave her hand a squeeze, and she turned her head to look at him, her eyes searching his face. What was she looking for? Why was she so troubled? His heart twisted. Didn't she know how much he cared?

After dinner, on their drive to the theatre, her continued silence unnerved him. During the meal she hadn't spoken much, but had eaten even less. Was she not feeling well? Her mouth turned down at the corners, and dark circles underlined her stormy blue eyes. She looked exhausted. No wonder she didn't have a lot to say.

He thought back over the past week. She'd worked everyday at the daycare, spent no telling how many hours at work downtown with the old geezers, and managed to spend more time with his parents than he had. Besides that, hadn't Mama Beth said something about Dani taking over her father's business? He made a mental note to ask about it later.

When they arrived at the movie theatre, Dani perked up. "*An Affair to Remember*! I love this movie." Her voice lilted, and her eyes regained a little of their familiar sparkle.

Though he enjoyed the show, Steve was more interested in watching her. As the night wore on her yawns grew more frequent, and during the last part of the show, when he was sure she was oblivious to everything except the movie, he leaned on one elbow to study her more closely. Her eyes were bright with tears, and she reached for a tissue during the final scene. His heart bounced to his throat. He'd never felt this strongly about anyone before, not even Lauren, and it terrified him. Like trying to walk a tightrope made of barbed wire.

The lights flickered on and revealed her tear-dampened face. She grinned sheepishly, still dabbing her cheeks. "I've seen this movie a thousand times and I still cry at the end."

He longed to dry her tears the way he'd done that night in the moonlight, but decided against it. His heart couldn't take it at the moment. Instead, he cradled Dani's soft hand in his own while they strolled through the parking lot. She didn't comment or try to pull away.

After he turned onto the highway to head home, Steve determined to re-light the spark of conversation they'd enjoyed earlier. He leaned toward her. "You seem a little tired tonight."

"I am." Her voice sounded weary in the darkness.

He rested his elbow on the console and peered at her, her face gently lit by the full moon. "Maybe you should slow down a bit."

Her laugh sounded hollow. "I'd love to."

Dani spoke the words like it was impossible. Did she have more going on than he was aware of? Or was she seeing Andy on the side? His jaw tensed. Even the thought of her with Andy made his stomach churn. A few minutes later he glanced at her. She was asleep.

He steered into Mama Beth's driveway and turned off the ignition. Illuminated by moonlight, her face held an innocence and vulnerability that gripped his heart. She needed him. He'd give anything to erase the years of pain and betrayal she'd endured. To show her what real love was all about. To show her not all men were jerks. He stroked her rose-petal cheek with the back of his hand.

Her eyes opened with apparent effort, and she sat forward. "I'm sorry I fell asleep."

"Don't be." He let himself out of the truck and sauntered to the passenger side to open her door.

As she climbed from the pickup, her foot caught on the carpet, and she tumbled into his arms. Their eyes locked, her fingers splayed against his pounding chest. Steve searched her face. It was time to show her how he felt. He bent toward her, capturing her soft lips with his own.

Palms pushed hard against his chest as she tore herself from his arms. Highlighted against her pale face, Dani's sorrow-filled eyes stared back at him, her voice coming in short gasps. "I'm sorry, Steve, I-I can't . . ."

His heart constricted, and then palpitated wildly against his ribs. This couldn't be happening. She fled through the gate and into the house, her final words tolling in his ears like death bells.

०४२3४०

Assumptions

Steve gaped at the smashed plate glass windows, his gut twisting. Who would do this and why? During the night, all the storefront windows had been broken, and owners had arrived this morning to shattered glass. In addition, materials and supplies worth hundreds of dollars had been stolen over the past few weeks, and someone had taken a can of spray paint to the historic buildings. Down the street, Ernie Talbot, dressed in his policeman blues, hunched over his clipboard and took a statement.

"So what are we going to do?" One of the Grannies planted both hands on her hips and glared at Steve.

"I'll take care of it." But how?

Otis grunted. "I think Dani and her lawyer friend had something to do with this."

Dani? No way. "What makes you say that?"

Otis advanced, his eyes bugged out, his breath foul. "A lot of us have seen the two of them down here at all hours of the night."

Hair rose on the back of his neck. Truth or town gossip? The Miller's Creek rumor mill had been known to operate faster than million-dollar satellites. "That's a mighty serious accusation." He thought back to Dani's actions the past few weeks. There were a lot of things that didn't add up, like where she'd been keeping herself. He yanked an arm toward the graffiti. "Have you actually seen them do any of this?"

"No, but I don't have to. Who else could it be?" Otis twisted his lips in a sneer.

"That's what I intend to find out. In the meantime, I suggest you not do any finger pointing unless it's backed up by fact."

The people grumbled among themselves and shook their heads as they dispersed. They looked ready to lynch someone. Otis' big mouth put him in a predicament. Now he had no choice but to find out what Andy and Dani had been up to. He sighed in exasperation and strode toward Ernie. They entered City Hall together. "What time did you find out about this?"

"Otis called me at seven this morning." The policeman tucked a pen behind his ear and headed for the coffee pot. "I got here as soon as I could to take pictures and statements."

A sick taste landed in his mouth. Why was Otis always the first one to find the vandalism? "This is the fourth time this week, Ernie, and the people are breathing down my neck. The work will never get finished with these setbacks."

Ernie followed him into the office and clicked the door shut. "I know, but I can't be on the lookout all the time. I do what I can."

Steve slumped in his chair. They were all overworked and cranky and ready for the work to be finished. "Sorry. I didn't mean—"

His friend waved a hand and took a seat. "Don't worry about it. Most people don't realize the amount of responsibility you've had to shoulder, and this latest mess hasn't helped any." He puckered his lips in a way that made his moustache look like a furry caterpillar. "I may have a solution. Otis offered to find men to patrol the area."

He mulled over the idea. "Sounds good. Why don't you put Otis to work finding volunteers, and I'll set the schedule." As if he needed something else to do.

Ernie rose to leave, but Steve stopped him. "Before you go, do you know the name of a good detective?"

"Yeah, a guy by the name of Mike Brady. Why do you ask?"

"Otis said Andy and Dani have been seen together—"

"Wait a second. You don't really believe they had anything to do with this?" Ernie's voice escalated and his bushy brows shot so high they sent wrinkles all the way up his bald head.

He clamped his lips together, not knowing what to believe. "I don't know. But apparently they've been seen downtown at odd hours."

"Andy lives upstairs from this office, remember?" Ernie leaned both hands on the desk, his gaze unfaltering. "With Dani seeing him . . ."

His heart sank like a cannonball in water. So it was true. Dani had flown straight from him to Andy, and he had no one to blame but himself. He raked a hand through his hair, frustration pushing words from his lips. "I have no choice in the matter. If I don't investigate this further, the people will string me up from the nearest tree. Everyone who just heard Otis' comment will assume I'm being soft on her because of . . ."

Ernie lowered his head. "Sorry. I know you and Dani—"

Steve held a hand up to stop him. The last thing he wanted was sympathy. "I need a phone number for Mike Brady." He was through with questions and ready for answers.

In the much-too-early hours the next morning, Steve rolled onto his side and punched the pillow. Every evening since his movie date with Dani, he'd dragged home, certain sleep would come, but it remained elusive. The problem was Dani, thoughts about her, questions. It killed him to stay away, especially in light of Otis' finger pointing. He'd do almost anything for the chance to talk to her, but every time he went to Mama Beth's, she was either gone or on her way out. And the few times he'd seen her in public, she avoided him like a dreaded disease.

He flopped onto his back with a frustrated grunt. Why had he pushed her? All he'd accomplished was to shove her farther away. Farther from him and closer to Andy. He released a weary groan and rubbed his eyes. Her rejection was bad enough, but seeing her and Andy together ripped his heart to shreds. And the latest development with the investigation would only drive the wedge between them even deeper.

The digital read-out on the alarm clock grinned its big red numbers in the darkened room. Four o'clock in the morning. Way too early to be awake, especially on a Saturday, but maybe he could get some paperwork done before the meeting with Mike Brady, a much better plan than torturing himself with thoughts of Dani.

Steve showered and downed a cup of coffee, then climbed in his truck. As he pulled onto the main road, an orange glow lit the northern sky and set off chills between his shoulder blades. *God, please don't let that be what I think it is.* He punched the accelerator.

As he neared town there was no longer any doubt. The glow intensified, and his nostrils burned with the acrid smell of smoke. Angry flames licked the darkened sky and poured a cloud of gray smoke and ashes into the night. He raced the truck to Mama Beth's house in a cold sweat, his mind and stomach agitated.

The strong west wind gusted and showered the sky with sparks. When he topped the hill, Mama Beth's house came into view, and he blew a relieved sigh from his cheeks. No fire at the house. The lights were on, which meant they were safe. He jerked the steering wheel to turn into the driveway, left the truck running, and sprinted to the door.

Mama Beth met him, dressed in her housecoat, her eyes round.

He hugged her close and tried to slow his breathing. "Thank goodness you're okay."

When he pulled away, her lips worked, but no sound came out. He grabbed her shoulders. "What is it?"

Her face went ash white. "Dani."

His heart leapt to his throat. "What about her?"

"She's gone. I don't know where. Her bed hasn't been slept in." Her words came out in a raspy whisper.

The air thickened and his leg muscles liquefied. Where was she? He ran full speed to the truck and tore out toward town.

As he reached downtown, the view brought on nausea. Miller's Creek was engulfed in flames, and Dani could be somewhere in the middle of this furnace. He stopped at the roadblock Ernie had set and opened the door. A blast of heat hit him in the face, and the fire issued a monster-like roar.

Ernie shouted to make himself heard. "The fire department is—"

"Have you seen Dani?"

"Huh?" Ernie cocked an ear toward him.

He fought back a wave of panic and yelled louder. "Dani, have you seen Dani?"

"Yeah, she and Andy came through half an hour ago. I tried to stop 'em—"

He didn't wait to hear more, but sprinted toward the fire. Half an hour? Anything could've happened to her in that length of time. *Lord, help me find her.* His eyes watered, blinded by smoke. The chalky taste of ashes filled his mouth and set off body-racking coughs. Fire trucks parked at odd angles in the street outside Granny's Kitchen, and Will Coleman, the fire chief, barked orders to the volunteer firemen.

Steve rushed to him. "What happened?"

The wind carried Will's voice. "Too early to tell, but we think a fire at Granny's spread to these other buildings because of the wind."

"Have you seen Dani?"

Will motioned with a jerk of his head. "She and her lawyer friend went that way."

Sprinting to the corner, the scene that lay before him plunged a knife into his heart. Both sides of the creek smoldered in the wake of the fire that still burned brightly on the other side of the creek, the new pavilion now reduced to a pile of metal, rock and ashes. Icy tentacles wrapped around his throat and threatened his ability to breathe. Was she lying somewhere hurt? He searched the area around the depot where a large blaze still lingered. A lone figure fought against the fire. Dani!

The heat warmed his feet as he darted to the bridge through smoking grass. Giant flames threatened the old train depot where Dani fought the blaze like David against Goliath. Rivulets of sweat rivered down her soot-darkened face, and she swung at the flames with a wet burlap bag, the fire hissing angrily with each hit. Another bag lay on the ground at her feet. He grabbed it and joined the fight. "Where's Andy?"

"Went for help." Her words came out in wheezing gasps.

The wind picked up and sent flames spiraling higher. Black smoke filled his lungs, and the heat and ashes stung his eyes. The whine of the fire truck siren ripped the night air. Steve motioned for Dani to quit, but she refused. There was only one way to stop her. He flung the bag to the ground, picked her up by the waist, and dragged her from the fire.

"No. Put me down." She two-fisted his chest, but he didn't release her.

Once safety was certain, he set her feet on the ground, her blond curls clinging to her face in damp tendrils. With her gaze wild and focused on the flames, she continued to struggle. Only when he pointed to the fire truck, did her body relax and crumple to the ground. He knelt beside her and grabbed her shoulders. "You okay?"

She nodded, breathless. "The depot?"

"Fine, thanks to you." He drew her close to his thudding chest, kissed her forehead, and rocked her in his arms, the realization of what might have happened sudden and strong. *Thank you, God, that she's okay.* He placed a finger under her chin and tilted her face to him, his tone husky with pent-up emotion. "What were you doing down here this time of night?"

Dani lowered her head, but didn't answer.

"She was with me." A terse voice sounded behind him. Andy strode toward them, his expression somber except for the fiery flames reflected in his eyes.

Dani wrapped her arms around her waist, her vision blurred by tears, all their hard work . . . gone. The air reeked of smoke, and the park lay in heaps of gray ash. Blackened rock columns, which once supported the roofs of the shelters and pavilion, bore silent witness to the devastation of the fire.

Behind her, footsteps crunched the charred grass. Andy sidled up and rested an arm across her shoulder, pulling her to him. "You all right?"

She nodded her head once, too tired to shrug off his arm, too numb to speak.

"The meeting's about to start. We should head that way."

Dani trudged beside him to the town square, her legs leaden. All she wanted to do was sit down and cry, not for herself, but for Steve and the people of Miller's Creek. They'd sacrificed so much to have their dream reduced to nothing but a pile of ashes.

He took her hand and rubbed it with his fingers, his sea-green eyes focused on her. "Dani, I think it's time for you to pull out."

She yanked her head around and gaped at him. After all that had just happened?

His lips were pinched. "As your attorney and friend, I advise you not to spend any more of your money on this town."

"Nothing like kicking them when they're down." Her anger spewed out, unrepressed.

He shook his head, his mouth set in concrete. "It's called cutting your losses."

"It's not *my* losses I'm concerned about at this point." She quickened her pace and left him behind. How could he make such a suggestion? He knew how much this meant to her. How much it meant to these people. To Steve.

A minute later she arrived at the square. The townspeople gathered near the gazebo, waiting as Steve plodded up the steps. Loving concern for the town shone from his face, weary lines carving the skin around his eyes. Miller's Creek surely flowed through his veins like the creek flowed through town. He momentarily met her stare then averted his gaze.

Her heart crumpled like a piece of paper. Had pushing him away been a huge mistake?

The microphone squealed for a moment. "Thanks for being here, folks." Steve's expression wore a mixture of sorrow and exhaustion. "We're all struggling with what's happened. We've put in long hours and now some of our work has been wiped out. Repairs will be costly, and it'll mean more hours of hard work." He paused, his chest rising and falling with a heavy breath. "It's normal at a time like this to question whether or not the effort will be worth it. But I want to remind you we've never been the kind of people who quit."

She eyed the crowd. Many members of the community nodded in agreement. Not only did Steve love these people, they loved him.

"This town has survived in spite of difficulties. Some of you have seen seven or eight decades here. You've weathered lots of storms." His words grew more forceful. "We face a tough problem, but we're tough people, and we're going to finish what we started."

The crowd responded with applause, whistles, and shouts as Steve shook hands with the city council members. He was no ordinary man and as different from Richard as a horse was from a cow. She struggled against the sudden lump of pain in her throat. Could he ever forgive her and let her close again? Or was it too late? Her thoughts traveled to the feel of his arms around her last night at the fire. How cherished and loved she'd felt. But when Andy showed up, he'd stood and strode away in the fire-flickering darkness, leaving her on the ground like discarded trash.

An unexpected longing to connect with her new friends surged through her. She had to let them know where she stood. Let them know they could count on her. She turned to the people nearby, but her "hellos" seemed to fall on deaf ears. No one responded or made eye contact. Something wasn't right. She spotted J.C. and pressed toward him through the throng. "Hi, J.C."

"Miss Dani." He bobbed his head at her with a sad smile, ambled straight past her, and disappeared in the crowd. What had she done to offend him?

"Dani!" Mama Beth shouted from across the street where she stood with the Millers and motioned for her to join them.

She hurried to her aunt and enveloped her in a hug. "I'm so glad you're okay."

Mama Beth didn't answer, but pivoted away and spoke to Trish instead.

Was fatigue playing tricks on her? Even her aunt's kind eyes held an angry distance.

A minute later the older woman faced her, lips compressed. "Let me say a quick word to Steve and then we'll go."

Dani watched her walk away then turned to smile at Trish and little Bo. "Hey, Trish."

Without glancing her way, Trish grabbed her son's hand and moved away. "See you around. We were just leaving."

More tears surfaced, and she blinked against them. What was happening? She made her way to Steve and Mama Beth. His wary eyes scanned hers momentarily then flitted away. The emotions reflected there pierced her heart. Sadness. Hurt. Disappointment.

Dani rubbed her forehead. She wasn't imagining this. Her friends were upset. *At her.* Mama Beth tugged on her arm. "Come on, we need to talk."

"What's going on? Why is everyone treating me like a pariah?" Her voice cracked.

Her aunt's lips thinned as she opened the car door. "Well, it may have something to do with your behavior the past couple of weeks."

The anger and displeasure on Mama Beth's face cut into her like a filet knife. "My behavior? What are you talking about?"

Her aunt glared and started the car.

Dani studied Mama Beth's drawn profile as they drove toward the house. "I'm sorry, but I don't understand what's going on."

"I can't talk about it right now. I'm too angry. Let me get home and get a cup of coffee to settle my nerves. Then we'll talk. You obviously still have a lot to learn about living in a small town."

She did have a lot to learn. Like what rule she'd broken to make them treat her this way. The stabbing pain in her heart worsened. Had she lost her only chance at home and family?

∞24∞

Nightmares

Later that same day, Steve wandered Main Street and surveyed the devastation from the fire. Half a dozen buildings had sustained serious damage, and Granny's Kitchen was completely gutted. He reached the corner, his heart taking a dive as he viewed what was left of the city park. Many of the ancient oaks were charred, and the thought of having them removed sickened him.

He tucked his bottom lip between his teeth and dropped his chin to his chest. Could Miller's Creek recover from this? Would the donor be willing to give more money to rebuild, or use this as an excuse to pull out? Would insurance cover the loss? How many of these people even had insurance? The questions churned in his brain and tangled in a giant knot.

With a heavy exhale, he pinched the bridge of his nose and turned to join Ernie and Will in front of Granny's. "Well, guys, how bad is it?"

Ernie's eyes narrowed and his mouth formed a grim line. "You're not going to like what we have to say."

He tried to bolster himself for whatever news they had, but his reserves were bone dry. "Let me have it."

Will and Ernie exchanged looks. "The fire wasn't an accident." Will's expression matched his matter-of-fact tone.

Steve groaned and lifted his gaze to the clear blue morning. What had happened to their peaceful little town?

The fire chief continued. "See these?" He pointed to a clump of burned rags lying right inside what used to be the front window. "They were most likely soaked in an accelerant and used to start the fire."

Ernie stepped to the end of the sidewalk and pointed down the alley. "Whoever did this broke in through the back door leading from the alley, laid out the rags, and then caught it on fire. That explains why it went up before anyone could get here." He jerked his head toward Will. "These guys arrived quick enough to dowse the rags in front. I've already called for an arson investigator."

Investigator. He'd forgotten his appointment with Mike Brady. He checked his watch. Still a few minutes to spare, but only if he hurried. He offered a handshake to his two friends. "Thanks for all your work, guys. I have a meeting to get to, but if you need me, you know where to find me."

He strode down the street to City Hall. Who set the fire? He pushed on the old wooden door and headed for the coffee, pouring himself a cup of the aromatic brew. The front door opened, and a tall, bowlegged cowboy entered, removed his hat, and sauntered toward him, the heels of his boots scuffing the floor, and an arm extended. "Mr. Miller?" His drawl was slower than a blue-haired driver.

Steve grabbed his hand. "You must be Mike Brady." The man looked as if he'd just returned from a cattle drive, cheeks bronzed and leathery, with a forehead as white and smooth as baby's skin where his hat had protected it from the harsh Texas sun. He blended in so well everyone would assume he was a local cowhand. "Care for some coffee?"

"You betcha."

After he handed the steaming cup to Mike, Steve motioned him to the office. He offered the detective a chair and moved around behind the desk, gathering his thoughts.

Brady initiated the conversation. "I noticed y'all had a big fire. Last night?"

Steve gave a tired nod. "Yeah."

"Accident?"

"Nope." He plopped down into the desk chair and leaned back. "We've had an outbreak of vandalism here lately."

"Is that what you want me to investigate?"

He considered the question. Yes, he needed to stop the vandalism, but he also had to find out what Andy and Dani were up to. Besides, Ernie had already called an arson investigator. "Yes and no."

Brady didn't speak, but his heavy eyebrows rose slightly as he slurped from his cup.

"I don't know for sure, but there's a chance your investigation might lead to the vandals." Steve leaned forward, rested his elbows on the desk, and entwined his hands, plowing through what he didn't want to say. "I want you to investigate an attorney, Andy Tyler, and a woman by the name of Dani Davis."

Half an hour and several questions later, Steve saw Detective Brady to the door. He returned to his desk and took a drink of the now-cold coffee, not near as bitter tasting as what he'd just done. Though he still couldn't bring himself to believe Dani had anything to do with setting the fire, she had been downtown at an unusual hour. He rubbed his eyes, gritty from ash and lack of sleep. It didn't make sense for her to set the fire, and then place herself in danger in an attempt to put it out, but what were she and Andy doing roaming the town in the middle of the night?

Hands folded behind his neck, he lifted his head to gaze at the ceiling. Why would Dani tell him she wasn't ready for a relationship then veer straight into one with Andy? He shook his head. It didn't matter. For whatever reason, she'd chosen Andy, not him. Without warning, his prayer from the night of the movie date with Dani entered his mind. He'd prayed for God's will, and God had answered. The One who controlled the universe also controlled this situation. It was something he needed to accept.

Ignoring the mound of paperwork on the desk, he dragged himself to his feet and gathered his things. He'd grab a meal and a quick nap then tackle the work this afternoon. As he reached the door the phone jangled.

"Your Mom's leaving us, son." The urgent cry in his father's voice snatched the air from his lungs. "You need to get here quick."

Nothing made sense.

Dani attempted to glean answers from her fog-stricken brain, but the fatigue made it impossible. She'd done something to upset everyone, but what? More tears leaked from beneath her eyelids and made their way to her chin. Why had her efforts to help landed her in such a predicament? Surely there was a way to clear up this misunderstanding. Then again, it might just be further proof of what she'd suspected all along. She was impossible to love.

Haunted by Steve's expression from last night at the fire, she rubbed at the furrows on her forehead. The hurt and disappointment in his eyes when Andy had stepped from the shadows ripped through her like a chainsaw. She'd longed to tell him the truth, to explain, but she couldn't. Not without giving away the very secret she'd worked so hard to keep.

She laid a hand across her chest, her heart feeling like someone had mistaken it for a bug and squished it under the toe of their boot. Last night's fire was a tragedy, but she couldn't deviate from the original plan not matter how much she missed Steve.

Dani brought her wrist close to check the time. Almost an hour had elapsed since Mama Beth stormed into the house to make coffee. What was she doing? Roasting and grinding her own coffee beans? As if on cue, the door squeaked and slammed. Mama Beth bustled onto the porch with two cups of coffee and sat on the swing next to Dani, her expression drawn and angry.

She swallowed against the emotion clumped in her throat. Mama Beth's fury only made everything worse. Dani took the cup her aunt offered, but her empty stomach reeled at the smell. "I'm sorry for whatever I've done to make you upset."

Mama Beth's eyes searched hers. "You honestly have no idea why I'm angry, do you?"

"No, but whatever it is I want to make it right." Tears filled her eyes, threatening to spill.

Her aunt studied her for a moment, then scooted closer and wrapped an arm around her neck. "It's all right, sweetie." She crooned her words, and pulled away. "I know this is none of my business, but what's going on with you and Andy?"

Dani uncrossed her legs and shifted uncomfortably. Had she learned the truth? "We're just friends."

"Then why have you been sneaking off in the middle of the night? Last night wasn't the first time your bed hasn't been slept in."

Her eyes widened. Surely her aunt didn't think . . . oh no, and the rest of the town, too! No wonder they were upset. They thought and believed the worst. Acid coiled on her tongue, and her brain accelerated. "It's not what you're thinking. Andy's helping me with some private business." She frowned. "Is that what this is all about?"

Mama Beth lowered her head, peering into her cup. "Not entirely." A weary breath escaped her. "You're not going to like hearing this, and there's no easy way to say it." She raised her gaze. "Everyone in Miller's Creek knows you and Steve were seeing each other, and now—"

"—and now we're not." The truth had finally come out. She took a long slow sip of smoky air to fight the sudden rush of anger. They still felt entitled to stick their noses in her personal affairs.

Her aunt's expression hardened. "I don't think you understand how much Steve means to this town. How much he means to me."

She turned her head to watch a couple of squirrels at play in the oak tree then faced her aunt, struggling to keep her ire in check. "I do understand, but this is my private business." Her voice trembled. "No one else, including you, has the right to meddle in my life. The decision not to see him was my choice. Not yours. Not Steve's. Not the people of Miller's Creek."

Mama Beth's eyes grew sad, and she glanced away, staring into space. "I tried to warn you about what living in a small town would be like." She brought both hands up and smoothed her silver curls. "Miller's Creek is a tight-knit community. When you hurt one, especially one as highly regarded as Steve, you hurt us all." Her gaze turned back to Dani.

"This isn't about Steve. I think he's wonderful. It's just . . ." How could she make Mama Beth understand her trust issues when she didn't fully understand them herself? No one could comprehend how much suffering she'd endured because of Richard.

"What is it?"

She looked away. There was no use in explaining. "Never mind."

"I think it was rather cruel to go out with Steve two nights in a row and then dump him for Andy. Don't you?"

Dani snapped her head around to view her aunt's cold anger, and her fingers fisted. Back in the same familiar spot—alone— with no one to take her side. Just like her parents and Richard.

She planted an elbow on the arm of the swing, and rested her forehead against her open palm. If only her muddled brain could function.

Mama Beth let out a ragged breath, her eyes bright with tears. "Sorry, I'm just tired. I don't understand any of this, but it doesn't change how I feel about you. I love you."

The pain in her throat made it impossible to reply.

Vehicle tires crunched in the driveway drawing her aunt's attention. "I wonder who that is." Mama Beth pushed herself from the swing and hurried to the corner of the porch.

The gate creaked, followed by the sound of boots on the wooden steps. "Hey Mama Beth, I'm here to see Dani."

Ernie? She moved to the front. Her life experience had taught her that a personal visit from a policeman was never a good thing.

He saw her and removed his hat. "Mornin', Miss Dani. Mind if I ask you a few questions?"

"No, not at all. Is something wrong?"

Casting a glance at Mama Beth, he sent a close-lipped smile, but didn't answer.

Her aunt stepped close and squeezed her hand. "I'll be inside. Ernie, would you like a cup of coffee?"

"Yes ma'am, please."

Mama Beth bustled away, and Dani took a seat in the rocking chair, her knees wobbly with fatigue. "Please have a seat, Ernie. You look ready to collapse."

He nodded and plopped into the other rocker. "I am. This shouldn't take long." He rolled his lips. "Several people saw you downtown late last night. Can you tell me why?"

Dani's heart lurched at the implication of his words. "I was visiting Andy." Her befuddled brain grappled with the words. "H-he's helping me with some legal matters."

The door squeaked. Mama Beth shuffled onto the porch, handed Ernie his coffee, then re-entered the house. He took a sip, his blue-gray eyes searching her face over the edge of the cup. "What time did you get down there?"

"I'd guess around ten. I know that's late, but I was working on some paperwork here then left to meet him. Mama Beth might know the exact time. She was headed upstairs to bed about the time I left."

"Did she know you were going?"

"Yes."

Ernie stopped to scribble a note on a notepad. "And how long were you there?"

She caught her breath. This wouldn't look good, but she'd tell the truth no matter what happened. She took a slow breath to steady her nerves. "The last time I remember looking at a clock it was 2:30 in the morning."

He didn't respond as he jotted down the note, but judging by the set of his jaw he disapproved. "Did you see anyone else downtown?"

"No, but Andy and I both heard glass breaking. We looked out the window, just as Granny's Kitchen went up in flames. That's when we called the fire department—"

His head shot up, his eyebrows raised. "You called the fire department?"

"Yes."

He lowered his head to write. "And then?"

"We left the building to see what we could do to help. We reached the area just as you were setting up the roadblock, remember?"

"Yes, I remember." He finished writing, clicked his pen and stuffed it in his front shirt pocket. "The fire was set on purpose, Dani."

Her mouth sagged open. Who would do such a thing?

"I've called in an arson investigator. I'm sure he'll have more questions for you."

Numb, Dani shook her head. "I'll help in whatever way I can, and I'm sure Andy will do the same."

"Thanks for your time." He stood, placed his hat on his head, and clomped down the steps, his notepad tucked under his arm.

She watched him drive away, her mind in upheaval. Ernie suspected her. Did everyone else in town feel the same way? Lowering her head to her hands, she rested her elbows on the arms of the rocker, attempting once more to understand. It was no use. The fatigue was too strong. Maybe a shower would help.

After showering, she sank onto the feather mattress in her room, every muscle in her body rebelling, the fog around her brain as thick as a fall morning. All she'd wanted was to help these people. The dam of tears she'd held back all morning burst open, and she covered her face with a pillow to mute her sobs. What had possessed her to think she could pull this off? The distant and distrusting faces of the townspeople replayed in her mind. Had she already outstayed her welcome in this place she'd grown to love?

She flopped onto her back and pleaded for her brain to stop its relentless pursuit of unanswerable questions, swiping tears from her cheeks. The simple and ugly truth was that Steve belonged here, and she didn't. It was only natural the townspeople would see things from his perspective. Dani let out a choked breath. Right back where she started, on the outside looking in, wanting to belong, but knowing she never would.

When she finally dozed, her sleep was restless. The acrid smell of smoke, Mama Beth's angry face, and the sadness in Steve's eyes all melded into a nightmare. A tall fence stretched skyward. Between the pickets she could see the people of Miller's Creek. They needed her help, but there was no way in. From out of nowhere, an urgent voice ripped her from the hands of sleep, jolting her into an upright position.

"Dani, wake up. Evelyn Miller passed away."

ⱷ25ⱷ

Death and Destruction

Another funeral.

Dani slumped in the pew next to Mama Beth and stared bleakly ahead, her eyes dry and gravelly. In front of the wooden pulpit, and adorned with an arrangement of white roses, sat Evelyn's casket. On both ends, several large flower sprays spewed their hot house fragrance into the air. Was this all there was to life? Hurt upon hurt, sorrow upon sorrow, and then you died?

The pallbearers passed, attired in an odd mixture of dark suits and carefully pressed blue jeans. From behind her, the family members entered and were ushered to their seats. The sight of Trish and Doc, followed by Bo and Steve, caused her throat to clog with tears. Though their sorrow was evident, their faces were enshrouded with an indescribable peace.

She concentrated on her breathing to hold the threatening tears at bay.

As the last gentle tones of the piano prelude ended, Steve made his way to the podium. He shuffled his notes, swallowed hard, and raised puffy eyes to the crowd. "My family and I want to thank you for being here today. Even though Mom wasn't originally from Miller's Creek, y'all made her feel welcome, and she considered you her friends." Light radiated from his face. Hope?

Dani's compassion swelled. How did he have the strength to speak? Especially after losing someone he loved.

"Words can't express how much we appreciate the visits, phone calls, cards, and food. The outpouring of love we've experienced over the past few days has been overwhelming, and we thank you."

She thought back to last night's visitation. Never had she seen a community rally around a family with so much love. She'd give almost anything to belong to that kind of community. Anything, that is, except her privacy. But would the cost of that privacy be more than she could bear?

Steve cleared his throat and shared memories of his mother, eliciting intermittent bouts of laughter and teary sniffles, and yanking at her heart until it felt ready to burst. He paused, choking back emotion, his eyes watering. Dani ducked her head against the sight, but not soon enough. Tears spilled down her face, leaving a salty residue on her lips.

"We want this service for Mom to be a time of rejoicing. She's at home now, resting in the arms of the One who loves her completely." His voice cracked then leveled out. "We'll miss her, but she's finally experiencing total peace and joy, and that's cause for celebration." He made his way to the front pew, responding to the loving hugs and touches from his family.

Why was she the one crying while the Millers held up like soldiers? Dani scrounged through her purse for a tissue, dabbed her cheeks, and studied the people in the congregation, their belief in heaven evident and strong. She fought the same old thoughts and feelings, afraid to give in. What did God expect from her? Brother Mac said salvation and heaven were a free gift of grace—something she could never earn—but if they were free, why was it such a struggle to accept them?

Mother's words hammered in her head. *If something sounds too good to be true, it probably is.*

Three days later Dani gulped in the hot dry air and settled, bone-weary, against a boulder near the creek, the gurgling water a blur. She'd made up her mind. Quitting wasn't an option. From the beginning, she'd determined to see the renovation through to completion no matter what. Anything beyond that was unknown, especially now.

The locusts' song rattled from the trees, sometimes soft, but more often a climactic crescendo, echoing her rising anguish. She had to find a way to repair her relationships with the people of Miller's Creek and Mama Beth. It might not get her anywhere, but it was worth the effort. These people mattered too much not to try, and so did her dream.

She lifted her gaze to the old oaks overhanging the banks of the creek then followed the drooping branches to the stony surface. The once-crystal-clear water now consisted of nothing more than a few murky puddles amidst water-worn rocks. For the past three days thoughts of Steve had bombarded her brain. She'd attempted to banish them from her mind, but to no avail. Puzzling over her contradictory feelings, Dani squeezed her eyes shut, her forehead tight and furrowed. The scared-little-girl part of her wanted to hang on for dear life to her self-inflicted ban of allowing her heart to fall in love. A different part—the last molecules of hope left buried inside—dared to believe that Steve was better than any man she'd ever known. But what if she was wrong? And worse yet, what if he didn't want her anymore?

Dani hugged her knees to her chest. No matter what happened, she had to find a way to make him understand how she treasured his friendship. The problem lay in getting close enough to express those feelings without sending mixed signals or endangering her resolve.

The hairs on the back of her neck tingled, though the air was breezeless. She glanced up. On horseback Steve stared back from the other side of the creek, causing her breath to rattle in her throat. How long had he been there? The distance between them shrunk as if their souls somehow intertwined.

After a moment both eternal and far too short, he broke the gaze and eased Biscuit into the creek, the horse's hooves slosh-clopping along the rocky creek bed. Head down, Steve's body shifted in rhythm with the gait of the horse, until he came to a stop nearby. He dismounted and tied Biscuit's reins to a low-hanging branch, and ambled to her, the area around his eyes swollen. "Hi."

"How are you?" Even as she asked the question, she realized its absurdity.

His shoulder-sagging sigh carried the weight of his burden in one swish of sound, and he squatted beside her, his pained expression sending stabs of hurt to her heart.

Dani scooted over to make room, and he joined her on the craggy sandstone. "I'm so sorry about your mom." She tried to look away, but couldn't drag her eyes from his face.

A weary smile tugged at one corner of his mouth. "Thanks. She's better off where she is. I'm glad her suffering is finally over."

"I am too, but that doesn't take away the hurt."

He moved his gaze to the creek. "No, it . . ." A shudder claimed his voice.

"I know how it feels."

"I know you do." Agony drenched his eyes. "I have so many regrets. I feel guilty—"

"Why? You were a wonderful son."

"Not at the end. I didn't spend time with her like I should have."

"But you were busy."

"That's no excuse." His face twisted in grief. "I ran myself ragged under the guise of working for Miller's Creek, when in all truth I was running from her illness and using it as an excuse to stay away. You spent more time with her than I did." He picked up a stone near his foot and hurled it into the deepest part of the creek, where it landed with a *kerplunk*. "The sad truth is that none of us are guaranteed another breath. We should take advantage of the time we have instead of shying away from people and situations because of our fears."

Her pulse thundered in her ears. He had no way of knowing how closely his words mirrored her thoughts. In a move she didn't fully understand, she wrapped him in an embrace and laid her head against his chest, the beat of his heart solid and steady.

He sat unresponsive and silent, the scent of his cologne wafting to her nose with each breath. What was she doing? She needed to move away, but found it impossible to let go. Instead Steve released a weighted sigh, and averting his gaze, gently pushed her away. He hauled himself to his feet and trudged to where Biscuit stood. "By the way, I never got the chance to say thanks for saving the train depot."

Why wouldn't he look at her? Dani swallowed tears and willed him to turn her way. "And I never got to say thanks for saving me."

He hoisted his lanky frame onto Biscuit and clopped past her to the cloudy water. With no further comment he rode away, her heart shattering in a million tiny pieces.

Dani's legs reduced to jelly. She lifted a hand to her face, collapsing into a chair at the daycare as the kids lined up for time outdoors. Their cheerful chatter made it difficult to hear, so she pushed the door closed. Surely she'd heard Andy wrong. "Say that again."

"Steve just called. He came back to work today and found the construction crew loading their equipment on the truc—"

"But why?" Even as she voiced the question, she knew the answer. Howard had to be behind this, and it couldn't have come at a worse time. With Steve out the past two weeks, she'd logged triple overtime taking care of funding requests, and trying to keep the work moving ahead. The finish line was in sight, but not if they didn't have a crew.

"That's why I called. I thought you might know." Andy's frustration flowed through the phone.

"No, I don't. Let me give Howard a call. I'll meet you at Mama Beth's in fifteen minutes."

Her hands trembled as she punched speed dial, the queasiness in her stomach shoving its way to her mouth. After the last conversation with Howard she should've seen this coming.

"Hampton Enterprises."

She nibbled her thumbnail. "This is Dani. I need to speak to Howard, please."

"He's in a meeting, Mrs. Davis. Can I have him return your call?"

Her temper rose, and she struggled to keep her voice calm. "No, I need to speak with him now."

"Yes ma'am."

A minute later Howard picked up. "I'm busy, Dani. Can I call you back later?" The edge to his voice revealed his agitation.

She took a deep breath to slow her racing pulse. "I need answers and I need them now." Muted voices sounded on the other end. What meeting was he in?

"I'm transferring your call to my private line." A few seconds later he came back on the phone, his tone now loud and belligerent. "I know what you want, Dani. This is about the crew I pulled, isn't it?"

"Why are you deliberately going against my orders?" She tugged on her ponytail with her free hand.

"Because your pet project has run up thousands of dollars in unnecessary expenses. As CEO, I have to act in the best interest of this company. Giving away our services hurts the bottom line. Didn't you learn that in Business 101?" His tone held a swagger.

"Careful, Howard, would you like to lose your job?"

He laughed. Not a joyful laugh, but one of sarcasm and ridicule. "Go ahead and try. We'll see who the executive board endorses—you or me."

Her brain raced. He was right. The only way to get rid of him was to go through the board, and based on the current membership, she'd lose. She tried to feign an advantage she knew she didn't have. "You won't get away with this."

"Don't be so sure." The phone clicked in her ear.

After checking out at the daycare, she sped toward home, knowing she had no time to waste. The sooner they got a new crew on the job the better. Five minutes later she steered into the driveway, Andy right behind her. She bolted from the car and hurried to him.

"Well?" His green eyes held worry.

"Howard yanked the crew. I'd fire him, but I can't make that decision without board approval. I'm certain they'll support him, not me."

Andy's forehead wrinkled. "What about getting rid of the board?"

"That will entail a meeting with the shareholders. I don't own enough of the company to make that call on my own."

He groaned and raked a hand through his sandy curls. "Now what?"

"I'm going to give him a fight." Dani shook her head at the thought. "I don't know how I'll be able to handle it and take care of business here, but I don't see that I have much choice."

"And the next step?"

"Call a board meeting. But in the meantime, we need to find a construction crew for the park. We'll just have to pay them out of the foundation funds."

"Do you have any idea how costly this little battle could be?" He grimaced, his mouth taut. "Just for the record, I think you're making a huge mistake."

The exasperation and fatigue lining his face tugged at her heart. How would she have made it this far without him? She grabbed his hands and peered into his eyes. "Thanks for hanging in there with me and being such a good friend. I couldn't have done this without you."

Andy glowered, leaving no doubt about how he felt.

A diesel engine roared behind her, and Steve pulled into the driveway. She stepped away from Andy as Steve climbed from the truck and approached them. His eyes, dark and brooding, skipped past her to Andy. "What did you find out?"

"We'll have a new crew before the week is up." Andy's tone and stance expressed disapproval.

Steve let out a puff of air between pursed lips. "Well, that's a big relief." He pointed over her shoulder. "Whose car is that?"

Dani turned to see the little red sports car and her stomach rose to her throat. *Oh no, it couldn't be.*

⊂ঽ26ড়঩

Hurricane Cecille

Her skin stinging like she'd bedded down with a bunch of red ants, Dani entered the front door of Mama Beth's house. She stared at her mother and aunt, so much alike and yet so different. Mother circled, a lion going in for the kill, while Mama Beth's face contorted with a myriad of emotions.

Mother waltzed across the living room and gave her a light hug, flaunting practically every piece of jewelry she owned. "Darling, I've missed you." In her cultured socialite voice no less. Who was she trying to impress?

"I've missed you, too." *Like a toothache.*

Next she gravitated toward Andy, plunging Dani's heart rate to sub-zero. "It's good to see you again, Andy. I must confess you're the last person I expected to see here."

"Hello, Cecille." Andy seemed unperturbed by her mother's theatrics.

Chomping on her lip, Dani glanced at Mama Beth, whose eyes held troubled confusion. Steve put an arm around her aunt's shoulders, his expression darkening like a black thundercloud. The stormy glare he sent made her knees go limp. Now he knew the truth. But it wasn't like she'd lied. She just hadn't corrected his assumptions, and with good reason.

A frown crinkled Mama Beth's forehead. "You two know each other?"

Mother had the gall to appear surprised, her eyes wide. "Well, didn't Dani tell you? She and Andy are old college buddies." Her saccharin voice matched her saccharin smile.

Dani went cold all over and hurried to her aunt's side. This information could ruin the fragile trust they'd rebuilt over the past week. "I can explain, Mama Beth."

"Mama Beth?" The cold anger on Mother's face was enough to freeze an entire lake.

"J-just a name Steve gave me when he was younger." Her aunt stumbled over the words and wrung her hands. "Cecille, this is Steve Miller, Bo's son."

"We met at the hospital." Mother stalked toward him, her expensive perfume cloying, and her glittering fingers extended, obviously very much enjoying the havoc and upheaval her presence caused.

Steve maintained a calm façade, but Dani sensed his tension. Like a guitar string about to snap. "Nice to see you again, Mrs. Hampton."

"I can tell we're going to be good friends, Steve." Her mother purred the words and narrowed her eyes to tiger slits, sending Dani a knowing glance.

She shrank back, daggered by the insinuation. Her relationship with Steve was already in jeopardy. Would her mother intentionally destroy the tenuous threads of hope she'd discovered in Miller's Creek? Did she want her back in Dallas that badly? Dani's blood steeled, and she straightened. Well, she wouldn't go down without a fight. "May I speak to you alone, Mother?"

"But of course, dear." She smirked and lifted a painted-on eyebrow.

Dani stormed to the porch, her mother's heels clicking behind her. Moving to the side yard so they wouldn't be heard, she pivoted, her fists clenched in two tight wads. "Exactly what are you trying to prove?"

"I'm not trying to prove anything. I came to talk some sense into that addled brain of yours. This little game has gone on long enough."

A tremor started in the pit of Dani's stomach and sent the tinny taste of acid to her mouth. She gulped in the dry August air. "What are you referring to?"

"I know you've been funding renovations to Miller's Creek, using company resources and money from the inheritance."

"And how would you know that?"

"Howard."

The tremor traveled to her legs. So Howard had decided to exact revenge through her mother. Or was it the other way around? "Howard should be careful before he loses his job."

"But you can't make that decision, can you?" A wry smile curled her mother's blood red lips. "Your father never meant for you to have the company—Richard, yes—but not you. Why, you never even had an interest in the company until a few weeks ago."

Words intended to hurt. They had. "What's your point?"

"I will not stand by while you run your father's company into the ground and spend your inheritance on this dried-up little town." Fine cold lines developed around her mouth like cracks in a glacier.

A shiver inched up her back. There was more Mother wasn't saying, but what? Her mind traveled to the last time she'd seen her, the disheveled lawn and absence of servants. A light bulb flickered on in her brain. She relaxed her stance, and her voice softened. "You've already spent the money Father left you."

Crimson flooded her mother's face.

So it was true. Dani shook her head with a cynical snort, then pivoted and strode toward the porch.

"We are not through discussing this." Mother's voice rang out behind her.

She kept walking. "Oh, yes, we are."

"Would you like me to inform your new friends you're the one financing their little fix-up?"

Like molten lava, fury bubbled to the surface. Would she be so cruel? The answer landed in her stomach like a brick. Well, one thing was about to change. She'd no longer back down. No longer stand there and take it. It was time her mother got a taste of her own medicine. Dani strode back, cheeks on fire and fingernails cutting into her palms. "That's it! I've had it!"

Mother's eyes rounded.

Dani didn't give her a chance to speak. Instead she stalked closer, allowing the repressed anger from thirty-five years to flow from her lips. "I'm tired of you treating me like a five-year-old. I'm not your punching bag or your bragging rights. I'm a person, and I will not let you treat me this way anymore."

The words seemed to bounce off her mother. "I know about your little foundation, though I can't for the life of me understand why you'd want to keep it a secret."

"Because I refuse to buy my friends like you do." She wished the comment back in her mouth, but it was too late.

Mother's eyes glowed, her face now inches away, her breath hot on Dani's face. "You'd better watch your step, missy, or I'll tell them everything I know."

The tremor inside burgeoned into an earthquake. "And you'd better watch yours, or I'll be out of your life so fast you won't know what hit." Her heart thumping like drums at a Friday night football game, Dani stomped up the steps and into the house, making her way to the kitchen. When she entered the room, Steve and Mama Beth immediately stopped talking.

A look of saddened betrayal resided on her aunt's face. "Where's Cecille?"

"Outside." The sullen silence in the room made her antsy. "Where's Andy?"

"He left."

Dani brought both hands to her temples and closed her eyes. *Think, Dani. Crew. Howard. Shareholders. Mother.* So much to do. Where did she start?

Steve rose to his feet, the chair scraping over the wood floor. He hugged Mama Beth, planting a kiss on her curls. "I've got work to do, but I'll call you later."

He exited with no acknowledgement she even existed.

Steve strode from the pickup to City Hall, his mind in an uproar over Dani's deceit. His blood alternately ran hot, then cold. The guilty look on her face when her mother revealed the truth about her friendship with Andy was all the proof he needed. Why had he been so foolish to fall for her lies in the first place? Mike Brady would hear about this.

Dani's face flashed in front of him, pale, like the night of the rodeo, her eyes bluebonnet blue in a field of white when she'd asked to speak to her mother privately. One second earlier she'd been a wilted daisy, but before his eyes had morphed into a steely ball of resolve. Maybe there was more to the story he didn't know. Once he calmed down, he'd at least offer her a chance to explain, that is if he could ever rid himself of the fiery anger which currently threatened to burn him alive.

A voice called out his name and he turned. Cecille Hampton climbed from her sports car and sashayed down the sidewalk, her smile glinting like her gaudy rings. The physical resemblance to Mama Beth was uncanny, but the comparison stopped there. He didn't trust this she-cat for one second. On the other hand, if it helped him find answers he'd gladly play along. "Hello, Mrs. Hampton."

The scent of her overpowering perfume bowled him over with an instant headache. "Please call me Cecille. I insist." She lifted her gaze to the buildings. "I cannot believe all the work that's been done here. Why, it almost looks the way it did forty years ago." Her voice dripped honeyed hypocrisy.

"Yes ma'am. The people have worked hard."

Her complexion turned pasty in the glare of the noon-day sun, her lips dark red in contrast. "Improvements like these don't come cheap. How did the people ever come up with that kind of money?"

He forced a polite smile. "Donations."

Cecille angled her head. "I'm very impressed." She hooked an arm in his like they were best friends and pulled him down the sidewalk. "Beth told me you're the mayor. I can tell you're doing a marvelous job."

Alarms clanged in his brain. Did she really think he couldn't see through her flattery? He'd met rattlesnakes he trusted more. "Thanks. Would you like me to show you around?"

Her mouth curled in at the corners. "I'd be delighted." They strolled down Main Street toward the park. "Now tell me, what do you think of my daughter?"

He struggled to keep his composure. Where did he begin? Imposter? Pretender? Hurting seeker? "She's nice." He kept his comment and tone intentionally vague.

"That's all?" Her perfectly arched eyebrows rose.

"Should there be more?"

"Well, an available man about the same age as my available daughter . . ."

What game was she playing? He maintained a straight face. "I've been very busy with this renovation project, as I'm sure you can imagine. I don't have time for a relationship at this point." And even if he did, there was too much polluted water between him and Dani. The thought sobered him, and he steered the talk to the renovation instead.

They reached the corner, the blackened park and piles of debris stretching out before them, and Cecille gasped. "Beth told me about the fire, but I had no idea it was this bad." Something akin to a smirk landed on her mouth, but quickly dissipated, like the changing colors of a chameleon. "Do they know what caused the fire?"

Her look of pseudo-innocence made Steve's skin crawl. "It's still under investigation." He turned around, and they ambled back to the car with her still latched to his arm like a bad case of the hives.

"No suspects?"

"A few."

Cecille came to a stop beside her sporty car. A strange glow flickered in her eyes, and she placed a well-manicured hand on his arm. "I want you to know Dani isn't . . ." Her bottom lip quivered then disappeared behind her teeth.

Steve's interest piqued. "Isn't what?"

A frown lined her forehead as if what she was about to say actually bothered her. "I don't know how to say this without sounding like I'm taking sides against my daughter. I assure you, I'm not. It's just that . . . well, Dani's not always as innocent as she appears to be."

A knot formed in his gut. Poor Dani. What kind of mother said those kinds of things about her daughter? "What do you mean?"

"I'm sorry. I've probably said too much." She seemed flustered. "I just don't want to see her take advantage of the people in this town, especially Beth."

A minute later, when Cecille backed the red sports car away from the curb, he still hadn't been able to unravel her comment or the motivation behind it.

Maybe Mike Brady could.

∝27∝

Buried Treasure

"**W**ell, where are they? I've had three people here in the last ten minutes asking if their applications have been approved."

Dani flinched at the barrage of angry words sounding through the cell phone, Andy's implication smarting. "Sorry, I'll look again, but I don't think the papers are here."

She winced at the loud click and yanked the phone from her ear. He obviously needed sleep as much as she did. As the renovation neared completion, everyone existed on caffeine, adrenalin, and precious little sleep. Keeping up with the applications was difficult enough, but factoring in the expense accounts made life sheer craziness.

Dani stuffed the cell phone in her pocket and rifled through piles of papers stacked around the room. Andy had given her the applications weeks ago, right after the rodeo, but she'd laid them aside because of other priorities. No papers meant no money. No money meant disappointed people. No, make that *angry*, disappointed people.

The headache that seemed to be her constant companion hammered out a dull thud between her eyes. If only this nightmare would end. After several minutes of searching, she plopped onto the bed and rubbed her forehead. A big part of her wanted to quit, give up, and walk away. Life would be so much easier without this hassle. Dani considered the option then shook her head. She committed to this project, and she'd see it through to the bitter end.

Then she'd return to Dallas. With everyone's continued suspicions it was the only thing that made sense. At least Mother would be happy. She huffed a puff of air through loose lips. Fat chance. Mother's presence had everyone on edge. Already here over a week, she showed no sign of leaving, though thankfully she spent much of her time away from the house. Unrest niggled at Dani's brain. Mother must have a reason for sticking around so long, but whatever it was, it couldn't be good. Maybe it was best that she remained out of the loop when it came to her mother's plans and motives.

Her gaze traveled the cluttered room, and she wrinkled her nose at the locker-room smell, disgusted at the mess. What had happened to her once orderly and peaceful life? Then she spied a manila envelope peeking from beneath a picture frame on the dresser. The papers!

She signed them quickly, grabbed her purse and keys, and rushed downtown to deliver the papers in person. Several minutes later she stood in Andy's office, a still-warm cup of coffee perched on his desk, but no Andy. Maybe he'd gone for a walk. As she scurried from the room, she rounded a corner and collided with Steve. The papers they both carried scuttled to the floor.

"I'm so sorry." Dani knelt to help gather the strewn papers, his nearness wreaking havoc on her maxed-out nerves. She rapped the stack of papers against the floor and handed them to him with a tentative smile, their fingers touching.

They rose at the same time, Dani searching his face for any sign of friendship. Nothing.

"What are you doing here?" His accusing eyes mirrored his gruff tone.

"Looking for Andy. Have you seen him by any chance?"

He shook his head and stiffened, his lips thin. "No. If you'll excuse me, I have work to do." Steve pivoted and strode toward the mayor's office, his boots thudding on the wooden floor.

His cold behavior undergirded the sting of her isolation, draining away her last shred of hope. Heavy-hearted, she departed City Hall with her mind on Steve. He hadn't been to Mama Beth's house in several weeks, at least not while she was at home. Red-hot needles pricked her eyes, the thought of what she'd lost growing more unbearable with each passing second.

The weather only reinforced and reflected her misery. In spite of a gray canopy spanning the sky, the late August day was another hundred-degree scorcher. The cloud cover spiked the humidity, her clothes clinging like plastic wrap. Coot and Otis lollygagged outside the post office in spite of the heat. As she approached, their expressions warned her away, but she set her jaw and advanced anyway. It couldn't hurt to try. She plastered on a friendly smile. "Hi, guys."

Otis grunted.

"Well, well, if it ain't Miss Dani." Coot boomed the words, but not in his once-friendly way.

She moistened her lips, her mouth drawing up as if she'd eaten an unripe persimmon. "What's going on?"

"Not much." Coot dug a knife from his pocket, opened it and cleaned beneath his nails. "How's that lawyer friend of yours?"

"He's fine, I guess. I was actually looking for him." The sneer plastered on Otis' face was enough to make her want to turn tail and run. "Have you seen him?"

"Walked past here a while ago headed to the creek." Coot stuffed the knife back in his pocket and gestured in the direction of the park, leaning against the building, arms crossed. "It'll sure be interesting to find out how that fire got started."

"And who's been breaking windows." Otis glared from beneath skewed eyebrows.

Their insinuations piercing deep, she squared her shoulders. They could believe whatever they wanted. "Andy and I had nothing to do with the fire or vandalism." Neither one spoke. They'd already assumed the worst. Pleading her case was pointless. "Please know I'd never do anything to hurt this town." She did her best to keep her tone level, but the tremor in her words belied the hurt in her heart. Both men focused their eyes on the ground, so she pivoted and left.

As she stepped away, Otis groused, raising his words within earshot. "Even Cecille thinks they might've had something to do with it."

Her stomach twisted. So that's where Mother had spent her time. Spreading lies.

A weight crushed against Dani's chest. She passed other people she knew, but they returned suspicious stares for her smiles. Mother's lies had spread like cancer, and she was the tumor.

She found Andy near the creek perched on one of the new park benches, this one metal and impervious to fire. He bent from the waist, elbows on knees, head lowered. Trotting over to him, she plopped down on the bench, breathless. "There you are. I found the papers."

"Thanks." He didn't look at her, but snatched the envelope she dangled in front of him.

"Sorry I misplaced them. There's just been so much going on."

"You're not the only one with a hectic life, you know." His crisp words were razor-edged.

"You're right. Being busy is no excuse."

The silence grew thick between them until finally Andy spoke. "Dani, I can't do this anymore."

Her heart plummeted to her stomach. "Can't do what?"

"All this." He waved the rolled-up envelope over his shoulder in the direction of downtown. "I can't do it anymore."

"You're quitting?" How would she ever manage alone?

"It's not like that. I'm not quitting. I just can't continue to do this and keep up my practice. I've put other matters on hold as long as I can." Andy faced the creek, his profile stony.

"We're all tired and discouraged, but we're almost finished." She placed a hand on his arm. "We can't let these people down."

He yanked his arm away as if her touch burned. "Why should you care about them? Do you know what they're saying about you? About us?"

"I'm not blind or deaf." At one time it had mattered what they thought, but not anymore. All that mattered now was finishing what she'd started. "I take full responsibility—"

"Then tell them the truth. Tell them what you've done for them." He finally faced her, his eyes blazing with desire for justice.

"And what good would that do?" She gripped the edge of the bench.

He gazed at her a second more, then rubbed his clenched mouth and turned toward the creek.

A hot tear escaped down her cheek and she whisked it away before he could see. "I'm not going to tell them anything." She shoved away the sob that rose in her throat. "I understand your concerns, but telling them about my involvement won't help. It might stop their suspicions, but it would create a different set of problems." Did she have the strength to speak the words in her heart? Dani inhaled deep and released a slow, shaky breath. "I hope you choose to stay, but I understand if you can't. I intend to finish this work with or without you."

Andy pursed his lips and nodded. Without a second glance her way, he tucked the envelope under one arm, stuffed his hands in his pockets, and plodded away like an old man. She watched his retreating back until he reached Main Street then gave in to the tears.

Dani dragged herself to an upright position and squinted at the alarm clock. She'd forgotten to set it again. Though still dark outside, the sun would soon be up. Her last day in Miller's Creek. With a groan she crawled out of bed, her achy muscles protesting. Two weeks had elapsed since Andy had returned to Dallas, during which she'd used the daycare fax machine at night to take care of foundation business. She massaged the area around her eyes. Four hours of sleep per night just wasn't enough.

She drifted to the lace curtain, lifted it to peer out the window, and noticed her mother traipsing toward the Thackers' house. Mother hung on in Miller's Creek like the unwelcome heat of summer, but not for much longer. Once she returned to Dallas, Mother would follow, having achieved her goal.

Dani weaved between suitcases and boxes on her way to the bathroom, and gasped at her reflection in the mirror. No makeup concealer in the world could cover those bags. After a quick shower, she lumbered downstairs, not bothering to fix her face or dry her hair. Not like it mattered. She'd become the invisible woman.

As she descended the steps her heart lightened momentarily, the sun casting a golden glow across the rustic surface of the old farmhouse table. It bounced off the glass panes of the dish cabinet where Mama Beth's dishes lined up like toy soldiers afraid to break rank. Her aunt scurried around the kitchen banging cabinet doors, the leftover smell of bacon permeating the air.

"Morning, Mama Beth. Why the big hurry?" She grabbed a banana from the counter, peeled it and took a bite, its creamy sweetness filling her mouth.

"I thought I'd work at the daycare today." Her aunt bustled to the sink to rinse out a sponge.

"Are you sure you feel up to it? You know I don't mind—"

Mama Beth raised a hand. "I'm going and that's it."

"But I enjoy working at the daycare."

"You have too much on your plate right now." Her aunt's gaze raked over her. "Just look at you. You're not eating or sleeping." Her eyes held hurt and concern. "What time did you get home?"

Dani pushed a breath between her lips and averted her gaze. "Four." She yearned to tell her that she wouldn't be a burden much longer, but how she dreaded it. How could she leave the one person in her life who loved her just because? They'd had their share of differences, the last few weeks particularly rough, but when all was said and done she knew Mama Beth loved her. Loved her like no one else in the world.

She swallowed the pain welling up in her throat and met Mama Beth's questioning eyes. Her aunt rubbed her arms and shuddered, then trained her gaze out the window above the kitchen sink. "I wish you'd tell me what's going on."

Dani couldn't answer.

Still in profile, Mama Beth continued to speak. "It'll do me good to be around the kids. You stay home and rest."

She had no strength or desire to argue, but even if Mama Beth assumed her daily responsibilities at the daycare, there was too much to do to sleep. Becky Morgan had cornered her at church to see if she had any old furniture to sell on consignment at Unique Antiques. Her aunt mentioned the attic, and Dani had promised to look. After Mama Beth left for the daycare, she'd check out the attic and load the car before heading downtown one last time.

Stabbing pain seared through her heart. One last time to listen as the old geezers cracked their goofy jokes, to walk the streets of the town she'd grown to love, to glimpse the accusations in Steve's cinnamon-colored eyes.

Mama Beth's irate voice brought her from of her thoughts. "Dani! I've asked you the same question three times. My goodness, but you're tired. Do you want me to bring you a plate lunch from the daycare?"

She shook her head. "No, thanks, I'll grab something on my own."

"Okay, I'll see you later." The door slammed behind her, and she clonked down the back steps.

Dani made her way up two flights of stairs to enter the musty-smelling attic. Sunlight streamed through a small window and illuminated the dancing dust. Old furniture and family heirlooms lay scattered about, ancient relics to a time past. Her shoulders slumped at the magnitude of the task. This place was a gold mine, but going through it would take forever. Mama Beth had enough stuff to start her own antique store.

An upright dresser stood to her immediate right. Maybe Becky could use this piece. Dani ran her fingers over the hand-carved detail then opened the top drawer. A stack of old letters tied with a faded ribbon caught her eye. With a gentle tug, she untied the bundle and picked up a letter addressed to Maisie Adams in Miller's Creek. The return address was Mona Beth Adams. In Dallas?

Yellowed and fragile, she pulled out the letter and began to read. Apparently Mama Beth had stayed with Mother and Father at the time the letter was written. She laid it aside for later. Maybe it would offer a clue about the rift between the two sisters.

Less than half an hour later, she placed the assorted papers and knick-knacks from the dresser in a stray box, one furniture piece now ready to go. Groaning as she rose to her feet, her fatigued muscles voiced their complaint, and she stumbled against the trunk behind her. With a large humped lid and leather straps, it reminded her of what an immigrant from Europe would use on a ship voyage to the new country. A grin snaked across her face. What if it contained buried treasure?

Chiding herself for an overactive imagination, she lifted the lid and peered inside, the scent of cedar and mothballs overpowering her nostrils.

Baby clothes? And not just any baby clothes, but beautiful, hand-sewn garments embroidered with dainty stitches. Dani fingered the delicate fabric. What baby? She removed the clothing carefully, uncovering old photographs atop two crocheted baby blankets, the picture on top of a handsome young man. She gasped at the likeness. Steve? No, the photograph looked too old. Dusting her hands against her jeans, she picked up the photo and flipped it over. *"Dearest Beth, All my love forever, Bo."*

Had there once been some kind of relationship between Bo Miller and Mama Beth? She puzzled over the question for a minute then dug further. There had to be a clue about the baby clothes somewhere. A few minutes later, ready to abandon search, her fingers landed on a book at the bottom right-hand side of the trunk and she carefully removed it. Made of leather, with ragged and well-worn pages, the old journal looked ancient. Dani cracked open the cover and glimpsed the hand-penned words written within. Mama Beth's writing, but it would have to wait. Tucking the journal beneath her arm, she slammed the trunk lid and hurried to her room, already dreading what lay ahead.

After washing the gray dust from her fingertips, she moved to her laptop to deal with urgent e-mails, but instead the old book once again captured her attention. She glanced at the clock. Time to leave for downtown, but something about the journal cried out to her. Oh well, a few more minutes wouldn't matter.

Within two pages, a knot lodged in her throat and refused to budge.

❖   ❖   ❖

Steve lounged on the sofa with an opened Bible on his lap in the quiet hush of a new day. *Bear with. Be patient. Forgive as Christ forgave you.* He knew what he needed to do. The words were clear and unrelenting.

Laying aside his Bible, he shifted to the window, the pink blush of dawn barely visible. A subtle change had come over Dani. The recent times he'd seen her at church or downtown, she'd been lost in thought, her light blue eyes troubled, tired and restless.

He rubbed a hand over his head. Trying to think through everything was pointless, like swimming in a haze of feelings and events which made no sense. He wanted to trust her, but there were so many unanswered questions. Andy had moved back to Dallas two weeks ago, their business dealings now transacted by phone and fax. Was his absence the reason for her distant look?

His chest collapsed as a heavy sigh escaped. Dani wasn't the only one who had changed. Mama Beth seemed bothered by something, and that worried him. In her condition the last thing she needed was stress, and if he had to venture a guess, her worried look most likely had something to do with Cecille.

Steve returned to the couch and picked up the Bible, the word forgive leaping from the page.

Forgive her.

There was no mistaking the message or the messenger.

↩28ↂ

A Secret Uncovered

Tears streamed down Dani's cheeks and plopped onto the journal's time-worn page. With a thumb and the corner of her shirt she blotted it dry. She couldn't read more. She wished she hadn't read any.

Did Mama Beth still love Bo? According to the journal, her aunt had once believed they would marry someday. Instead he'd returned from college with a wife and child. Evelyn and Steve. She used the palms of her hands to wipe her dampened face, overwhelmed by her aunt's heartbreak. To see the Miller family around town must have been so painful for Mama Beth. How could she live in Miller's Creek with such unrequited feelings for a man who belonged to someone else?

The last question landed with a thud in her stomach. Her affection for Steve could have headed that same direction. She cared more than she wanted to admit, more than he or anyone else would ever know. The heart-rending distance between them was for the best, but that knowledge provided no comfort against the pain, the same sort of pain her aunt had endured for decades.

Dani's shoulders slumped as unbidden images rose to the surface, a younger version of her aunt in love with a childhood sweetheart, and him married to another woman. To ease her broken heart, she'd resolved to go on with life by dating other men, and had ended up in the clutches of a monster. The journal didn't name the man who had stolen what never belonged to him—what hadn't been offered—leaving in his wake more pain and destruction.

She laid the old book on the bed and hugged her knees to her chest. Mama Beth had been too embarrassed to speak up, unwilling to bring disgrace on her family. Instead she'd moved to Dallas to live with Dani's parents until the baby was born. Her gaze flitted to the next entry in the opened journal. Each word echoed with Mama Beth's sweet voice.

> *I love this new life stirring inside. How I wish I could keep this baby to love and mother. But I can't.*
>
> *I've prayed for God to make a way for this child, and I believe He has. My brother-in-law, Daniel, is a good man and doing well in his business. This morning he suggested I give the baby up for adoption. Oh, God, give me strength!*
>
> *I know I can't give this baby the life it deserves. I belong in Miller's Creek, and without a father this child would be an outcast. I'll never be able to provide the advantages this precious baby deserves.*
>
> *This is the best thing I can do for my baby, but it breaks my heart.*

Fresh tears overflowed and Dani grieved. Grieved for her lost childhood, the children she'd never bear, and for the sacrifice her aunt had made on behalf of her nameless child. The baby clothes in the trunk, never worn, made for a baby she'd never know. No wonder she often seemed far away, in another time and place.

She released a shuddering breath and closed her eyes. Teardrops squeezed out and slipped down her face. This new information made the decision to move back to Dallas even more difficult, but leaving Miller's Creek was the right call. With her tumor gone, Mama Beth could resume a normal life, perhaps with the man she'd loved her entire life. The last thing her aunt needed right now was an unwelcomed guest or an unwanted burden.

Closing the book, she padded to the attic to return the journal to its rightful place, then hurried downstairs, an hour late for one last task.

From atop an aluminum ladder, Dani rolled paint onto the walls of the last building scheduled for renovation. She had hoped the physical labor would provide a welcome respite from her tortured thoughts, but staying focused proved impossible. Thanks to the old journal, her insides tangled in tight knots.

To make matters worse, Steve was here, bringing with him the familiar turmoil. Why did relationships have to be impossibly complicated? She tightened her lips. Not that it mattered. She'd soon be gone.

J. C. stood back to survey their work. "Lookin' good, fellas. I'm glad the last old lady is getting fixed up."

"Yeah, and the building, too." Coot blared the comment then dissolved into wheezing laughter.

Dani smiled in spite of the dark cloud hovering over her spirit. The old geezers and Steve continued to jabber like a bunch of crows. Their jokes and laughter bounced off the cream-colored walls and into her heart. Already she missed their camaraderie.

She scanned the room, her arm at rest on the top rung, the smell of fresh paint saturating the air. They'd done a good job of repairing and cleaning the building. A new tin ceiling gleamed above her head. Once they finished painting, the oak floors would be stripped and refinished like the other buildings in downtown Miller's Creek. Only a handful of unoccupied stores remained, the others now filled with various new businesses, including a florist, boutique and an old-time general store. With Granny's Kitchen and Creekside Park rebuilt, the last vestiges of the fire had been erased.

In spite of the ache in her heart, she had no regrets. She hoped the improvements would make a difference for the town's people. Advertising and promotional work still loomed ahead, and had she stayed, she would've gladly taken on the task. But someone else would have the responsibility and honor now, her time in Miller's Creek finished.

Her ladder jostled and rattled, sending her heart into panic mode. She grabbed hold with both hands, glancing toward the floor. Steve grinned back, a shock of his dark hair belligerently refusing its normal confines. She returned a weak smile and resumed painting, her thoughts confused. He'd ignored her for weeks, and today—of all days—he wanted to play?

Steve positioned his ladder next to hers and scaled it until he stood beside her, his expression and words friendlier than they'd been in a long time. "Looks like you're having trouble reaching the high spots."

She kept painting, her gaze trained on the wall. "Yeah, even with the roller extension, my arms aren't quite long enough for these high ceilings."

"Tell you what. I'll take care of the places you can't reach, okay?"

Dani nodded, but no, it wasn't okay. She didn't want him that close. Didn't want his stare fixed on her. Under the ruse of getting more paint on the roller, she descended the ladder then stayed on the floor, away from his probing gaze.

An hour later, Steve sauntered toward her, his once-white T-shirt speckled with flecks of beige paint. "I'm going to Granny's for burgers. You want one?"

"Yes, please. Thanks."

"Let's see if I remember. You like mustard, all the fixings, and no cheese, right?"

Her throat burned. "Very good." She tried to keep her voice light.

"I'll be back in a few minutes." He hesitated, his brows knit together in the middle. "You okay?"

"Just tired."

His cinnamon eyes sparked hope. "It's almost over."

"Yep." As if she needed a reminder.

Steve touched her arm gently, drawing her eyes to his face once more. "Thanks for all you've done to make this possible, Dani. You've worked hard on this project and I appreciate it." His words were soft and sincere.

Tears threatened and she turned away, pretending she had a speck of dust in her eye. "No big deal. Now would you go after those burgers before I starve to death?" Pent-up emotion wobbled her words.

He laughed, loud and hearty, the sound and his dimpled grin slashing through her. "Okay, grouchy. I'll sure be glad when this over so you can catch up on your sleep."

Without further comment, he ambled out the door with a cheery whistle, taking her heart with him.

Not two minutes after he left, overwhelming nausea descended and she pressed a hand to her abdomen. Her head hammered furiously, and her mouth watered, but not in a good way. A short time before she'd felt fine, but now feared losing the meager contents of her stomach, probably a combination of no breakfast and paint fumes. She snatched her purse from the work table and pulled out a ten dollar bill. That should cover lunch. With a quick word of explanation to J. C. she left for home.

A few minutes later Dani pulled under the carport, her head feeling like someone had buried a hatchet in her skull. As she entered the back door, raised voices spewed from the living room and stopped her cold.

"Cecille, you have to believe me. I haven't told Dani anything—" Mama Beth's words sounded strained. What was she talking about?

"Don't give me more lies, Beth." The hostility in Mother's tone produced chills throughout her body. "You must have told her something or she wouldn't have stayed in Miller's Creek this long. I want the truth and I want it now!"

Mama Beth spoke again, and behind the words Dani heard tears. "I made you a promise thirty-five years ago and I've kept it. I kept it even when I wanted to tell her the truth. She deserves to know—"

What promise?

"Oh, please. I'm sick of your Little Miss Innocent act. If people only knew the truth about you."

Dani's anguish built and pounded against her already throbbing temples. Her stomach lurched, and the room began spinning. Mama Beth needed her help. She gripped the cool stone counter, bent at the waist, and prayed for the dizziness to end.

Mother's harsh tirade continued. "I never believed your story. Not for one minute. It was all just an act to protect your precious reputation, wasn't it?"

"That's not true. How could you say something so cruel?"

Dani pressed a hand to her spinning head, her vision blurring as Mama Beth sobbed.

"If I find out that Dani knows you're her mother—"

A roar rumbled in her ears and drowned out the rest of the words. Mama Beth? Her mother? Stormy waves of pain surged, threatening to drown her in their undertow. More betrayal at the hands of those she loved. Why hadn't they told her the truth?

The bitter contents of her stomach rose to her mouth and she raised shaky fingers to halt its progress. She needed to escape, and time to think. A voiceless word exploded in her head. *Run.*

Shivering uncontrollably, she attempted to leave the rotating confines of the kitchen, but as she pivoted a glass on the counter toppled, crashed to the floor, and shattered into a million tiny shards. The room spun out of control again, and Dani grabbed one of the pine stools at the island to steady herself.

Mama Beth and Mother scurried into the room.

"Dani." Mother's ashen face registered shock and fear.

"Are you okay?" Mama Beth came toward her, cheeks wet, eyes full of sorrow and concern. She laid a hand on her arm. "Let me help you."

Dani yanked her arm away and lifted a trembling hand. "Stop, I . . ." Body-racking sobs tore from somewhere deep inside, a keening wail. "I—I've heard all I want to hear."

Wild panic swirled through her. She needed out. *Now.* She backed toward the door, twisted the knob, and stumbled down the back steps. Five minutes later she left the Miller's Creek city limit sign in her rear-view mirror.

Steve leaned against a wall in the newly renovated Granny's Kitchen, waiting for the burgers, when his cell phone rang. He flipped it open and brought it to his ear. "Hello?"

"This is Mike Brady."

"Hey, Mike, glad you called. I've been meaning to let you know. I decided to call off the investigation." He glanced around to make sure no one was listening. "Just let me know how much I owe you."

"That's actually why I called. I uncovered some information you might be interested in. Want to discuss it sometime this afternoon?"

Steve pursed his lips. What information? It wouldn't hurt to at least listen to what the man had to say. "Okay. Twelve-thirty work for you?"

A minute later he hung up the phone, uneasiness hanging over him like a buzzard. He'd finally get some answers, but at what cost? The sizzle and smell of fresh burgers on the grill momentarily distracted him, and then his thoughts turned to Dani. Maybe over lunch they could find a quiet spot near the creek to talk.

She'd kept a healthy distance between them all day, quiet and withdrawn. Gray shadows of fatigue parked beneath her eyes and her mouth tilted down at the corners. When was the last time he'd seen her smile? He clenched his jaw. This was his fault. If he lost her he had no one to blame but himself. He had to find a way to mend fences, and better yet, a way to tear them down. A smirk landed on his face. Knowing Dani, that wouldn't be easy.

Above the normal restaurant babble, he heard her name mentioned at a nearby table. "Otis thinks Dani is the one behind the vandalism. I wouldn't be a bit surprised if Mama Beth didn't throw her out."

Otis and his thoughtless words. Sudden remorse rained down on him, seeping into his spirit. He'd questioned her behavior too, declaring her guilty until proven innocent. Steve rubbed a hand across his face, his mouth dry. No wonder she seemed withdrawn and sad. She'd worked as hard as any of them, maybe harder, and people treated her worse than an outsider. The thought soured his stomach.

One of the Grannies plunked four white sacks on the counter and rang up the total. He paid, grabbed the sacks, and headed to the door, his mind racing. On one hand, Dani's behavior had been suspicious. But he and the rest of the town had made the situation worse by their judgmental attitudes. Why hadn't he just gone to her and asked instead of harboring doubt?

Now it might be too late. What were her plans once the work was finished? His chest tightened. No one had given her a reason to stay, but they'd all given her plenty of reason to leave. He quickened his pace and lengthened his stride, reaching the building a short fifteen minutes after he left.

Dani was already gone.

Shoulders heavy, Mama Beth collapsed in a chair at the kitchen table, her soul troubled by all that had transpired. She'd prayed for years for Dani to know the truth—even allowed herself to dream about it—but never could she have imagined it would be like this, as if the very air she breathed disappeared with Dani. There was nothing she could do but pray. Tears sliding down her face, she bowed her head. *Lord, watch over Dani. Be near her and turn her to You. If it be Your will, bring her back home.*

Cecille paced the kitchen, her shoes clicking against the wooden floors, her face twisted with emotion. Clearly she loved Dani, but based on what she'd seen, their relationship was in serious trouble.

A patch of sunlight fell across the table, bringing with it a bittersweet joy. God specialized in hopeless situations, and if ever a situation seemed hopeless, this was it. Mama Beth hauled herself to a standing position, feeling old beyond her years, and headed to the living room.

"Where are you going?" Her sister's voice shook, her eyes rounded with pain.

"To call Steve and let him know what's happened. He might know what to do or where to find her."

Wavy lines creased Cecille's forehead. "Don't you think she'll come back after she's had a chance to cool off?"

Mama Beth considered the question, remembering Dani's dazed expression. She glanced down at the furry kitten Dani had so carefully tended the past several weeks. No, she wouldn't be coming back, at least not for a long time. And maybe not ever.

○○29○○

Finding Home

Words scattered like a covey of quail at the crack of a shotgun. Dani financed the whole project? Steve sensed the truth before the question finished reverberating in his brain. Dumbfounded and slack-jawed, he sat at his cluttered desk grappling with the news Mike Brady had just announced. He blinked hard and scratched his head. Why had she kept her involvement a secret, especially once the entire town turned against her?

"There's more." Brady spoke in a drawling monotone, a western-style robot delivering factoids.

"Go on."

"For the past month, Mrs. Davis has been involved in a battle for control of her father's company. That's why the construction team pulled out of the park when they did. They worked for the company. The last crew was paid for by foundation funds, which of course she provided." He stroked his handlebar moustache. "Seems like the woman has plenty of money and plenty of trouble to go along with it."

The detective's words slammed into him, and the thought of her solitary struggle minced his heart in fine pieces. Questions continued to tumble inside like cement in a mixer. He needed to apologize and quick. But could she ever forgive him?

Brady cleared his throat. "There's something else that might be of interest to you."

More? Steve leaned forward. "What's that?"

"She's adopted."

Air dammed up in his throat. No way. She looked too much like Cecille and Mama Beth. "That's not possible."

"It's the truth."

He let the news sink in, compassion for Dani welling inside, then rose and stretched a hand toward the detective. "Thanks for all your work, Mike." He patted the bill in the front pocket of his shirt. "I'll get a check in the mail to you right away. Now if you'll excuse me, I have somewhere I need to be."

Steve escorted him to the door then re-entered the office to grab his things. J.C. had mentioned that Dani left because she hadn't felt well. He'd make a quick run to Mama Beth's to make sure she was all right. Just as he reached the door the phone rang. Muttering under his breath he returned to the desk and grabbed the phone. "City Hall, Steve speaking."

"I'm so glad I caught you." Trish's urgent tone captured his full attention. "Dad fell off a ladder. I'm following the ambulance to Morganville."

"I'm on my way."

As he reached the door a second time the phone rang again. This time he let it ring.

She'd already left? The air whooshed from him like someone had punctured a lung, his knees buckling beneath him. "What do you mean, she's gone?" He stared into Mama Beth's tear-filled eyes. "When?"

"About one this afternoon. I tried to call."

Still stunned, he attempted to quell his shock with a slow breath. "Dad fell off a ladder. I was at the hospital with him, or I'd have been here sooner."

Her eyes rounded until worried brows pushed them down. "Is he okay?"

"A little bruised, but other than that he's fine. He's at home resting. Why did she leave?"

Mama Beth struggled to speak. "She overheard a fight between me and Cecille. Things she shouldn't have learned that way. Oh Steve, if you could have seen her." She buried her head in her hands, gut-wrenching sobs filling the room.

He hugged her, his heart heavy. Where would she have gone?

The creek.

With renewed hope, he placed his hands on Mama Beth's shoulders and peered in her eyes. "I'm going to check a couple of places, but I'll be back."

Steve sprinted to his truck then tore out of the driveway, his mind reeling. This couldn't be happening. Life without her would be so empty. The thought sent jolts of disappointment and fear coursing through him, and he pressed the accelerator to the floor and raced to the park. He screeched to a stop in the parking lot, shining the truck headlights in the direction of the creek. She wasn't here. Only one other place she might be, but only if she hadn't already left town.

As he whipped the pickup in reverse, his headlights revealed a lone figure on the sidewalk skulking into the shadows of the store awning. The person shrank back further into the darkness as he passed. Herman Talley? Why would he be in downtown Miller's Creek this time of night? He lived in Morganville. Steve thought back to the last time he'd seen the man. He'd been none too happy that another contractor had been hired to take care of repairing the mortar on the buildings.

Motive. Could Herman Talley be the vandal? The arsonist? Though protecting Miller's Creek mattered, finding Dani mattered more. He sped down the country road and punched Ernie's number.

"Sorry to bother you, Ern, but I just saw someone downtown that you need to check out." He relayed the details of what he'd seen. "Oh, and if you see Dani would you let me know?"

By the time Steve reached the pasture gate it was almost too dark to see. He rolled down the window to get a closer look. A late summer rain from two days earlier had muddied the area and left an earthy scent in the air. His pulse beat faster at what he saw. Fresh car tracks pressed down the grass. Someone was here. Or had been.

Nearing the water, his spirit deflated. No vehicle. He grabbed his flashlight and hurried to the bank, the creek's familiar gurgle spilling its song into the night. Shining the light on the ground at the creek's edge, he spied fresh tracks made by small feet.

Dani had been here.

He ripped the hat from his head and let out a groan. So close to finding her, but not close enough. Where could she be, and was she okay? What was the fight between Cecille and Mama Beth about? What had Dani heard that made her run away? Was it about the adoption? How could he ever tell Mama Beth about the investigation?

Questions attacking him like a pack of bloodthirsty mosquitoes, he hurried to the truck and started the engine. Maybe she'd gone back home while he'd been out looking for her.

He steered into the driveway a few minutes later, his frail hope dissipating like dew on a hot August day. She hadn't returned. Instead Mama Beth waited for him at the gate, her eyes expectant. As he climbed from the truck, he met her gaze and shook his head.

Her expression fell, her face lined and weary. "You have time for a cup of coffee? I have something I need to tell you."

"Sure." He had something to tell her too, and she wasn't going to like it one bit.

Dani plopped onto the beach and gazed across the crashing waves of the Gulf of Mexico, its waters green-gray and murky from last night's storm. She leaned back and locked her elbows into place, allowing the breeze to sweep through her hair.

What had prompted her to turn south instead of driving to Dallas? Maybe the prospect of being in proximity to her mother—correction, her adopted mother—had subconsciously steered her away. No, it was easy enough to get lost in the city. Divine intervention? She licked her lips, salty from the ocean breeze. Was God's hand at work in all this?

She peered down the beach at the imposing structure nearby. The ocean-front condo on Mustang Island had definitely been a godsend. With the start of school the beach was cleared of summer crowds which made this the perfect time to visit.

Dani dug her fingers into the soft sand and held up a handful to watch it slip to the ground. Funny how time and dreams were the same. They both trickled by as fast as sand through her fingers. A couple strolled by, their arms linked, and an ocean of hurt broke against her heart. Steve's face appeared in her mind, and she allowed the image to linger. If only things could've been different. She closed her eyelids and bathed herself in memories, his lopsided grin and lanky saunter, those cinnamon-colored eyes of his, always full of questions.

Sea foam splashed her toes then dashed away, teasing her with a game of tag. She needed this time to think. To make sense of all that had happened. Dani faced the breeze, inhaled deep, and let it out in a heavy sigh. In a single heartbeat, she'd been transformed from wealthy heiress to adopted child, a lifetime of questions answered in a tick of the clock. And what about her father? What had happened to him? Had criminal activity become a way of life for him? A chill tingled down her arms and she hugged herself until it passed. Mama Beth should have told her the truth. But then again, how do you tell someone their whole life has been nothing but a lie?

A rumble erupted from her stomach, demanding food, but she wasn't ready to leave the quiet peace. She lingered as the sun sank lower in the sky and watched the seagulls make their dives and swoops toward the waves, their cries haunting and lonely.

With a last long look at the churning water, Dani picked herself up, dusted off crumbs of wet sand, and made her way to the room. Once inside, she dialed room service then dropped to the bed to wait for her meal. She pulled the hotel Bible to her lap and picked up where she'd left off, the words continuing to provide an unexpected comfort.

Dani started when a knock sounded at the door several minutes later. "Room Service." The voice called out in sing-song style. She opened the door to a short older woman with salt-and-pepper hair. "Where you want me to put your food, hon?"

"On the balcony please." Dani held the door open wider and moved aside. The smell of fresh seafood hit as the woman passed, sharpening her hunger.

"I see you're reading your Bible." The woman set the tray on the patio table. "What book?"

"John, I think."

"One of my favorites." The woman with kind brown eyes faced her. "The other night when you checked in, you looked like you'd had a pretty rough day. You doing better?"

Her cheeks flamed and she lowered her eyes. "Yes, thank you. Let me get you a tip." She moved through the sliding glass door to get her purse, the woman close behind. Rifling through the contents of her bag, she located a couple of ones at the bottom, smoothed out the wrinkles, and handed them to the woman.

"Thanks for the tip, hon." Her voice was warm, like hot chocolate on a frigid winter night. "Mind if I give you one?"

Dani twisted her head to one side and puckered her eyebrows. "I'm sorry?"

"Here's my tip for you." The woman pointed to the Bible. "Any answers you're looking for, God can give you in that book. Keep searching." Then she patted Dani's arm. "And don't be afraid to trust any man whose heart belongs to God." With that, she let herself out the door with a wave and a smile.

Dani moved to the balcony overlooking the ocean, the sun-drenched water now molten gold as the last semi-circle of sun made its final descent. The woman's words stuck in her head. She did need answers, but a man whose heart belonged to God? The phrase turned her thoughts to Steve. Why would anyone like him want someone like her?

She placed a napkin in her lap and uncovered the dish, the tantalizing aroma rising to her nose. Delving into the food with an appetite she hadn't possessed in days, the first delicious bite of grilled amberjack dissolved on her tongue, nourishing both her body and spirit. But a minute later, she pulled back a linen cloth to reveal a batch of warm biscuits. The fork slid from her fingers and clanked against the plate. Mama Beth. She should at least call to let them know she was okay.

Dani padded into the room, retrieved her phone and dialed her mother's number first. She picked up on the second ring. "Dani! Are you okay? I've been worried sick."

"I'm fine."

"Where in the world are you?" Her voice took on its typical demanding quality. "Why didn't you return my calls?"

Her stomach turned. She couldn't deal with a barrage of questions right now. "I'll call you later." Hands shaking, she clicked the cell phone shut and tossed it to the bed. That had been harder than she expected. Breathing deep, she closed her eyes. Calling Mama Beth would have to come later. An image of her aunt at the farmhouse table, hands folded in prayer, appeared in Dani's mind and brought with it comfort.

Mama Beth, her birth mother, a woman she cherished in spite of all that had happened, would pray for her. She sensed that she'd been immersed in a mother's prayers, not just today, but every day of her life. Her eyes opened in wonder. The same presence she'd experienced in Miller's Creek was here.

God.

If she ever needed His help in figuring out what to do it was now. She raised her eyes to the ceiling. *God, I've tried to make it through life without You and made such a mess. So I'm asking for Your help. Please show me the way.*

A peace beyond comprehension trickled over her like soothing balm. She flipped a page in the opened Bible, her gaze drawn to a verse from one of Brother Mac's sermons. *"I am the way and the truth and the life. No one comes to the Father except through me."*

The way. That's what she'd just prayed for, and something she'd searched for her entire life. The road of living to please her parents had proved to be a dead end. Then she'd tried to find the way on her own, but that path only brought pain and confusion. It was time to try a different road. She lifted her gaze heavenward and cried out to God again. As she prayed, a long-buried seed of hope grew inside and branched its way through every part of her.

Dani awakened the next morning to a shaft of sunlight stretching golden fingers across the room. Squinting groggily against the brightness, she mulled over the change in her, like she'd found...

Home.

The inaudible word brought her to an upright position. That first Sunday at church in Miller's Creek, Brother Mac had talked about Christ being her home. She hadn't understood then, but now it made perfect sense. Not just something she believed, but something she knew in her heart. She'd been frantic in her search for home, desperate to make it happen, only to have it staring her in the face the whole time.

Joy bubbled up into soft laughter. She slipped from the bed and traipsed to the balcony to drink in the first rays of light. There was much to learn, but she didn't feel afraid. God would help her. And miracle of miracles, the home she'd longed for her entire life wasn't a place after all.

Jesus was her home now and for always.

ভ30ড়

The Search

Steve's neck muscles knotted as a car whizzed past on his right, horn blaring. He glanced nervously in the rear-view mirror. It would help if the lady riding his bumper would back off and put down her cell phone.

His mind flashed back to the summer after his senior year in high school. On a beautiful June day he and Lauren had driven to Dallas to shop for things for their dorm rooms. One minute they'd been talking and laughing, the next minute a blur, as another vehicle crashed into them from behind, sending them into a tailspin that ended in a seven-car collision.

The image of Lauren's lifeless body on the pavement had been forever imprinted on his brain. He tightened his grip on the steering wheel. There weren't many reasons he'd venture in to Dallas and face traffic. In fact there was only one. Dani. He had to find her, not only for Mama Beth, but for himself. He'd called Cecille last night after church and arranged to meet with her today. Maybe between the two of them they could locate Dani and convince her to come home.

He exited the interstate onto Mockingbird Lane breathing a sigh of relief. Though there was still a lot of traffic, at least it was slower-paced. How did people survive with all the noise and miles of concrete?

A few minutes later, he turned onto Preston Road, following the directions Cecille had given him over the phone, his mouth swinging open like an unlatched barn door. Compared to these houses, his mother's Southern mansion looked like a miniature dollhouse. With manicured lawns and sculpted gardens, the neighborhood dripped wealth. The house on his right stretched on for what seemed like two blocks before the road turned and he could view the front. This was the place. Looked like some kind of modern-day castle.

He parked his truck in the large circular drive and strode to the house. Before he could even knock, Cecille opened the door, a changed woman from the last time he'd seen her. The dark area beneath her eyes hinted at sleepless nights. He could relate.

"Hello, Steve. Please come in."

Hat in hand, his boots thudded on the shiny marble floor as he followed her through the massive foyer, down a long hallway, and into a kitchen that would hold his entire house. She pivoted toward him. "Please have a seat. Would you care for a glass of tea?"

"Yes ma'am, please." He perched at the counter and pulled at the collar of his polo, wondering if he'd ever felt so out of place.

She placed the glass in front of him, her expression subdued, her fingers devoid of the gaudy rings she'd worn during her stay in Miller's Creek. "I appreciate your concern for Dani, but I'm not sure I'll to be able to help you find her." She lowered herself to the ornate bar stool.

"Any idea where she might've gone?"

Her head moved from side to side then lowered. "No."

"Has she been in contact with you?"

"Last night."

His pulse quickened and he leaned toward her. "And?"

"She just wanted me to know she was okay." Her voice cracked and her eyes, so much like Mama Beth's, flooded with tears that spilled over and slipped down her cheeks. "Will she ever forgive me?"

No matter what she'd done in the past, she clearly loved Dani and felt remorse for her behavior. He draped a hand across hers. "I believe she will. She loves you."

Cecille pulled her hands away and wiped her tears. "I don't know why. I don't deserve it."

"You must've done something right. You raised a mighty special lady with a heart of gold."

The woman managed a weak smile. "She is special. I'm just not sure I can take credit."

"Would any of Dani's friends know where she is?"

"Maybe Andy."

Steve stiffened at the familiar fingers of jealousy clawing his insides. This might not be pleasant, but he had to know. "Can you give me directions to his office?"

"I can do better than that. I'll take you." He glimpsed in her expression the same determination he'd seen in Dani on more than one occasion.

After Cecille gathered her purse and keys, he followed her to the garage, struggling to keep his jaw from hinging open like some hick from the sticks. Folding himself into her little red sports car proved to be an even bigger challenge. With his knees riding near his chest, he grabbed hold of the arm rest and clung to it for dear life as she zipped in and out of traffic. The only thing worse than driving in Dallas was riding with someone who's crazy driving contributed to the problem.

They pulled up outside a fancy stone building with Tyler & Coleman Law Firm plastered on the front in big black letters, self-doubt seeping into his psyche. No way could he ever compete with this kind of money. Why would Dani choose him when she could have this? Especially after the way he'd treated her. He crawled from the confines of Cecille's sardine can of a car offering up a quick prayer for things to go smoothly. Regardless of past hard feelings between him and Andy, the last thing he needed to do was alienate the one person who might know where she was.

The receptionist at the front desk smiled as they approached. "Welcome to Tyler and Coleman. May I help you?"

Steve was relieved when Cecille answered. "My name is Cecille Hampton. I don't have an appointment, but it's imperative that we see Andy Tyler. Is he in?"

A minute later they were ushered in to Andy's office, surprisingly simple for a big city lawyer like him. When he saw them he hopped to his feet, coming from behind his desk to hug Cecille. A friendly smile on his face, he offered Steve his hand. "Hey, Steve, glad to see you. I hear things are basically finished in Miller's Creek. Congratulations."

Taken aback at Andy's relaxed friendliness, he nodded. The last time they'd spoken in Miller's Creek, the tension between them had been so thick a chain saw couldn't have ripped through it. Steve shook his hand. "Yep, almost done. Thanks for seeing us on such short notice."

"I must admit, I never expected to see the two of you together." Andy moved to the group of wing chairs nearby and motioned for them to sit. "Let me guess. This has to do with Dani."

He and Cecille nodded at the same time. "Have you seen her or heard from her?" Steve tried to squelch the anxiety in his voice, but to no avail.

"We've been in touch."

Lowering his gaze, he let out a shaky breath. So they were still together. No wonder Andy seemed so happy. "Do you know where she is?" He kept his eyes trained on Andy.

"No." His direct gaze never wavered.

Cecille released a heavy sigh, her shoulders sagging. "Well, thanks for your time." She stood. "We won't keep you."

Steve rose to his feet. The trip to Dallas had been a waste of time. Dazed, he turned to follow Cecille, but Andy laid a hand on his shoulder. "Could I speak to you alone for a moment?"

He glanced at Cecille, who nodded. "I'll wait in the lobby." She closed the office door behind her.

Andy offered a close-lipped smile. "Please have a seat." They both settled into the chairs then Andy leveled a green-eyed gaze his direction. "You're in love with her aren't you?"

His brows shot up, and he released a short laugh. "That obvious, huh? What about you?"

The lawyer shook his sandy curls. "Let's just say I've moved on. Dani made it clear she wasn't interested in me right after the rodeo."

The rodeo? That was weeks ago. "But I thought—"

"Yeah, you and the rest of the town." He laughed good-naturedly. "Dani and I are friends and always will be. Don't give up on her. She might come around."

Steve leaned forward, elbows on his knees, and busied his hands with his hat. "I know she's the one behind the foundation."

Andy leaned back in his seat, eyes wide. "Really? Well, it's about time someone knew."

"Why'd she keep it a secret?"

"Her parents."

His eyebrows wrinkled. "Sorry, I'm not following you."

Andy raised both hands, his expression serious. "Based on what Dani's mentioned, I think they must've been the status-seeker-types who used their money to buy friends. She wanted the people in Miller's Creek to like her for who she was."

The words knocked the air from his lungs. Why had he been such a fool? He grappled with words. "She's a better person than I ever gave her credit for."

Andy smiled sadly. "Yeah, she is."

"Thanks for your help, Andy." Steve stood and stretched out his hand. "If you happen to hear from Dani again, would you tell her we all want her to come back home?"

"Sure."

Steve made his way to the door, but Andy's voice called out from behind. "Steve?"

He turned. "Yeah?"

"For what it's worth, I think she loves you, too."

Lips tight, he lowered his head. "After the stupid moves I've made—"

"Don't underestimate her. You've already done that once."

Steve nodded and walked from the room, his heart heavier than one of the boulders perched beside the creek.

Early Tuesday morning Dani clicked the cell phone shut, tears gushing down her cheeks as she weaved her way through the I-30 commuter traffic in Dallas. She glanced into the rear-view mirror and used one hand to wipe away tears. Calling Mama Beth had been the hardest thing she'd done so far. The sorrowful plea in her aunt's voice made her want to rush back to Miller's Creek immediately, but she couldn't make that kind of promise until she and Mother worked things out. Thoughts of Steve flowed to her mind, followed by a flood of feelings. She missed Mama Beth, but her heart ached for Steve, to see his face and hear his voice. *God, please help us.*

She'd left Mustang Island yesterday, hoping to make it all the way to Dallas, but road construction and snarled traffic had spoiled her plans. Instead, the late hour and fatigue from the difficult drive had forced her to spend the night in Waco. It was for the best. Feeling more rested could only be to her advantage when she confronted her mother.

As she pulled up to the front of Mother's estate several minutes later, she glimpsed a foursome of men at the Country Club across the street strolling back to their golf carts. Did they know? Lately the question was never far from her mind. The lady behind the counter at the gas station, the teenager in the drive-through, the homeless man crossing the street in front of her as she waited at the traffic light, did they each know how much God loved them?

Breathing a quick prayer for strength and wisdom, she opened the car door and headed up the massive steps to the front door. From outside she heard the chimes pealing her arrival. A minute later her mother opened the door.

"Dani!" Mother flew out the door, embracing her and sobbing. "I'm so glad you're okay. I've missed you so much and been so afraid . . ." She pulled away, resting her hands on Dani's upper arms, her eyes full of sorrow and tears. ". . . so afraid I'd never see you again."

She gave her mother another hug then grabbed her hand. "Let's go inside where we can talk."

Once in the living room, Dani glanced around. The place had been emptied of some of its furnishings, and less stuff cluttered the tables and walls. Her mother's gaze was fixed on her like she might evaporate.

Smiling, she placed a hand on Mother's knee. "Don't be afraid. I'm sorry I left the way I did, but I needed to be alone to think through things. I'm back to stay."

Her mother's bottom lip disappeared, and she sat quietly as if pondering what to say and how to say it. "I never meant for you to learn the truth about your adoption, but I was wrong. And I'm so sorry about the way you found out. Please forgive me."

"I already have, but I'm not sorry I learned the truth."

"What are you going to do?" Mother's face paled, her voice hesitant.

How would her mother react to her plan? She licked her lips. "First I want us to spend some time together, then I'm going to finish the work in Miller's Creek and do a lot of praying. God will show me the road He wants me to take."

Her eyes flickered with unspoken questions. "You sound as if—"

"As if I've found God?" She smiled, her heart full to overflowing. "Actually, it's the other way around. He found me."

"You look happy."

"I am."

Head lowered, her mother continued. "Then I'm happy for you. There was a time when I believed."

Heart bursting, she knelt in front of her mother. "It's not too late to try again."

Mother smiled then reached a hand to cup her face. "Oh, my darling, I'm so sorry for what I've put you through. For making you feel like a thing instead of a person. I wouldn't blame you if never had anything to do with me as long as you live."

Dani shook her head. "That will never happen. You'll always be my mother." She hugged her again then sat beside her on the couch. "I want to help with your bills."

Her mother raised a hand and gave her head a vehement shake. "I've already sold my jewelry and a few other things and found a buyer for the house. That gives me more than enough to live on."

Frowning, she studied Mother's face, not sure she recognized the changed woman in front of her. "But where will you live?"

"A nice town home close to my friends. I've already moved a few of my things." A sad smile trembled on her face. "I want you to go back to Miller's Creek."

Her heart thudded to a stop. "What makes you say that?"

"Because you were happy there, at least until I came and messed things up." She reached for a tissue and swabbed her eyes which had filled with fresh tears. "Beth and I had a chance to get to know each other again after you left. I'd forgotten how sweet she could be."

"She is wonderful. I wouldn't have found my way to God had it not been for her." Dani ducked her head, the tormenting questions still rolling in her head. "Did you know the man who...?"

Mother nodded her head. "Your biological father? Yes. Beth and I had a long talk and she told me the whole story. He was later imprisoned for doing the same thing to someone else. He's dead."

A breath shuddered from her. The decision about whether she should contact him had been taken from her. Dani searched her mother's face. "Thanks for telling me. As for returning to Miller's Creek, God's plan may be for me to stay in Dallas."

Her mother's smile was genuine, her eyes crinkling at the corners. "I don't think so, dear." She patted her hand. "There's a very special man who needs you in Miller's Creek."

௸31 ௸

Full Circle

Steve traipsed up the steps to the front porch of Mama Beth's house early Tuesday morning, not surprised that she wasn't in her usual spot in the rocking chair. Since Dani had left, she rarely ventured out of the house, choosing instead to stay inside close to the phone. He couldn't blame her. Thoughts of Dani consumed him, made worse by yesterday's pointless trip to Dallas. Not knowing what had happened to her was the worst possible torture. *Lord, keep her safe and draw her close to You. And let her call soon.*

He found Mama Beth in the chair next to the living room window, her eyes distant and swollen. Peering across the room at her the ache in his heart grew heavier. She'd aged at least a year in the past week.

The phone shrilled, shattering the silence, and she dragged herself from the chair. "Hello?" A trembling hand fluttered to her chest and tears slipped down her weathered cheeks.

Dani? He moved to Mama Beth's side and braced her up with an arm around her shoulders.

"I'm so sorry, Dani. Please forgive me. Please come home." Mama Beth's voice trembled with emotion then her muffled sobs answered the question in his heart. She wasn't coming back. Her tear-stained face took on numb resignation. "I understand.

Please know I'm praying for you." She hung up the phone, her face ashen gray.

"You okay?"

She shook her head. "She's hurting and I'm to blame." Her tears started again and she laid her head against his shoulder.

Dani was safe, but not coming back. No chance to apologize, to tell her how much she was missed, to tell her how he felt. Resolve straightened his spine. He'd travel wherever to make things right. "Where is she?"

Mama Beth dabbed her cheeks with a tissue, her voice void of hope. "She didn't say." She took two steps toward the chair then stopped and clutched her head. "Steve, I—"

The last words she spoke before she crumpled to the floor.

Dani checked the gas gauge and steered onto the road which led to Miller's Creek—half a tank—more than enough to get home. A late summer batch of Black-eyed Susans dotted the roadside. Laughter gurgled in her throat as a pasture of cows came into view. She rolled down the window and allowed the rich earthy scent to filter through the car.

A smile planted itself on her face as she remembered the first trip to Miller's Creek and the dirty cowboy who'd rescued her. A brief moment of apprehension shuttled through her system. It was time to be completely honest with him, but would he understand why she'd tried to cover up her involvement in the renovations? Her deception had been wrong. She knew that now. A choice she'd made based on fear and self-protection.

Half an hour later, she drove into Miller's Creek, her heart lighter than it had been in weeks. The familiar country cottages, decked in fresh paint, lined both sides of the road like old friends waiting for her return. Colorful banners for the Autumn Daze Festival traversed the road announcing the dates for the upcoming event. The irony of the moment sent off waves of gratitude. Reborn and renewed, she and Miller's Creek had both risen from the ashes to a new life.

Dani pulled into the gravel parking lot of B&B Hardware, half in dread, half in anticipation. A couple of bottles of root beer for her and Mama Beth might make the task before them a bit easier. She gulped a deep breath, praying this visit would open the door for mended friendships.

The bell clanked to announce her arrival, and she blinked to adjust to the darkness. She took a tentative step forward, the wooden floors creaking out a welcome.

"Miss Dani!" She heard J.C. before she saw him. "Boy, are you a sight for sore eyes."

She threw herself into his outstretched arms. "Oh, J.C., I've missed you, too." Smiling, she drew back to peer into his kind eyes. But instead she saw worry.

"I guess you came because of Mama Beth. The whole town is praying for her."

Her breath froze in her throat. "What are you talking about?"

"I'm sorry, I thought you knew. She collapsed yesterday, but thankfully Steve was there when it happened. They rushed her to Morganville."

She didn't wait to hear more.

Dani reached Morganville General in record time, the prayer she'd prayed all the way still reverberating in her brain. *Lord, help me not to be too late.*

Her cheeks damp with tears, she hurried inside and made her way to the nurse's station. "Can I help you?"

"Yes, I'm looking for Mona Beth Adams' room."

"Dani?"

At the sound of Steve's voice her heart quickened and she pivoted to meet his gaze. He towered in the doorway of the waiting room, a tortured expression on his fatigue-lined face, a day's worth of stubble shadowing his jaw. With long strides, he closed the distance between them and enveloped her in his arms, his lips against her hair. "I'm so glad you've come home."

She allowed herself to enjoy the strength and security of his embrace before she tugged herself away and searched his eyes. The sorrow she glimpsed there sent rivers of fear pulsing through her veins. "Mama Beth? Is—?"

"She's okay."

Dani closed her eyelids, her knees like rubber. *Thank You, God.* Her eyes fluttered open to find his steady gaze trained on her face. "What happened?"

He positioned an arm around her and helped her to a chair in the waiting room. "She collapsed yesterday morning. The doctor thinks it's just stress-related, but they're running some tests to make sure. He's in with her now. They ran me out of the room until they're finished."

With a groan she brought a hand to her mouth. "This is my fault."

Steve grabbed her shoulders and forced her to look him in the face. "No, it's not. If it's anyone's fault, it's mine." With surgical precision his long-lashed eyes probed hers, the intensity both thrilling and excruciating. "I'll be right back." His words husky but determined, he strode from the waiting area and returned with two cans of soft drink.

She stared at the can he offered then tilted her head toward him. Did he remember the day of Mama Beth's surgery?

A tender hint of a smile played on his lips. "It's my turn."

He *did* remember. Overcome with emotion, she managed to croak out a "thank you" before she popped open the drink and took a sip, the fizzy liquid tickling her nose. She let out her typical carbonated drink hiccup. "I'm so relieved you were at her house when she collapsed." She shivered. "I don't want to think about what might have happened if—"

"Don't play the what-if game. God put me there at the right time. That's all that matters." A nerve pulsed in his jaw and his Adam's apple bobbed, revealing the depths of his concern.

"Thank you for taking such good care of her. It means a lot to me."

"I wouldn't have it any other way."

She smiled remembering her trip into town. "Miller's Creek looks great."

A frown creased his forehead and he lowered his head. "Yes."

She puzzled over the change in his demeanor. Had there been more trouble? "Is everything okay? Has there been any more vandalism?"

A half smile softened his face and he shook his head. "No. We caught the guy. Seems he was a little miffed he didn't get the bid for some of the construction work."

The silence grew thick then he cleared his throat and looked her in the eyes. "I know she's your mother."

The softly spoken words unleashed a flurry of unexpected feelings, and she ducked her head to escape his scrutiny. Mama Beth had told him, but not her? She steadied her nerves with a deep breath and turned to face him. "It's wonderful and scary at the same time. I mean, who wouldn't be delighted to have Mama Beth as their mother? It answers so many questions, but it—"

"—also creates more?" Compassion and understanding shone from his expression.

She nodded, momentarily unable to speak, amazed at how he knew her thoughts. "At first I was just so hurt and confused."

"I can understand that." He tucked a stray curl behind her ear then crumpled his dark brows. "I know it's none of my business, but where did you go? I even went to Dallas to find you."

Her heart seized then lightened. He hated the city—the traffic, the noise—everything about it. She tilted her head to one side trying to glean meaning from the light in his eyes. "You went to Dallas for me?"

His sheepish smile confirmed her thoughts.

It was time to tell him the news. "I went to Mustang Island. I know I should've called, but I couldn't."

"Hey, it's okay." He squeezed her hand in encouragement. "You needed that time."

"I did a lot of soul searching." She left the words hanging intentionally. He of all people should know.

"And?" Like melted caramel candy his eyes softened.

Her heart flooded with assurance, pushing a smile to her face.

Steve twisted his head to one side then grinned and dragged her into his arms. "Oh Dani, I'm so glad. I've prayed for you to know Him."

Her spirit took wing, and she momentarily allowed herself to relax in his embrace. If things worked out like she hoped, there would be time enough later to shelter in his arms. She forced herself to move away, but her joy turned to confusion at his troubled expression.

"What's wrong?"

He grabbed both her hands then wet his lips. "There's something I have to tell you, but I don't know how to say it." Remorse colored his eyes chocolate brown. "I found out you were adopted before Mama Beth told me. I also know you financed the renovation."

She searched his face, not understanding.

"I'm sorry." His voice quaked and his eyes glistened. "I thought you were taking advantage of Mama Beth and trying to sabotage the renovation, so I had you investigated."

Investigated? She averted her gaze. Though his confession surprised and hurt, his actions were justifiable. He'd only been trying to protect those he loved, and she'd given him plenty of reasons to suspect her.

"Excuse me. Are you here with Miss Adams?" A doctor stood nearby.

"Yes." Steve spoke, his tone oddly strangled.

"Miss Adams is doing fine. We were concerned about her heart, but all the tests came back negative. We're going to keep her one more night, and if she does okay, we'll let her go home in the morning. You can see her now."

Without a second's hesitation, Dani broke into a run down the hallway.

Mama Beth stared at the giant oak tree out the hospital room window, the steady beep of the heart monitor already grating on her nerves. The doctor said he thought it was only a scare. A scare? No, a scare was having the daughter you loved ripped from your life forever. She struggled to breathe, her heart heavy. Where was Dani? Would she ever come back home?

Let it go.

She let out a sigh and prayer. *Yes, Lord, I know I need to let it go. Help me.* She'd clung to the pain with both fists, afraid of releasing the only part of Dani she still had left. Eyes closed and fingers spread wide, she lifted shaky hands to the ceiling then let them drop to her side, the situation with her daughter in God's capable hands.

The door opened and closed, probably the doctor again, or maybe Steve. She opened her eyelids and turned her head, her breath ratcheting in her throat. "Dani." She could only whisper her name, afraid the vision would dissipate. But in less than an eye blink, her daughter rested in her arms, tears flowing freely. It wasn't a dream. Her little girl had come home. She stroked Dani's golden curls suddenly aware of the miracle. Thirty-five years ago in a hospital room much like this one they'd been separated, but their lives had finally come full circle.

ᑫ32ᑅ

Dreams Fulfilled

Steve dismounted and sauntered to the creek, the crisp fall weather leaving a nip in the air. Steam rose from the water and added to the haze of the morning, the fog on his heart just as heavy. He kicked at a stone with the toe of his boot and sent it flying through the air. It landed in the creek with a *plop* and sent ripples scurrying along the surface of the water.

He heaved a disgruntled sigh and parked himself on a large boulder. Dani was finally back in Miller's Creek after several weeks in Dallas taking care of what Mama Beth called loose ends. At church yesterday, Dani had sent him a smile from the choir loft, but left church without saying so much as a word to him.

How did you tell a woman you loved her so much you could taste it? Steve hurled a rock into the water. Why bother? Why should she trust him again after the way he'd treated her?

A twig snapped behind him and he turned his head.

Dressed in an old pair of blue jeans and a pullover sweater, Dani ambled toward him, smiling at him in a way that sent his heart on a journey to his throat. "Mind if I join you?"

"Not at all."

She scooted onto the rock beside him, her arm brushing against his. Having her close twisted his insides.

"Pretty day." She flashed him the look that always made him feel like she knew him better than anyone else.

"Yep."

Dani whistled then stopped in mid-tune. "In fact, it's a good day for a barn cleaning, don't you think?"

He jerked his head toward her, frowning. "Huh?"

A playful grin turned up the corners of her mouth. "Well, you should know what a barn cleaning is. Didn't you grow up on a ranch?"

Something told him her words had nothing to do with cleaning a barn.

"Well, didn't you?"

"Look, I don't know what kind of game your play—"

Dani gave him a stern teacher look. "I'm not playing games, Mr. Miller. Answer the question. Did you or did you not grow up on a ranch?" The left corner of her lips twitched, but she maintained firm control.

He sighed and shook his head, unable to keep the grin from his face. "Yes, teacher."

"Good. We're making progress. Now, can you tell me what happens at a barn cleaning?"

A chuckle erupted and rattled his chest. "Well, you, uh . . . get rid of some pretty smelly stuff."

"Precisely."

"So you're saying we need to get ready of some smelly stuff?" He raised an eyebrow and gave her a sideways glance.

She flashed a smile so bright his throat cinched up like a lasso. "You catch on quick, mister. Why don't you go first?"

He tipped his hat. "Yes ma'am."

Dani twisted around and sat crossed-legged facing him, her look suddenly serious.

Steve took one look into her blue eyes and shot a quick plea to heaven for help. "I'm an arrogant old fool, Dani. When you first came here, I was jealous. The whole town fell in love with you, and your ideas for Miller's Creek were so smart." He grabbed one of her hands and sheltered it in his own. "I was torn in my feelings toward you. I saw one side of you I loved, but there were so many things that made me doubt you." He let out a shuddering breath. Could she find it in her heart to forgive him? "I feel horrible for the way I've treated you and for having you investigated. I don't deserve your forgiveness or your friendship, but I'm asking for them all the same."

She lowered her head for several minutes, her lips pursed. As the silence lengthened, his fear mounted.

When Dani raised her gaze, a storm brewed behind her troubled eyes. "I don't know how to say this other than to just say it. I've been hurt by every man I ever trusted, so I shied away from you, afraid you'd break my heart. I acted in secrecy to protect myself and I know that made you question my motives. I do forgive you, and I ask for your forgiveness in return." Her eyes flooded with sorrow and her voice softened to a whisper. "But as for being your friend . . ."

His heart plummeted at her silence, and he braced himself for the words to come, already feeling their sting. He couldn't blame her for rejecting his friendship.

"I think it's only fair to tell you . . ." She paused again as if searching for courage.

He closed his eyes and steeled himself against the prick of her daggered words.

". . . that my feelings go a little deeper than friendship."

His eyes and mouth flew open, the air around him suddenly thin as he took in her precious smile.

A tender light shone from her face. She inched closer, touching her lips to his, their silky softness sending a tremble across his shoulders. How long had he waited for this moment? With a groan, he hugged her closer to him, the hurt, confusion and doubt melting away like a day-old Texas snow.

When they pulled apart a minute later, her eyes glistened with tears. He moved fingers to her dampened cheeks, longing to erase the years of hurt she'd endured. *Lord, help me to be the man she needs me to be.*

She giggled through the tears, pointing to his smile. "What's that for?"

Laughter spilled out of him. "I never knew barn cleaning could be so much fun."

In what felt like slow motion, Dani climbed from the car, her mouth hinging open. Paralyzed with delight, she stared out over the hordes of people in downtown Miller's Creek for the First Annual Autumn Daze Festival. She moved to the middle of Main Street, brought both hands to her face, and circled around. Shoulder-to-shoulder they walked, the sounds of their laughter and chatter carried on the cool breeze.

Around the town square, craft booths rested beneath brightly colored awnings, and the tempting aromas from the food vendors wafted through the air. "You won't believe it 'til you see it, folks." The radio announcer's voice blared from his station in the gazebo. "Downtown Miller's Creek is bustling once again, just like the good old days. These kind folks have rolled out the red carpet and let me tell you, they know how to throw a party."

"Hey Dani!" Coot yelled at her from across the street. He and the rest of the Old Geezers congregated outside of Granny's Kitchen. She waved, gratefully remembering how they'd come to her in the past few weeks with their apologies.

"Have y'all seen Steve?" She raised her hands to megaphone her mouth.

"Sure have." Ernie called back, but gave no further explanation. After a brief pause, all the men started laughing.

Hands akimbo, she shook her head in mock exasperation. "Very funny. You know what I mean. Now where is he?"

They laughed again and J. C. hollered. "He's at the creek."

She sent them a happy wave and set out for the park, the cheerful sounds of the carnival reaching her ears from two blocks away. How was she supposed to find Steve in this throng of people?

Her eyes came to rest on the bridge and her heartbeat settled into a rhythm of peace. She knew right where to look.

Pushing her way through the crowd, she made her way to the depot. By next year, if all went according to plan, the passenger train would be restored, and Miller's Creek could add an old-fashioned train ride to its list of growing attractions.

She spied Steve's lanky frame leaning against the old train station and stopped to watch him, amazed by the difference his love had made in her life. He stared across the full parking lot, a contented smile at rest on his face. Her heart danced knowing she'd helped bring his dreams to fruition.

Resuming her walk, she reached calling distance within a few steps. "Hey, stranger." He looked up, smiling his pleasure. She angled up next to him and threw her arms around his neck.

A happy light shone from Steve's cinnamon-colored eyes, his lazy grin accelerating her pulse as his arms encircled her waist.

She smiled up at him, tilting her head to one side. "What are you doing over here? Don't you know there's a party going on?"

He chuckled, a thrilling melodic sound that curled her toes. "Yeah, it's kind of hard to miss. But I can't help thinking that none of it would've happened had it not been for a certain woman I know."

"Oh really? And who might that be?"

Steve's lips brushed hers with a tender touch. "You know who." He pulled her to his side, one arm still around her waist, and used his other hand to point. "See that spot right over there? That's when I first knew."

"First knew what?"

"That I loved you." His eyes took on a distant look. "The night of the fire I was so afraid something had happened to you." A host of emotions traveled across his face.

"You weren't worried for Miller's Creek?"

"Of course I was, but I was more concerned about you. That's how I knew. Any woman who made me care more about her than I cared about this town had to be a pretty special gal, even if she was a city woman."

She yanked on the brim of his cowboy hat, pulling it down over his eyes. That would teach him to call her a city woman.

He laughed, readjusted his hat, and pulled her back in front of him, his hands resting lightly on her hips. For a moment he didn't speak, just stared into her eyes. It was something he did frequently and she never tired of it. His expression softened. "You ever wonder where this road's going to lead?"

"Not any more."

His eyes filled with questions.

Inexpressible joy started in her toes and worked its way to her face. "I used to wonder about what road I was on all the time. Now I don't, because God is with me."

He scooped her up in his strong arms, her pink Ropers barely touching the ground, and gave her a kiss she wouldn't soon forget.

A road stretched out before both of them. A road that led home.

About the Author

Cathy Bryant's debut novel, *Texas Roads*, was a 2009 finalist in the American Christian Fiction Writers' Genesis contest. A Texas gal by birth, Cathy lives with her husband in a century-old Texas farmhouse, complete with picket fence, flowers, butterflies, and late summer mosquitoes the size of your fist. Learn more about Cathy at www.CatBryant.com.

❖   ❖   ❖

Dear friends,

Dani's story was born from my own quest to find home. For years my husband, two sons, and I seemed destined to be wanderers, moving from one small Texas town to another. And just about the time we'd feel settled, God would move us again. I yearned to put down roots— to find a place that felt like home.

God used that time in my life to grow me spiritually and help me realize that for His children, home will never be a place. Instead our home is Jesus. Only He can fill that home-sized hole in our hearts.

I don't know where life's road has taken you, but I pray you'll discover the peace and joy of making Christ your home.

At Home in Him,
Cathy

Book Club Discussion Questions

1.   Steve struggled with his mother's illness and in knowing how to pray for the situation. Dani battled with trusting a God who allowed difficulty. In your opinion, what are some of the benefits of enduring hardship and suffering? How has hardship and suffering shaped Dani? Steve? Mama Beth? You?

2.   Dani and Mama Beth both harbor secrets. Why? How are their secrets different from one another? Their motives? How are their secrets alike? And their motives?

3.   Steve believes that he is inadequate and ineffective in his efforts to help Dani know God. Have you ever felt that way? Is Steve actually ineffective? How can you apply this to your life?

4.   What is the theme of this story? What symbols do you see used in the story? What is the main symbol, and how does it intertwine with the theme?

5.   Why do you think Dani struggles so much with the decision to move to Miller's Creek? Have you ever faced a decision where you felt nothing but opposition? How did it affect you? How did it influence your decision?

6.   Dani often questions God and His goodness. What are your thoughts and feelings about people questioning God? Is it wrong? Why or why not?

7.   We are all quick to make assumptions about others. What are some of the assumptions Dani and Steve make about each other? What are some of the assumptions you made about the characters as they were introduced? Name several places in the story where characters made hasty and often incorrect judgments. Why did they make these assumptions and with what consequences? Have you ever been on the receiving end of incorrect assumptions? How did it make you feel? How did it change you?

For more discussion questions, visit http://TexasRoadsbyCathyBryant.blogspot.com, where you will find a Bible Study that corresponds to the story, Mama Beth's recipes, and more!

SNEAK PEAK:
Book 2 in the Miller's Creek Series
(Working Title: *A Path Too Narrow*)

In spite of the thousands of winking lights that surrounded Trish James, weddings somehow lost their luster in the wake of death. She adjusted the tulle on the wedding arch, the soft netlike fabric billowing beneath her finger tips as she wrapped the twinkle lights. The church sanctuary had never looked better and she knew it.

As if on cue, Dani's next words echoed her thoughts. "This wedding must be hard on you after Doc's death."

Trish swallowed the knot that bounded into her throat. "I'm fine. It's not everyday that my brother marries the most wonderful woman in the world." She sent Dani a sincere smile. "I've never seen Steve so happy."

Her sister-in-law-to-be didn't smile back. Instead a frown creased the area right above her eyes. "You sure you're okay?"

"Yep." She bent low to snag a sprig of silk ivy from the box then focused her attention on inserting it in just the right place, forcing away stinging tears. "Are you all ready for the big day tomorrow?" She glanced at Dani.

Joyful light sprang to her friend's face. "And the day after that and the day after that. I think I've been getting ready to marry Steve my entire life."

"I'm happy for you both." Though the words were hard to speak, she meant it. It wasn't their fault her life was in the toilet right now.

Dani stood back to view the stage. "You have such a gift, Trish. Everything looks absolutely magical."

Trish gazed at the curly tree branches she'd ordered and spray-painted white, now wrapped with tiny sparks of light. The branches stretched across the expanse of the stage with matching trees at the back of the church for added effect. Once the ivy, ribbons and flowers were in place, and candles were inserted into the globes that stood among the trees, her vision would be complete. "I'm glad you like it. I hope it's what you wanted."

"It's better than I could've ever imagined." Dani hurried to her side and draped an arm across her shoulder. "You're going to get loads of business once the people in Miller's Creek see this."

A heavy sigh fell from Trish's throat before she could contain it. "From your lips to my bank account."

Dani's sky blue eyes clouded over again. "I don't know how to say this, so I'm just going to say it and get it over with. Are you doing okay? I mean, do you need to borrow money or something?"

No. Yes. Yes. She wasn't doing okay. She needed money. She needed . . . something. "I'm fine." Trish hurried to a large box perched by the piano to get a couple of the delicate cracked glass globes for the candle stands. The words "I'm fine" seemed to be her constant mantra these days. Who was she kidding? She closed her eyes and reopened them slowly, tired of pretending everything was good. Her eyes flitted to her wristwatch. She still had so much to do to make the decorations perfect. *God, please let this bring me some business.*

Dani perched on the railing and swung her short legs. "Is Little Bo doing better?"

Doing better? How could he be? "Sure, if you don't count the nightmares and barely letting me out of his sight." She left out the thumb-sucking and low grades, tucking more greenery into the arch.

"So the counselor is helping?"

The double white doors at the rear of the church swung open with a bang, and Dani let out a squeal. "Andy!"

Trish turned to watch Dani fly down the podium steps and into the arms of a man who looked vaguely familiar. The Dallas attorney had the kind of smile that could instantly brighten any room. "Hey, how's the bride-to-be?"

Dani pulled back to smile up at him. "Never better."

"Yeah, I can see that."

She tugged at his arm. "Come here. I want you to meet my sister-in-law."

His loose-limbed gait gave off the impression of someone who was always relaxed, like he'd just returned from a vacation at the beach.

"Andy, this is Steve's sister."

Sea-green eyes sparkled. "Well, does Steve's sister have a name?" He extended a hand toward her, his smile still toothpaste-commercial bright, a left dimple winking at her.

Trish laughed and shook his hand. "I'm Trish. Nice to meet you, Andy."

Dani's face took on a crimson hue. "Sorry. Guess my mind is elsewhere."

A door squeaked behind them, and the woman all of Miller's Creek knew as Mama Beth bustled into the room. The smell of fresh baked bread trailed her from the fellowship hall. "My goodness, if this isn't the most gorgeous thing I've ever seen. Trish, this is amazing." She moved to Andy's side and gave him a hug. "Hi, Andy."

He hugged her back and gave her a peck on the cheek. "Hi, sweet lady." Then he turned his gaze turned to Trish. "Looks awesome. You did all this?"

She ducked her gaze, pushing a strand of hair behind one ear.

"All of it." Dani practically bubbled. "And wait until you see the fellowship hall."

"Speaking of fellowship hall, I could sure use your help in the kitchen." Mama Beth's voice took on a commanding tone as she bustled toward the door. "We've got enough work to do to keep an army busy before the rehearsal dinner tonight."

Dani looked torn. "But I can't leave Trish down here to do this by herself."

Andy placed his hands on his hips in mock protest, his tan corduroy jacket pulled back at the bottom. "What am I? Chopped liver? I'll help Trish. You go help Mama Beth." He held up a hand.

"Trust me when I say I'll be more help here than in the kitchen."

"Good point. I've had your cooking." Dani gave him a triumphant gloat and hooked elbows with Mama Beth. "Y'all know where to find us if you need help."

The two women hurried from the room chattering like two sparrows fussing at one another.

Andy chuckled then turned his friendly Florida ocean-colored eyes her way. "So, Steve's sister, what can I do to help?"

Trish laughed. "I was actually waiting for a man to come around. I have a box full of candles I need brought in." She pointed toward the side exit door. "My SUV's right out there and it's unlocked."

He gave a cocky mock salute that bounced his sandy curls.

"Yes ma'am. Your wish is my command." Andy trotted down the steps, his stocky frame disappearing through the door.

She watched him go then stepped down the stairs toward the box of greenery on the front pew, her eyebrows raised. Dani's friend was more handsome than she remembered. How had a man his age managed to evade walking the aisle? She burrowed through the box looking for more sprigs of ivy for the arch and remembered the promise she'd made Dani yesterday to entertain Andy and make him feel welcome. She heaved a heavy sigh. The last thing she needed in addition to her other responsibilities was a man to take care of.

The exit door opened, and Andy entered, the only portion of him showing above the bulky box his eyes and forehead. She hurried over to him. "Can I help? I know that box is heavy. I loaded it this morning."

"Nah, I got it." The words wheezed out. "You loaded this by yourself?"

She ignored the question and pointed to the stage. "Can you bring it up the podium steps?"

He shot her a you've-got-to-be-kidding look then labored up the steps, his face red, and his breath coming in agonized spurts. As he reached the last step, the toe of his shoe caught against the extension cord that snaked along the edge of the stage. Trish saw what was about to happen, but words congealed behind her clamped lips. He stumbled, the box flying from his arms, candles launching through the air like small missiles. Andy hit the floor, the box landing at the base of the first tree.

In slow motion, like carefully-placed dominos, one by one the trees rippled to the floor in a staccato of crashes and crunches. Then, as if to punctuate the effect, the white metal archway in the center teetered, then toppled forward, landing with a bang.

Her mouth hinged open as her hands made their way to her cheeks. All her hard work. Ruined. Trish stood dazed, until she realized Andy was still flat on his back. She hurried over to him. "Are you all right?"

He pushed himself up on all fours and surveyed the devastation around them.

Once she assured herself he was okay, she plopped down on the top step. The scene replayed itself in her mind, and a giggle gurgled out of her, bursting forth in an almost-maniacal laugh.

Andy's laughter joined hers, and he crawled over to sit beside her.

Without warning her laughter turned to sobs, and she covered her face with her hands. Now she'd never be ready on time. No one would be impressed. No one would want her services. No business, no money. How would she pay her bills?

"I'm sorry. I'm so sorry." Andy slid a hand down her arm. "I'll fix it, Trish, I promise. I'm so sorry—"

Trish came to her senses and swatted at the tears on her cheek. "Will you stop apologizing?" Her voice snapped like a snarling dog. "It was an accident, for Pete's sake. I promise not to press charges." She clenched her teeth, rose to her feet, and moved up the steps to stand among the ruins. Blinking back tears, she knelt to retrieve shattered slivers of glass from the broken globes. These weren't even paid for.

Andy knelt beside her, his focused attention boring a hole through her skin. "Here, let me get that. You start putting things back where you want them."

Trish could only nod at his softly-spoken words, a knot of tears wedged in her windpipe. She moved to the white trees and started the tedious process of lifting them back into place, the strands of lights now dripping from the branches like a child had thrown them in place.

Coming Soon